A Gangsta's Karma 2

Lock Down Publications and Ca$h
Presents
A GANGSTA'S KARMA 2
A Novel by *Flame*

Lock Down Publications
P.O. Box 944
Stockbridge, Ga 30281

Visit our website @
www.lockdownpublications.com

Copyright 2021 by Flame
A Gangsta's Karma 2

This is a work of fiction. Names, characters, places, and incidents either are products of the author's imagination or are used fictitiously. Any similarity to actual events or locales or persons, living or dead, is entirely coincidental.

Lock Down Publications
Like our page on Facebook: Lock Down Publications @
www.facebook.com/lockdownpublications.ldp

Book interior design by: **Shawn Walker**
Edited by: **Kiera Northington**

Stay Connected with Us!

Text **LOCKDOWN** to 22828 to stay up-to-date with new releases, sneak peaks, contests and more…
Thank you.

Submission Guideline

Submit the first three chapters of your completed manuscript to ldpsubmissions@gmail.com, subject line: Your book's title. The manuscript must be in a .doc file and sent as an attachment. Document should be in Times New Roman, double spaced and in size 12 font. Also, provide your synopsis and full contact information. If sending multiple submissions, they must each be in a separate email.

Have a story but no way to send it electronically? You can still submit to LDP/Ca$h Presents. Send in the first three chapters, written or typed, of your completed manuscript to:

LDP: Submissions Dept
Po Box 944
Stockbridge, Ga 30281

DO NOT send original manuscript. Must be a duplicate.

Provide your synopsis and a cover letter containing your full contact information.

Thanks for considering LDP and Ca$h Presents.

Flame

Prologue

January 3, 2011 12:09 am

Vero Beach, FL

"Yeeeaaaahhhhh," the raspy-voiced person said, breaking the conspicuous silence. "Oh, let's do it!"

The lone headlights suddenly broke through the darkness upon entering the vacant parking lot, causing the furiously blood-pumping organ in Devon's chest to skip a beat. Whether it was fear or eagerness that caused the dramatically fluctuating heartbeat was totally irrelevant at the moment. What mattered most was there was no calling off the murderous plot now.

Hell, even if something offhand were to occur that could lead to them aborting the mission now, Devon certainly knew there was not a damn thing that could be done or said by anyone to deter her rage-filled accomplice who was squatting in the darkness nearby. *Fuck it, it's kill or be killed*, Devon reasoned, while looking to the left and observing, with no small measure of contempt, the sinister expression of a killer's face. Devon instinctively knew not to try to wear the mantle of the victim tonight … or any other night.

Flame

Chapter One

March 11, 2010 12:02 pm

Sanford, FL

Unbelievable. It was truly difficult for Bizzy to believe a whole year had passed since his father's murder, and the killer was still on the streets ... somewhere. Being that it was exactly one day after the one–year anniversary of his father's death, it still seemed like it was just yesterday when he attended the philanthropic, yet infamous, Demetrius' funeral. Demetrius was the head and mastermind of the notorious RockBottom Family Enterprise or RBF, as they were also referred to. Although Bizzy had an extremely troublesome time during the last year coping with the loss of his father, he'd had an even more troublesome time during the last five months trying to reunite and reorganize the nearly billion-dollar organization his father had built from nothing and left behind.

At first, he was too engaged in trying to track down the bastard that cut his father's life short to think about running a crime mob that dealt with multiple legitimate and illegal businesses. But after he began remembering all the straightforward talks he had with Demetrius about life in the wicked game, Bizzy's determination to find his father's killer gradually diminished as the days went by.

The two indelible quotes he remembered vividly from his father were, "When the game is over, the king and the pawn go back into the same box," and "When money is involved, bullshit is an equal opportunity employer." His father's words of wisdom helped him to refocus on the grand scheme of things.

In truth, Bizzy didn't know what the grand scheme of things really was, due to him being a spoiled and ignorant person before his father's untimely death. Yes, he knew how to make money by

8

hustling, but Demetrius tried to get him to learn every business aspect of RBF without forcing it on him. If he'd soaked up all the knowledge back then, he'd know exactly how to manage such a lucrative enterprise.

Now that it was all on him to keep his father's hard work afloat, and since he hadn't taken heed to his father's warnings or advice, he really didn't have the slightest idea of where to start. Eventually, though, he grew tired of constantly thinking about how to do things, and he started by making one call.

Feeling somewhat contrite for not wholeheartedly seeking to avenge his father's death, it was with much relief to discover that the first person Bizzy called was going through the same misery as he was. His cousin, Chad, was the closest person to Demetrius prior to his death. Chad was there for Demetrius when nobody else was at that time, not even Bizzy, so it was no surprise that Chad wanted to continue to build up on Demetrius' legacy by assisting Bizzy in whatever it took to keep RBF's name on top in the game.

Bizzy didn't plan on calling anybody else until after he met up with Chad. The meeting between the two second-cousins would determine if RBF could be salvaged, because Chad ought to know if it was worth the risk since he was Demetrius' right-hand man and protege throughout RBF's last major stint. They would deeply discuss the pros and cons before mutually deciding whether to carry the torch or to let the flame go out.

Knock at the door

Bizzy arose from the modest couch in the hotel's living room. He opted to convene with Chad at the Days Inn off State Road 46 in Sanford, which was about an hour northeast of South Orlando, because it was a neutral site located in a discrete area between Orlando and Daytona.

He then approached the door, peeking through the peephole before opening up for his guest.

"What's happ'nin', Cuzzo?" Chad greeted softly as he stood in the doorway.

9

Thirty-year-old Chad was was Bubba's son. Bubba was Obie's twin brother, and Demetrius' first cousin. Bubba and Obie were presently incarcerated in different federal prisons serving fresh, lengthy drug and gun sentences that stemmed from their involvement with RBF. He indisputably resembled both Bubba and Obie so much that when a majority of people saw the trio together, which was a rare sighting, they swore they were indeed triplets.

Born in West Palm Beach but raised in Orlando, Chad lived a similar carefree life as Bizzy growing up. Although Bubba tried stringently to keep him from gravitating towards the life of crime, it was only natural that he became a hustler himself, because the blood of a hustler flowed through his veins. Therefore, his destiny was manifested. Around the age of nineteen, he began bootlegging knockoff products.

He eventually became a big time bootlegger, and he perfected his craft up until Demetrius called upon him last year — almost ten months after Bubba, Obie and a few others in RBF were indicted by the feds — to help keep RBF from going under. He was ambitious, loyal, smart, and he was still learning the ropes of hustling narcotics. Overall, Chad was exactly what Bizzy needed right now, a family member that wore the same size shoe as he did.

"Ain't too much goin on," Bizzy finally replied in his deep voice. His six-foot-five stature towered at least ten inches over his older cousin. He shook Chad's hand and embraced him. He then moved to the side and said, "C'mon in."

After Chad entered the room, Bizzy quickly stuck his head out into the hallway and observed everything before closing and locking the door. He then walked over to an armchair adjacent to the couch Chad had settled down on. "Do ya burn?" Bizzy asked while sitting down.

"I know it's been … it's been," Chad rubbed his chin "like, five or six years since da last time we seen each otha, an' a lotta shit has changed since then, but smokin' like a wildfire is sumthin' that'll never change 'bout me." He grinned slightly. "I did stop smokin' fo' awhile tho' becuz ya ... becuz Demetrius wanted me ta leave petty shit fo' petty niggaz an' become a tycoon myself. "

Bizzy sighed. "Yeah, he tried ta get me ta stop burnin' fo' da same reason. I just kept on blowin' tho' becuz I thought I knew er'thang an' didn't need his guidance back then. Boy, how wrong was I? Becuz I realize now that I dunno shit an' that I shoulda listened ta my pops." He paused momentarily before changing the topic. "How come I didn't see ya at da funeral?"

"Ta be one hun'ed wit'cha, I was too paranoid. I still think da feds are two seconds from bookin' my ass. Cuzzo ... da last few days of Demetrius' life was so ... I didn't know what ta do once he was gone. Then, whoeva offed Demetrius, I swear that they're out ta get me, too." He lowered his head. "I know I shoulda stopped by ta pay my respects, but ... I was just too scared ta' do it, Cuzzo."

When it appeared to Bizzy that Chad was close to crying, he said, "Bruh, I understand."

"Cuzzo, I told Demetrius that a bitch was gonna get da best of him. I told him ova an' ova ..."

"What bitch?" Bizzy questioned with a raised brow.

"I dunno what da bitch name was or what she look like. I just know that whateva bitch he was fuckin' wit befo' he got murked, eitha set him up or clouded his better judgement. One way or da otha I told him that a bitch was gonna be his downfall. An' da crazy thing is that I feel like he knew a bitch was gonna get him killed."

Bizzy did know about a bitch his father was fucking with before he was murdered, but he wasn't sure if Chad was referring to the same female. The chick he knew a little bit about went by the name Beauti, and she was supposedly a sexy bitch, that's all he knew. He searched the entirety of Palm Beach County high and low for her, as well as social media, and wound up with no promising leads. *I'll find you, Beauti,* he said to himself, *and when I do, I'm going to show you an alternate ending to the Beauti and the Beast!*

11

Moving past that, Bizzy rolled up some loud, and they proceeded to watch TV and smoke in silence. Approximately ten minutes later, the blunt was a half-inch long roach sitting in the ashtray on the coffee table.

"I bet'cha ain't smokin' on nuttin' like that," Bizzy declared, looking like a sleepy Jet Li.

Resembling a drowsy Jackie Chan and smiling from ear to ear, Chad responded, "That shit … ai'ight."

They both laughed.

"Ai'ight," Bizzy said after the laughter ended. "It's time ta get serious." He stared directly into Chad's bloodshot eyes. "Now, it's a fact that'chu an' me combined dunno a quarter of what my pops knew, but wit da knowledge that'chu got from being 'round my pops befo' he passed, along wit da shit I know, da two of us togetha gon' try ta revive RBF. I'm pretty sho' da feds shut down all da legit businesses RBF managed an' I ain't trippin' bout that right now. What I wanna do first is get some of da illegal dealings that RBF ran back on point, 'specially da hustlin' division. Da only problem is that I don't have all da money or da few good men needed ta kick this shit off."

"Well, Demetrius left me wit a few contacts ta hit up when shit got like this. I never tried contactin' anybody on that list cuz I felt like da game was over. But, I think da people on that list will shoot us a few bucks, or help us ta get up an' runnin', becuz they were loyal ta Demetrius." He paused. "Now, as fo' da few good men ya lookin' fo', I can't help ya on' that becuz I have a hard time trustin' anybody after what happened ta Demetrius. An' ta be honest, I'm skeptical 'bout that list now that I said that."

"I feel ya," Bizzy said. "Hmmm … what about da last few niggaz that were helpin' y'all move all that work, like Virgil? Him an' my pops been cool since they were jits, so I know he'll help."

Chad slowly shook his head. "Cuzzo, you ain't heard what happened ta Virgil, huh?"

"Naw, what happened?"

12

"Cuzzo, yo pops fucked him an' this otha dude named Buckey up. Man, I was there when he had these four sadistic, crazy mothafuckas torture an' mutilate 'em both befo' feedin' 'em to da gators."

Shocked by the news, Bizzy asked, "What he did that fo'?"

"I know ya heard 'bout his last load gettin' jacked, rite?"

"Uh-huh."

"So ya heard them Triple S niggaz were behind it too, rite?"

Bizzy nodded with a fierce expression on his face. "Yeah, an' I'ma take care of 'em, too. They're on my to-do list."

"Well, Cuzzo, Virgil ran his mouth so fuckin' much that Demetrius knew he had to 'ventually put a handle on him befo' da wrong thang came out his mouth. Virgil was a key piece in our plan, however, an' we needed him at da time. So Demetrius decided to keep a close eye on him 'til da time was rite.

"Wheneva Demetrius had ta leave outta town ta handle bizness, he had me watch Virgil an' his peeps that were on our team. On a few occasions, I caught Virgil an' his peeps havin' secret meetings without Demetrius' permission. So, since I neva liked Virgil becuz of his big mouth, I told Demetrius what da play was.

"Then, all of a sudden, da biggest load in RBF's history gets jacked. Demetrius suspected Virgil had sumthin' ta do wit da lick, an' so did I. Demetrius then interrogated, tortured an' killed him an' Buckey. Virgil's otha buddy got away." He closed his eyes. "Cuzzo, they did er'thang unimaginable ta Virgil an' Buckey. They were fucked up!"

"Damn." Bizzy took a second to gather his thoughts. "Well, I guess that's that. RBF is no longer a factor. We can't do nuthin'."

Chad quickly sat up. "Hell naw, Cuzzo. I ain't 'bout ta let wha' Demetrius, my pops an' my uncle Obie started from nuttin' go down like dis." He paused briefly. "I ain't gon' lie, I ain't want ta deal wit this shit no mo'... I was movin' on. But after ya reached out ta me, an' I see ya gotta vision, I'm ready now. Demetrius ain't die an' my pops an' unc ain't get locked up fo' nuttin'. Listen… Demetrius," he leaned closer to Bizzy, "promised that he was gonna take care of his family as long as he lived. Now that he gone, it's up ta you an' me ta step up an' put da family bizness on our backs."

"I feel ya, bruh," Bizzy agreed," but it's just us two. We can't do this shit by ourselves, can we?"

Chad shook his head no. "But I got my dawg JuneBug ta hit up. I trust him. He most likely willin' ta tag along. Plus, we might as well see who is down on this list that Demetrius gave me. If he trusted them, I can too, I guess.

"Honestly tho, do ya think this worth it? We're just two sons of big-time dope boyz tryna take over a major operation we weren't deeply involved in."

Chad gazed seriously at Bizzy. "If ya satisfied wit workin' a nine ta five, like sweatin' in da hot ass sun or burnin' up while cookin' fries, then it ain't worth it. But if ya wanna put in a lil' hard work all day, er' day, ta eventually see mo Gz than a Gucci bag, then I'll tell ya ta stop actin' like our fathers produced two lames that dunno how ta be bosses, an' let's go chase this paper till our feet bleed!"

Bizzy weighed Chad's last statement in his mind. After about twenty seconds, he began examining his forearms and hands before looking towards the blazing sun shining through the hotel's windows. Then he replied, "Bruh, I hate walkin' in da heat fo' long periods of time, let alone workin' in it. An' da only thang I know how to cook is a bird, an' I ain't talkin' bout da kind that lays eggs."

They both burst into laughter.

"Cuzzo, since ya talkin' bout chicken, I'm hungrier than an Ethiopian lookin' at a Snicker's commercial." He smiled, then added, "Hungry? Why wait?"

"Well, I don't wanna hold ya up no longer, bruh." He stood up and Chad stood too. "Just text my cell when ya got them contacts fo' me an' after ya hit up ya dawg, okay?"

"I got 'cha."

The two embraced briefly.

"It's good seein' ya."

"Same here, Cuzzo."

As Bizzy walked Chad to the door, he said, "Oh, by da way, if we do decide ta set this off, we ain't fuckin' wit that white girl that much, eitha."

Chad turned around and looked at Bizzy. "If we ain't pushin' major powda, then what we sellin? Girl Scout cookies?"

Bizzy simply smiled, and said, "I'll get back wit 'cha on that after I make a few calls myself."

Chapter Two

March 11, 2010 1:30 pm

Wellington, FL

"Wake up. Devon, wake up, baby," Miracle insisted as she rubbed the back of her soft hand over Devon's cheek. "Dee, wake up."

While stretching and yawning, Devon awoke rather peacefully. "What 'chu want?"

"Eewww," Miracle suddenly said while frowning.

"What, girl?" Devon grumbled while squinting a bit. "What's wrong?"

"Wasn't nothin' wrong a second ago... until you blew that hot ass mornin breath in my face. Eewww!" She covered her nose and mouth with her hand. "You need to get up and handle that," she added, sounding muffled.

Devon quickly threw the bed covers back, reached up and grabbed Miracle. After yanking Miracle down onto the bed, Devon began to plant wet kisses all over Miracle's face.

"Eewww! Stop it!" she shouted in between laughing. "You're goin' to melt my face! Stop!" Although Miracle actively squirmed and kicked, Devon knew that she really wasn't trying to get away. Miracle was just seeking some TLC right now, and Devon didn't mind giving it to her. *My baby just needs me to show her love and affection every now and then*, Devon thought while simultaneously kissing and tickling her playfully.

After about thirty pop kisses, Devon concluded the romp by passionately kissing Miracle, and the kiss lasted all of a minute. Once their lips unlocked, Devon said, "Now we both got stank-ass mornin' breath."

"Damn you," Miracle proclaimed as she attempted to break out of Devon's embrace. "Now I have to go brush my teeth ... again!"

"No, you not!" Devon said, pulling Miracle back down so that they were body-to-body. During this kiss however, Devon's hands explored Miracle's scantily-dressed build, from her 38F breasts to her twenty-seven-inch waist, down to her forty-four-inch hips and ass. Still, after five years of being nearly inseparable, Devon couldn't help but to highly praise Miracle's five-foot-eight, one-hundred-and-eighty-pound Amazonian body that was covered with a rich dark-chocolate, which she inherited from being a mixture of Jamaican, Haitian and Cuban.

Devon unquestionably adored and loved Miracle to death, not because of her supernatural beauty. It was because Miracle was dependable and true, through thick and thin, which was why Miracle was the one and only for Devon.

Once they unlatched lips again, Miracle whispered, "I love you, Devon."

"I love you too, Marie." There was a pause. "Now, why did you wake me up from my beauty sleep?"

"Oh," Miracle said, propping up on her elbows about three inches from Devon's face. "Somebody been blowin up your phone this mornin'. You ain't hear it?" She paused briefly but continued before Devon could answer." Of course, you ain't hear it, because *somebody* was too busy partyin' till four this mornin'. I hope you had a damn good time without me!"

Devon grimaced. "You had to watch Kamani last nite."

"Sooo, that don't mean you leave me here." She got up and sat on the edge of the bed with her back to Devon. "We could've chilled and ordered a movie or two off of *Netflix* last night or somethin."

Ha, she need to quit all this Oscar-worthy acting, Devon thought. "Awww, I'm sah–wee, boo boo. I really didn't plan on stayin' out so late. I was just kickin' it wit Shan till I realized that yesterday was da one-year anniversary death of —"

"I know, I know." She cut Devon off. "Still… you could've —"

17

Returning the sassiness, Devon cut her off and asked, "Did ya answer my phone? I know yo' nosey ass did, so who was it?"

"You know damn well I ain't answerin' your phone." She turned to face Devon. "Da only person that has been callin' you lately is RahRah. He just …"

"Shit!"

"What?"

Devon's brother, Ronell, aka RahRah, who was five years older, was released from state prison a little over a month ago. Too busy to visit big bro that much during his two and a half-year bid, Devon really felt terrible about neglecting RahRah while he was down. Devon was feeling even worse now because he was home and was still being neglected, involuntarily. Devon owed him proceeds for putting money into Studio X and a life, literally, because if it wasn't for him, the two of them would be fertilizer for the cemetery grass somewhere.

On July 6, 2007, Devon stopped by Downtown Projects to holla at RahRah about business as usual. Unknowingly, Devon walked right into RahRah's crib being invaded by two thugs. After knocking on the door and being snatched into the apartment by one of the thugs, Devon had been taken into a room where RahRah was bruised and bleeding.

One thug searched the place for money and drugs while the other made Devon hand over personal money and jewelry. During that process of emptying pockets and removing jewelry, RahRah miraculously grabbed the concealed .380 on Devon's waist and shot both jack boyz dead. RahRah, unfortunately, had been hit in the thigh with a 7.62 round during the brief shootout and had bled profusely. Nevertheless, Devon remained with RahRah until the police showed up.

They both had been placed under arrest on the spot. After the police obtained Devon's and RahRah's statement, Devon got released from police custody in less than twenty-four hours, while RahRah spent two weeks in the hospital before being booked in the county jail with two first-degree murder charges.

But, after a thorough investigation showed that RahRah had acted in self-defense, he eventually got charged with possession of a firearm by a convicted felon, although the gun was legally registered in Devon's name. In the end, RahRah finally pled out to three years' state time. And RahRah did that time with little support from Devon, the one person he never thought would handle him like he was an off-brand nigga.

Sitting up in bed, Devon began to massage both temples. "Man, I promised RahRah yesterday that I was gonna pick him up at twelve."

"Where were y'all goin'? Was it somewhere important?"

"Naw, not really." Devon sighed. "I was gonna take him car shoppin'. It was a surprise. I know that big bro don't have any wheels, so I was gonna buy him a new school and get it done up fo' him." Devon winced. "Man, I been doin' big bro soooooo wrong."

"Well, you need to call him and tell him you overslept, that's all. He should understand." Miracle grabbed Devon's phone off of the nightstand. "Here. Call him now."

"Naw, I'ma get my ass up an' shoot downtown ta pick him up." Climbing out of the bed, wearing a black wifebeater and gray sweatpants, Devon then walked towards the bathroom. Just before entering the bathroom though, Devon spun around and asked, "Where Rhapsody at?"

Miracle frowned. "Hmph."

"What's that supposed ta mean?"

"Ugh, Dee. You know I don't care too much about that girl. It's bad enough that you got her livin' here with us." She folded her arms over her chest. "So, I don't know where she at, and I can care less where she at." She sucked her teeth, then mumbled, "I hope she headfirst in a dumpster somewhere."

Devon stared at Miracle for a few seconds before smirking. "Marie, I dunno why you don't like that girl. She like ... hmmm... she like a puppy. She loves her owner ta death, which is me, an' she'll do whateva ta keep me happy."

19

"Yeah, and I'm just waitin' for ya lil' puppy to shit on me so I can put that bitch to sleep."

Devon laughed. "That girl terrified of you … fo' some reason." Devon then shrugged. "She ain't gonna do nuttin' an' ya' know this. An fo' da record, we … you an' me … both agreed that it was cool fo' her ta live here. She's our maid, babysitta, errand runna and sex toy." A smile spread across Devon's face. "You gotta admit that she know how ta suck a mean—" With eyes closed, Devon shuddered. "That girl hella talented!"

Miracle was shocked to see that simulated gesture of pleasure, along with the delightful look, on Devon's face. So she angrily grabbed a pillow and threw it as hard as she could. The target was Devon's smiling face, and she landed a direct hit.

"What da?!" was all that Devon could get out before being hit by another pillow. Without hesitating any further, Devon turned around quickly and retreated into the safety of the bathroom. Right as the door was being closed, another pillow hit the door like a missile. "I'm sorry," Devon yelled through the door. "But y' know it's true!"

"Fuck you, Devon! You betta stay in there all day! I swear, I'm goin' to get you when you come out!"

Damn, I'm going to be real late now picking up RahRah, Devon thought with a grin before undressing to hop in the shower. *I'll just have to come out with my surrender flag up once I'm done and suffer the consequences, because she's going to be waiting right there on the bed until I come out.*

"I'm sah-wee, Marie baby! I love you!" Devon concluded in an attempt to bring peace to the situation at hand. "I'ma take ya shoppin' when I get back, okay? Whateva ya want, I'ma get it."

"I want you to kiss my ass, Devon!"

March 11, 2010 1:48 pm

West Palm Beach, FL

The pleasant, breezy day was perfect for dropping the top and putting the dro in the wind. Smoking and cruising the streets without a destination in mind was a pastime that Bumper and Skat did quite often, and it was exactly what they planned on doing for a few hours on this beautiful afternoon.

However, during their aimless expedition, Bumper and Skat ended up with an unexpected itinerary while on their outing when they crossed paths with RahRah, who was sitting on his baby mama's porch on Spruce Avenue in Pleasant City (aka Da City) with a mean mug on his face.

RahRah had been on the porch for the last two hours, waiting patiently for Devon to scoop him up as promised. He had no clue whatsoever where Devon wanted to take him, nor did he know whether Devon was coming or not. He did know that he was almost to the point of saying "Fuck Dee," because he was unable to get in touch with Devon on the phone. He ultimately told himself that he was going to chill another ten minutes before calling someone to pick him up from his aggravating, money-hungry BM's house.

Approximately five minutes later, Bumper rolled down Spruce in his outrageous, burnt orange '74 Caprice, squatting perfectly on twenty-eight-inch Forgiatos with the top peeled back. In his passenger seat was Skat, and in the air when they pulled up and stopped was the smell of exotic. With the twelve dimes quaking in the trunk, both Bumper and Skat mean-mugged RahRah while showcasing the sixteen luxuriant 22-karat gold teeth in their respective mouths, all the while bouncing energetically to the lyrics of Young Jeezy's "White Girl."

Rather than take offense or feel threatened by the menacing display and looks on their faces, RahRah merely laughed at the spectacle his homeboys were putting on for him. The energy emanating from both Bumper and Skat, along with the music that shook the entire block, caused him to eventually start bouncing in the chair on the porch. And since he had no gold in his mouth, he just showcased his pearly whites. He was really beginning to feel better until...

"Arr you nigguhz fuckin' stoopid?" RahRah's BM, Quinterria, shouted as she burst out of the house. Quinterria was one of the jazziest broads in the hood. She kind of resembled Lauren London in the movie *ATL* as far as looks. But she was far from being the sharpest knife in the kitchen drawer. "My damn babee in hea sleepin' an' y'all stoopid-ass nigguhz out hea thowin' a fuckin' block pahty!" She then looked at RahRah. "You'se a fuckin' dummee, ya' know that rite? Yo' broke ass out hea dancin' an' shit. You wanna dance, then you kneed ta go shake yo' ass fo' a dolla, Mistah Chippendale."

Shortly after Quinterria burst out of the crib and began speaking, Bumper had turned the volume down enough so that both he and Skat could hear clearly what she was saying. They both began laughing hysterically once she was done snapping.

Although Quinterria undeniably feared RahRah, she just loved putting him on the spot in front of anybody. So her latest rant was of no surprise to him, because he knew her like the back of his hand. Nevertheless, she should've known the back of his hand would meet her face after showing her ass. Pronto!

SMACK!

"Ratchet bitch, take yo' ass in da house!" he yelled, with his nostrils flared and teeth clenched. "Befo' I beat yo' dumb ass out here!" Seeing that she was taking her sweet time to do as he instructed, and although she was holding her stinging face and sobbing, he grabbed her firmly by the upper arm, opened the house door, shoved her inside and slammed the door. "An' ya betta stay in there, bitch!" He then looked at Bumper and Skat to find them dying laughing at his expense.

Without warning, the house's front window flew open and Quinterria said somewhat tremulously, "I bet'chu won't be out hea when I call my brudda. Punk ass!"

The window slammed shut.

RahRah instantly ran towards the door. Like a mad man, he turned the door knob a few times while yanking the door. After unsuccessfully opening the door, he walked to the window and screamed, "Call yo' brotha! It ain't like I'm scared of da fuck nigga, so call him, bitch!"

Looking at RahRah from the safety of the other side of the window, Quinterria was giggling and sticking her tongue out at him. She then mouthed all types of obscenities at him, calling him everything foul she could pronounce in her limited vocabulary.

Right as RahRah drew back to hit his BM through the glass, Bumper hollered, "Rah! C'mon, let's peel! You trippin' now, Durt!"

RahRah bit his bottom lip and pointed at his BM before pivoting to head in the direction of Bumper's 'Vert. "Ain't been out a good two months an' this bitch 'bout ta make me catch a fresh body," he professed as Skat opened the passenger door and leaned forward for him to climb in. "Da only reason I come over this bitch house is ta—"

"Smash her fine ass," Skat interjected.

Ignoring what was said, RahRah continued, "I only come over nowadays to chill wit my fifteen-month-old lil' girl."

"My bad fo' gettin' ya in trouble, Durt," Bumper said with his signature devilish grin on his face.

Dread-headed Jarvis Clemmons, aka Bumper, was thirty-two years old and the heart of downtown West Palm Beach. He was one hundred percent African, meaning there was no additives running in his veins, and his matte pitch-black skin proved his blood was uncut. If it wasn't for the white of his eyes and the golds in his mouth, his face would be the same as staring into an empty black bucket.

Nobody knew for certain how he wound up with the nickname Bumper, but rumor was that he had been bumped on his head one too many times as a toddler and wasn't "wrapped too tight" in the head. He was in the same class as those Al-Qaida boys in the Middle East. Although he was the streets worse nightmare since

Freddie Krueger and over-respected since the age of fifteen, he was the most down-to-earth, ready-to-give-his-life breed of nigga around his real homies. They consisted of the niggas that managed to survive the terrorist-type of violence that transpired in the streets during the last seventeen years, and RahRah just happened to be one of the niggas that rode with him from the beginning.

"Here, hit this shit an' calm yo' nerves, Durt," Bumper insisted, holding the blunt over his shoulder for RahRah to grab as he slowly pulled off from Quinterria's crib.

Faltering to grab the blunt, RahRah stammered, "I... I... I can't be smokin', dawg. I'm on these papers fo' da next ..."

"Ha!" Skat sneered. "Nigga, you ain't worried 'bout no fuckin' papers, so stop frontin'. You just smelled this shit from a mile away an' got scared ta hit this strong becuz this wasn't out here befo' ya left ta do ya bid, that's all. You and yo' lungs scared of this potent tree."

Keyshon Nesbitt, aka Skat, was a little nigga standing every inch of five-foot-three. Light-skinned like Michael Jackson with braids that touched his shoulders, he was the kind of nigga that misled many to believe he was "all play," because he was always trying to openly clown people, even strangers. Naively believing the twenty-nine-year-old jokester survived this long through his silliness was a misconception that left many taking permanent dirt naps. However, that was just the tip of the iceberg when it came to him putting niggas to rest, because his little man complex and high-yellow skin, not his jokes, played a major part in him earning the street name Skat.

Around the age of sixteen, he finally blanked out when niggas in the hood refused to respect him or take him seriously, mainly because of his height and light complexion. He went on a daily rampage for nearly a year straight, by "chopping at" (he was infatuated with AK-47's) every crowd of niggas that mocked and fucked with him in the past, causing them to "scatter" like roaches when that AK's muzzle light flashed on and off. He still made niggas scatter to this day, but it was primarily for fun now since

24

people in the hood knew not to talk about him or try him in any kind of way.

The two childhood friends, Bumper and Skat, were a deadly combination. Even though it might not   seem   the duo were heartless thugs just by looking at them now, they paid their dues in full, respectively. For instance, Bumper amazingly survived being hit eight times with a carbine fifteen and being shot three times with a MAC-11 less than two months apart from each other. And Skat, by some means, beat four separate first-degree murder charges during the last ten years. People in the streets truly began to think they were Satan's Angels, and they'd both lived up to those expectations since Bumper survived that first attempt on his life and Skat beat that first body.

By 2004, the destructive duo had such a massive following of down-ass niggas throughout downtown West Palm Beach, they decided to give their band of misguided ruffians a title. After a few hours of smoking and joking, the two chose to name themselves the   SunSet Syndicate, aka Triple S, with the word SunSet signifying death. Things in the area suddenly seemed to have gotten worse once the group had a name to represent and they upheld the SunSet Syndicate title to the fullest.

In good time, Triple S were being compared to the Possum Boyz, the ultimate family of hood terrorists and self-made millionaires that conquered downtown West Palm Beach from the seventies until 1988. However, Bumper and Skat both knew when they spawned Triple S, they were not worthy of being mentioned in the same breath as the Possum Boyz, because they had yet to be recognized for doing something diabolical to make South Florida take notice of them. Simply killing petty niggas for no valid reason and selling a brick or two at a time wasn't going to gain them the notoriety they knew they desired.

Nevertheless, that all changed for Triple S during the early morning of March 6, 2009, in Homestead, FL, with the unforeseen and valuable help of their dawg, Devon. Triple S presumably pulled off the biggest drug heist by a small group of goons in

Florida's history when they came up on three hundred and forty-seven bricks of that Tony Montana.

But the best part about the lick, though, besides the amount of work they'd obtained, was that Triple S had jacked their rival. Demetrius, aka Kilo, was the head of RBF and a legend from the very streets they roamed. A week after that robbery, Demetrius got whacked out of the blue. Then, after a twenty-one-year tenure in the game, RBF, for the time being, folded due to infrastructure problems, leaving the precious streets of West Palm Beach for Triple S to take over with little to no resistance.

Now, Bumper and Skat were balling out of control and expanding their operation with the niggas that had been through hell and back with them since day one. They had officially become millionaires in the hood, and they were no longer disclaiming the rumors they'd surpassed the Possum Boyz. Yeah, they were recognized and rising now. And they were quietly and patiently waiting for any opposition to rear their heads so they could readily chop them off.

Phone rings and vibrates

"Aye!" RahRah yelled at Bumper before tapping his shoulder. Once Bumper looked over his shoulder, he motioned for the music to be turned down. Bumper promptly cut off the subwoofers and lowered the mids and highs just enough to hold a conversation. RahRah finally answered his phone. "What's up, Dee? I'm wit Bumper an' Skat ... we just slidin' an' smokin' in West Palm Beach... Naw, I ain't smokin' ... I know, but never mind that. Why ya left me hangin' earlier? I'm startin' ta feel like ya tryna duck me, like ya ain't fuckin' wit'cha boy... ya' know what? I ain't trippin' ... I dunno when I'ma be back ... A car? ... It's all good, you can keep ya money ... listen, I ain't tryna go through this wit'cha rite now ... holla."

"I don't mean ta be in ya B. I., Durt," Bumper blurted out as he looked over his shoulder once again, "but it sounds like Devon been dodgin' ya lately." He paused. "Ta keep it a hun'ed wit'cha,

I ain't seen you two niggas togetha since ya jumped. What up wit that?"

"Man, we were ... down fo' each otha, know what I'm sayin'? When I got jammed this last time, Dee came ta viso *every day* da jail had visitation while I wuz at Gun Club an' had my books fatter than Mo'Nique. We were ... straight then. We had plans ta put down da pack an' invest our bread into a business. Dee used da money I put up ta open Studio X." RahRah inhaled deeply before exhaling. "But shit changed when I finally went up da road in da panhandle wit those redneck-ass crackas. Its's like Dee fa'got all about a nigga until I was nine months from da door. An' during those nine months, Dee finally hopped on da road ta come see me an' started sendin' me a few dollas again. Befo' then, if it wasn't fo' you two niggas, that time up da road woulda been real stressful."

"Nigga," Skat said before sucking his teeth, "you act like we some fuck boys that don't look out fo' our own. You knew we were gonna send yo' *scary* ass a bet er' week, nigga."

Before RahRah could snap, Bumper said, "If ya want, I can put ya on, Durt. Today! All ya gotta do is say so..."

"Cuz we sho' ain't finna beg yo' broke ass ta get this money wit us, homie."

Once again, Bumper cut in before RahRah could go ham on Skat. "Durt, I know how it is ta do a bid. When ya get out, ya lie to ya'self by sayin' how ya gonna getta job, how ya gonna stop smokin' while ya on papers, how ya gonna be there fo' ya lil ones, how ya gonna do this, how ya gonna do that. But all that positive shit go out da window, Durt, when reality hits ya ass an' ya see that'cha broke wit no car, no job, no place ta call ya own. An if ya do find a job, it's eitha one that's under da table an' ya have ta bust ya ass in da hot sun, or it's a legit one that ain't payin' nuttin'.

"I know this cuz I been there, Durt ... a few times. So, I'm tellin' ya ta keep it real wit ya'self an' let's eat, becuz as you can see, we tryna eat till our bellies burst, Durt."

27

"Yeah, nigga," Skat chimed in. "Becuz if ya ass dependin' on luck ta get'cha on ya Reebok Classic-wearin' feet this time, just rememba that dependin' on da rabbit's foot ain't work fo' da fuckin' rabbit, nigga."

RahRah nodded his head slightly in agreement. He knew what they were both saying was the God's honest truth. He could recollect how he lied to himself when he got out of prison in 2004, which was around the time Triple S was formed, after serving a tad bit over five years for armed robbery. He tried everything in his power to stay out of the streets back then, and he probably would've stayed on the straight and narrow path if Devon never proposed that they went into the hustling business together. Yet, he didn't blame Devon for putting him on, he blamed society for being biased because he wanted to do the right thing.

These two niggas are right, he thought. *I might as well get on my feet now instead of waiting to hop in the game later on down the road after becoming fed up with trying to do the right thing and nothing good happens for me.*

"I see it's on ya mind, nigga," Skat flippantly said. "So while ya thinkin' 'bout that, think about this." He turned his little body around in his seat to face RahRah. Then, in a serious voice, he said, "Nigga, we're livin' in a world today where lemonade is made from artificial flavors and furniture polish is made from *real* lemons."

Bumper quickly glanced at Skat with a confused look on his black face. He then slowly turned to look at the road ahead before shooting his eyes over to Skat again. "Durt, what da fuck that 'posed ta mean?"

"Yeah … what da fuck you talkin' 'bout?" RahRah asked with a puzzled look on his face as well.

With an expression on his face that said he didn't know what the fuck that meant either, Skat still confidently commenced to explain his off-the-wall quote. "Nigga … that shit mean …" he delayed for a second or three to think. "Yeah, I got it now … nigga, that shit mean … it mean da world is fucked up!"

Bumper and RahRah both burst into laughter.

"Durt, you gots ta be da smartest *dumb* nigga that I know."

While laughing, RahRah said, "Yeah, *you* need ta smoke some *weak* and leave that strong alone cuz that white boy in ya comin' out."

"Nigga, y' know I ain't ... ohhh, if I had my stick, I'd shot ya in da fuckin' face fo' tryin' me like that," Skat angrily said, damn near standing up in the passenger seat.

"I know," RahRah said while still laughing. "That's why I said it cuz ya stickless."

"So, what'cha finna do, Durt?" Bumper inquired, changing the topic. "You wanna sell bricks? Or do you wanna lay bricks?"

Without delay, RahRah answered, "Yeah, I'm down." He paused briefly. "But instead of bricks, I need ta start off wit a few zones. At least till I get back into my routine."

"That's what's happ'nin'." Bumper merely shrugged. "Now, don't even trip 'bout that chump change Devon owe you cuz you'll make that back in a few weeks. We damn near got da county in a chokehold. We got that work on deck. So I'ma bless ya wit' a few racks ta get'cha wardrobe on beat an' ta get a lil' place. An' it sounded like Devon was gonna buy a slider fo' ya today, but don't worry 'bout that either. I got'cha. You can borrow one of my *seven* whips till ya got enuff ta cop ya own." He spun around to face RahRah and added, "You Triple Snow."

"Whoa, I thought I been Triple S, nigga!" RahRah said. "Shit, I grew up wit y'all niggas, too. We put in alotta work togetha."

"Yeah, you always were Triple S. But when ya jumped from prison round '04, when we were really puttin' in work, you an' Devon had y'all own agenda then." He grabbed a fresh blunt from the ashtray and held it over his shoulder for RahRah to take. "Rite now tho,' this here diff'rent, this beyond what you an' da homie Devon had goin' on. *We* got da streets on smash now. It's just that I need all my real niggas wit me becuz, sooner or later, all this layin' back an' livin' good ... just know that this shit is gonna get

29

real *ugly*, Durt, an' I need ta know if ya gonna be ready when it does. So, ya ready, Durt? Fo' da good, da bad and da ugly?"

RahRah knew exactly how to respond. "From sunrise ... till SunSet."

Flame

Chapter Three

March 13, 2010 3:14 pm

Palm Beach Gardens, FL

Down to the last contact on the list Chad had given him, Bizzy was undoubtedly feeling as if everything Demetrius had accomplished with RBF was going to disintegrate in just a few minutes. The list contained five people that Demetrius knew he could depend on to manage all of RBF's businesses for him if he were to go on a long vacation, to jail, or the worst-case scenario, to the grave.

Unbeknownst to Bizzy, however, all but one of the five people on the list were bottom tier members of RBF. When Demetrius chose to give the list to Chad with that single high-level RBF member on it, he did so because he felt that one person would be intelligent enough to repudiate any illegal dealings between them if the police ever got a hold of his treasured black book which contained numbers and information about all of his dealings.

The first four people on the list he spoke to knew about Demetrius' tragic fate, of course, and were no longer interested in being linked to RBF. Out of those four, only one feared being indicted by the federal government. However, all four came clean and said they didn't respect or trust Bizzy, with all of them claiming he had no experience on how to run a billion-dollar outfit, due to his immature way of thinking and his absence during all the substantial business moves that RBF had engaged in over the years.

They were absolutely correct.

And Bizzy agreed.

What they said of him was dead on the money. He was in no way prepared for the task at hand, mentally or financially. Yet rather than give up after being disappointed, disrespected and rejected by the first four on the list, he nonchalantly called the last person on the list, expecting off the jump to be turned down for a fifth and final time. And the only reason he called the last person was at least then he could say that he called everybody and strived to keep RBF in the game, instead of not trying at all.

When he placed the final call, and informed the person who he was, he immediately heard how the man on the line became nervous. *Damn, another one that's scared of the feds,* he thought at that time, as the man proceeded to ramble on and on about nonsense. *I tried, Pops.*

However, the man promptly settled down and told Bizzy that he wanted to meet face-to-face to discuss things.

After a second of thinking it over, Bizzy ultimately agreed to meet up with the guy, and they hung up once they had confirmed a time and place.

It was now a minute until the time Bizzy agreed to confront this unknown man. As he waited impatiently, he gradually began to feel out of place, just sitting in his lightly tinted 2010 Cadillac CTS-V in the parking lot of a colossal marina. Whereas his car seemed to belong among the Beamers, Benzs and Bentleys that sparkled and shimmered in the packed parking lot, his black skin was in contrast to the white folks that were everywhere! On top of that, an ancient-looking white man, riding through the parking lot on a golf cart, had yet to pass by his car without staring long and hard.

"Man, where in da fuck is this guy?" he said to no one in particular.

He checked the time on the platinum Rolex that his father gave him two years ago on his twenty-fifth birthday. The watch read 5:20 pm. "Maaannnn, I'm 'bout ready ta haul ass."

Right when he finished talking to himself, the old white man in the golf cart was riding by again. But this time the man rode by twice as slow as before, while gazing at him through Coke bottle glasses.

"Fuck this," Bizzy said as he reached for the keys already in the ignition. "I ain't 'bout ta go to jail fo' …"

*Boom Boom Boom *

33

Ducked way down in the seat with a snug grip on the Glock 17 tucked between the center console and the driver's seat, Bizzy frantically scanned the windows. He upped his fire when he saw a young-looking white man with ghostly white skin, standing at his passenger window and staring uneasily at him. The man simply stood frozen in place as if paralyzed, before mouthing something to him. He was unable to hear the man clearly, so he reluctantly unlocked the door. He kept his Glock drawn and aimed at the man's face, however.

"Please, put that down," the white man pled as he sat down slowly in the passenger seat with his hands up by his face.

"Who are you?" Bizzy asked, gun still pointed at the white man's face.

"My name is Kelly Kronkite." He stopped to cautiously wipe the sweat that was forming on his forehead. "I'm a … pardon me, I *was* an associate of Demetrius. My condolences for your loss." The thirty-one-year-old Palm Beach Gardens resident, and the co-owner of Kronkite Konstruction with his father, Karl Kronkite, had been dealing with Demetrius nearly six years prior to his death. He used to purchase ten kilos weekly from Demetrius, until he agreed to assist Demetrius with his last scheme, which consisted of him moving a hundred and thirty kilos and paying for them later.

Selling a single brick for twenty-nine thousand was a piece of cake since he sold to his upper-class peers exclusively. He was a real intelligent man, a real business man, and he was a real pea in the same pod as Demetrius when it came to money. His favorite motto was, "Having money isn't everything, it's the *only* thing."

Bizzy slowly lowered his weapon.

"Aahhh, thank you," Kelly declared before rubbing his chest. After taking a few deep breaths, he said, "So, you must be Demetrius' son? It's funny how we have never met in person until now, being that your father always talked highly of you."

"What did ya have ta tell me that's so important fo' us to meet face ta face?" Bizzy asked, disregarding all that insignificant shit Kelly was saying and getting straight to the point.

"Well, I wanted to meet with …"

Kelly stopped talking, and he was no longer looking at Bizzy. Instead, he mutely looked past him.

Bizzy quickly turned around to find the old white man from the golf cart standing at his window.

"Let me handle this," Kelly said. "Roll down your window, please."

Bizzy covertly hid his gun first before rolling down the window.

Kelly then leaned slightly towards Bizzy and said, "Earl?"

"Mr. Kronkite?" Earl replied in a booming but dry voice.

"What seems to be the problem, Earl?"

Earl, sporting a prodigious pair of thick-lensed glasses resting on his abnormally big nose, looked down at Bizzy with a disgusted look and said, "I was just making my rounds when I spotted you. Is everything okay, Mr. Kronkite?"

"Yes. I'm just giving my … my friend here a pep talk before we board my boat. See, he's never been on the open water, and I was just telling him that open water is the most relaxing place to be on earth. Isn't that right, Earl?"

Keeping a steady eye on Bizzy with disdain written all over his face, he said, "Yes, it sure is, Mr. Kronkite." He suddenly began to cough explosively without even attempting to cover his mouth, causing Bizzy to recoil in disgust. After about fifteen seconds, as if nothing ever happened, he said, "Well, do you need me to fuel up your boat for you, Mr. Kronkite?"

"No, Earl. It's already full. Thanks."

"Well, since…since everything is okay here, Mr. Kronkite, I'll continue on with my rounds."

"Yes, Earl, everything is honky-dory."

"Okie-dokie." Earl finally looked away from Bizzy to wave at Kelly. Then, he looked down at Bizzy again with an expression on his face that said, "I'm watching you closely, nigger," and walked off while coughing again.

Bizzy rolled up his window.

"That was Earl," Kelly explained. "He's a retired veteran and he owns a couple of boats here. He has nothing but time on his hands, so he just patrols the parking lot as if he were patrolling the jungles of—"

"Fuck that," Bizzy cut him off, "get back to bizness."

"Right." Kelly cleared his throat before shifting into a more comfortable position. "Pardon me for being a nervous wreck. It's just that I hope I don't upset you by saying … well … *phew*… might as well get straight to it … I've quit the business."

"What?"

"Wait just a sec …"

"Man, you coulda tole me dis shit ova da phone! You got me …"

"Wait, wait, wait!" Kelley interjected. He didn't say another word until he saw that Bizzy had calmed down, then he continued. "I've quit the business … because of the feds." He suddenly began to look around. "Your father knew very well that the DEA was watching him after they were unsuccessful in removing him from the streets for good. When he contacted me after he'd won his trial, I told him right then that I was done because I didn't want to be involved with him no more … business-wise. However, your father, who was a very persuasive man, convinced me that the feds would never know I existed, he assured me of this." He sighed. "I trusted Demetrius …" He paused to look around again.

"What da fuck ya keep lookin' around fo'? You makin' me mo' paranoid than I already am!"

"Listen, and listen carefully," Kelly stated sternly, his grayish-blue eyes staring intently into Bizzy's pupils. "Do not pursue your father's dream of being the biggest drug dealer in the…just let it go. If you let it go now, then you won't have to look over your shoulder like I have to." He paused briefly. "And a federal agent by the name of Zimmerman won't have a reason to harass you."

"Huh?"

"I have to go," Kelly said as he opened the door. "He may be watchin' us now." He then climbed out of the car. Before he closed the door, he stuck his head in the car and said, "And just so you'll leave me alone forever, I left some money in a locker today at a bowling alley in West Palm Beach called All-Star Lanes. Do you know the place?"

"Yeah."

"Good. Now, because of the respect that I have for your father, consider this as me buying my way out." Kelly inconspicuously tossed a locker key on Bizzy's passenger seat. "And remember what I said ... let it go!" He then sighed. "But if you're anything like your father, I know you won't take heed to my advice." With that, Kelly closed the door, looked in all directions cautiously, and walked away as nonchalantly as he could muster.

Bizzy grabbed the locker key and stared at it as he twirled it in his fingers. *I hope this the key to solving all the problems I'm having,* he thought as he put the key in the center console and started the car. *There's only one way to find out, though.*

March 13, 2010 11:58pm

West Palm Beach, FL

Almost two years after the doors opened, StudioX was just as full, if not fuller, than its monumental grand opening night. Despite the return of hot spring weather, which ultimately brought the tricks that loved to blow money out from hiding, StudioX had indeed established itself as one of the swankiest, must-see gentlemen's clubs in the south. And the club wouldn't have attained the recognition it had if it wasn't for the ingenuity and boldness of Devon.

The four-hundred-person maximum capacity, fifty-two-hundred square foot building, in a busy plaza a stone's throw from

I-95 on Palm Beach Lakes Boulevard, was state-of-the-art and one-of-a-kind. The captivating facade was illuminated in animated, bright art-deco colors, and featured an entrance walkway lined with dancing, multi-colored landscape lights.

Upon entering StudioX, to the immediate left, there was a gift shop that sold G- to XXX-rated items and novelties. After walking straight ahead and going through a security check, there was an electric sliding door that led to a fifty-seat restaurant and bar that had large flat screens, dart boards, poker video game systems and pool tables. Another sliding door to the right in the restaurant-bar led to where the stripping took place.

At the back of this large room there was a huge stage with three poles. And on both sides of the stage were two large aquariums filled with exotic fish. Also, on opposite sides of the room were two smaller stages. Lining the walls were plush leather couches. On the floor, spaced out, were ten privacy booths with La-Z-Boy style chairs. The DJ booth was on a platform next to a large bar to the left of the room. And finally, the main attraction, behind sequin beads to the right of the huge stage was where the bubbly flowed and the pussy sold – the Champagne Room.

With every stripper doing what they did best and every tipper throwing money like it grew on trees, StudioX, for the umpteenth time, was the place to be tonight, and the night was still young. Devon and Miracle both had made their customary rounds separately, meeting and greeting all the fresh faces, familiars and celebrities before rendezvousing at the bar. They then ordered drinks and chatted with each other about business matters as usual since they were entrepreneurs, not patrons, whenever they were in their establishment.

During the middle of their conversation, however, DJ Knotty Head suddenly cut off the music and announced, "Comin' to da stage now, fellaz, is one'ah my favorite dancers in South Florida, fo' real! Shawty commands er'body's attention while on stage, an' she is indisputably goin' down in my book as the best ta work a pole – ever! Fo' y'all niggaz that come here er' nite know 'zactly who I'm talkin' 'bout. Becuz instead of y'all spendin' quality time wit da ol' lady an' kidz, you come out er' nite ta break y'allselves when this phenomenal female blesses da stage.

"An' fo' y'all new niggaz, y'all need ta start thinkin' of a great excuse now fo' ya ol' lady, becuz ya leavin' here tonite wit ya pockets on *E* afta shawty stops shakin' an' clappin' her trance-inducin' ass. So, witout furtha ado, y'all give it up fo' y'all girl … my girl…Rhap-so-dy!"

To the music of Ludacris' "My Bitch Bad," Rhapsody, wearing a yellow eccentric strappy bra and matching thong that complimented her Hershey chocolate complexion and honey blonde hair-do, magically appeared on the huge main stage. She immediately hopped on the pole, flipped upside down, did the widest split in the universe and slid down the pole ever so slowly while shaking her thighs.

After her opening signature move, she stood up and didn't waste any time strutting her 36 DD-25-44-inch frame to the edge of the stage where dozens of hands full of money waited impatiently to place a dollar, or fifty, in her thong or garter belt. The five-foot-two, one-hundred-thirty-pound Rhapsody then squatted down, spread her legs wide open for her frenzied fanatics, and literally swept the money on the stage with her juicy ass. Seconds later, she laid on her back, raised up on her neck and shoulders with her legs stretched out to the ceiling and began to p-pop, causing the mixed gender crowd to suddenly go into a chaotic struggle to rub on her fat cat through her barely-there thong.

With a few horny, raunchy partisans toiling to pull her tiny thong to the side and without hindering them from having their way with her cookies, she commenced to removing her top, exposing her perfectly round and soft double Ds. As if walking and chewing bubble gum were the most difficult things to do together, the crowd faced a mind-boggling dilemma when they had to choose between fondling her moderately wet pussy, or caressing her robust titties.

She didn't care what they did, however, she was simply eating up all the attention ... and the money! *Yeah, give me all y'all money*, she said to herself with a smile, as all types of bills covered the stage around her and filled up her thong and garter belt. *Get it in now*, she mused, *so I can get mines in later when I go shopping with all y'all money.*

"Damn, that girl sho' know how ta put on a show," Devon said, standing in place mesmerized. "She prolly got at least five racks on her rite now. ... an' she ain't been on stage three minutes!"

Miracle looked at Devon who was to the point of drooling and said, "Hmph, looks like she know how to be a nasty hoe to me. That's all she know how to do. Lettin' all those dirty, filthy niggas up there finger-fuck and rub... "

"Why you sound so jealous when half of that money she getting is ours?"

"Jealous?" Miracle sucked her teeth. "Why should I be jealous when she, not me, up there bein' a nasty hoe?" She then rolled her eyes. "I didn't have to do half of wha' she up there doin' and I was —"

"Rite," Devon interposed, "you were gettin' money like that —"

"Without havin' to do shit that a hoe does," Miracle added. "All she doin' up there is bein' a hoe, point-blank period!"

Devon smiled.

Although Rhapsody was hands-down the best in her class, which was the "anythang-goes" class, Miracle was arguably the best money-making dancer, when it boiled down to her performing for a crowd without all the extracurricular touching and groping. She earned the name Miracle at the age of nineteen, during her very first day of taking the stage when the DJ that day declared it was a "Miracle" how she made a section of the pole vanish between her ass cheeks.

She danced and held her own for a year until she met Devon, who became her pimp/manager at that time. She continued to strip until Devon fell deeply in love with her, and made her hang up her stilettos to help manage StudioX. She became the secretary and treasurer of the club and she still held those positions, along with others, to this day.

"Heeeyyy, Dee!" someone yelled from halfway across the room.

Devon could distinguish that unique voice from a mile away. "Wassup, Shan?"

"I almost didn't see you over here," Shan said in a cartoonish, high-pitched drawl before giving Devon a hug. "It's been two days since I last seen you. So what? You tryna hide from me?"

"Why would I do such a thang?" Devon said sarcastically. "Y' know I fucks wit'chu cuz you … you my bitch."

"I better be, dammit." Shan giggled. "Oh, I'm sorry, girl. How you doin', Miracle?"

"I'm fine, Shan," Miracle proclaimed flatly with a fake smile plastered on her face. Miracle didn't necessarily dislike or hate Shan, she just didn't appreciate how Shan was so… fake. Regardless, she understood how tight Devon was with Shan and she didn't mind their harmless friendship, so she merely kept the peace by being fake as well. "How you?"

"Girrrrlllll, I'm fine. I'm just getting' my drink on and …"

"I hope that'chu remBembera what happened da last time you were …" Devon changed voices to impersonate Shan's, "…just gettin' yo drink on."

Shan giggled again. "I know Dee, and I cannot say thank you enough. That's why you my dawg for life and I'll … ooohhhh, I'll … Giiirrrrlllll, don't get me started. And I promise that what happened to me will not ever happen again."

A little over two months ago, on the night of StudioX's New Year's Bash, at approximately four in the morning, Devon saved Shan's life. The two had never encountered each other until that night. It all started when Devon stepped outside of StudioX to get some of the fresh wintery air. Amazingly, Devon was the only person outside at that time. Then, all of a sudden, the loudest scream came from the parking lot. Devon, who was drunk as hell, absolutely had no intentions of checking out the scene. But the screaming persisted again a few seconds later and it didn't cease.

Devon cautiously peeped around to see if anybody else happened to hear the same screaming prior to going to investigate where the screaming person was. However, when the screaming ceased, a concerned Devon then untucked the trusty .380 and walked towards where the screaming came from. Carefully looking between the rows of cars that littered the plaza's parking lot, Devon stumbled across a man bent down over what appeared to be a female's body. Upon further inspection, Devon noticed the man was actually choking the quiet and unmoving female on the ground and initiated the intervention by busting twice into the chilly air.

The startled man quickly unhanded the female's throat after hearing the shots and hurriedly ran away once he saw Devon with the .380 fixed on him. After the man hopped into a car and sped off, Devon run over to the unconscious female and called the police.

"Hmm-huh, you say that now," Devon chided. Devon then finally noticed Shan's outstanding outfit and added, "What in da hell you got on, girl? See, that's exactly what I'm talkin' 'bout. Wit'chu drinkin' an' wearin' that shit, what happened last time is bound ta happen again."

"What? This ugly dress!" If there was a flyest-dressed competition in the club tonight, Shan would've took the trophy home without having to worry about any competition. The provocative, form-fitting red Vera Wang cocktail dress, with its plunging neckline and revealing cutouts, paired with stunning red Christian Louboutin peep-toe pumps, was a red carpet-worthy ensemble, especially since it was in conformity with Shan's caramel skin tone, slim shape and auburn-highlighted short, curly hair. "This is just my party dress, Dee."

"It looks more like your 'fuck me' dress," Miracle mumbled loud enough for only Devon to hear.

With a smile, Devon stealthily nudged Miracle with an elbow.

The trio then held a brief convo before Rhapsody came up on them in a hurry.

"Daddy, I have to talk to you," Rhapsody rapidly said, nearly out of breath.

"What's wrong now?" Devon asked full of concern, seeing how distressed Rhapsody was.

"I got …" she started, but she stopped after she saw Shan was standing there trying to be nosey … as always. "Scuse me, Shan, but …"

"Alright girl, damn!" Shan said with much attitude. "It's 'bout that time fo' me ta find me a baller anyway, so hi and bye, child!"

Rhapsody waited until Shan was good and gone before she continued. "Dee, I got … I got anotha one of those notes," she said with a terrified look on her baby doll face. "An' this one is worser than da last ones."

"Damn, that's da fifth one this week!" Devon declared.

"I know." She inhaled deeply and exhaled hard. "I know you said it was prolly a new nigga that's simply infatuated wit me, but … I'm startin' ta get scared now, daddy."

"Let me see the note," Miracle said.

With trembling hands, Rhapsody gave Miracle a folded-up napkin. She then looked around to see if anybody was looking their way.

Miracle casually unfolded the napkin and silently read the writing:

I Don't Apresheate How U Lettin Dem Niggaz Feel All Ova MY Body. I Kno U Only Doin It Bcuz U Lost. But Now Dat I Found U Im Gonna Reskue U.

Hold Tite, Ok? DADDY Got U!

Once she was finished, Miracle swallowed the lump in her throat and handed the note to Devon. While she read the disturbing note, Miracle asked Rhapsody, "Where did you find this note?

Was it wrapped in a fifty-dollar-bill and thrown on stage as the previous ones?"

Rhapsody shot her eyes to the floor and shook her head no.

"Where was it then?" Devon asked angrily while balling up the note. "Cuz this shit ain't amusin'."

"It was…somebody put…it was wit da money in my thong and taped to a hundred-dolla-bill this time," she said with tears forming in her eyes. "Daddy, I'm scared. What am I gonna do?"

"Well… I'm…" Devon sighed. After nearly ten seconds of quick thinking, Devon said, "I honestly dunno what ta do rite now."

Flame

Chapter Four

March 17, 2010 7:10 am

West Palm Beach, FL

Awkward.

It was still somewhat awkward, and taking a bit of time to get used to, but Devon decided to play the hand that was dealt. Instead of just having to keep in touch with one brother, RahRah, who was actually of no relation, except that they grew up together as orphans in the custody of RahRah's grandmother, Miss Candace, Devon had to now keep in touch with a newfound brother, Bizzy. They were informally reunited on March 14, 2009.

For Devon, having a new brother wasn't too bad. However, having to keep that brother from discovering who actually murdered their father, the man Bizzy loved more than anything, was occasionally nerve-wracking. Once again, Devon had a role to play. Rather than being someone else for days at a time, now, merely pretending to be clueless to certain things while in Bizzy's presence was fairly easy to do. And today, inevitably, was one of those days Devon had to put on the act.

Before heading to StudioX to oversee a few things this glorious morning, Devon was presently in a favored restaurant, Denny's, waiting for Bizzy. Although their individual busy schedules clashed, causing them to infrequently spend time together since their reunion, they had a mirthful good time when they were able to mingle and learn about each other. Their bond was certainly becoming stronger with each meeting, and Devon was unequivocally becoming more entangled in a web of deceit.

"Wassup, sis?" Bizzy greeted in his deep voice as he approached the table toward the back of the restaurant.

Snapping out of a daydream, Devon said, "Damn, I was slippin'." Devon blinked a few times. "Wassup, Biz?"

"Ain't shit," he replied as he sat down in the booth opposite Devon. "But I was thinkin' on the way ova here how I'm glad ta have a sista now, even if ya are ... diff'rent." He smiled. "It's just good knowin' that sumbody out here has da same blood as mine."

Bizzy was a handsome young man, resembling his late father from head to toe. He was tall, brown-skinned, wore a low 'cut with deep waves, and he dressed like an aspiring businessman. If he learned only one thing from his father, it was definitely how to look like the CEO of a successful corporation.

"Well, I was satisfied wit RahRah bein' my only brotha," Devon honestly said. "But knowin' now that'chu are my *real* brotha, it's ... it's sumthin' that trips me out er'time I wake up." She grinned. "But I feel da same way you do at da end of da day."

"How are you, darlin'?" the wrinkled, cigarette-smelling old white woman unexpectedly said. "Back again so soon, I see."

"Yes, Ms. Maggie, I am."

Ms. Maggie was Devon's favorite waitress at Denny's. Devon had been served by Miss Maggie every other morning for the last two years straight. She could distinctly remember how she gave Maggie the nickname "Agatha the Marlboro-Smokin' Witch" the first time they interacted. After eventually realizing how sweet a person she was, Devon made sure that Ms. Maggie – and only Ms. Maggie – served her, and she would leave a thirty-dollar tip every time. *Ms. Maggie probably just buys cigarettes with the money,* Devon thought with a smile – *cartons of them!*

"I'll have da usual, Miss Maggie."

"I already know what *you* want, sweetie. But what about your handsome friend?" She winked at Bizzy.

"I'll have steak an' eggs," Bizzy promptly said.

"Okay, I'll be back shortly, sweeties."

While waiting for their breakfast, the brother and sister entertained each other with small talk. During the chat, Bizzy curiously asked Devon why she was suddenly growing dreads, and if she was going to stop occasionally dressing up in casual women's clothes, too. Devon's response was that she missed her first set of "wicks," and dressing up femininely the last year felt like she was lying to herself.

Devon then asked Bizzy about their Aunt Sheryl.

"Da last I heard," Bizzy started, "Aunt Sheryl was home in Jacksonville takin' care of my … my bad, she's takin care of *our* granny, Louise. An if ya ain't know, G-Ma been battlin' brain cancer fo' da last coupla years. She in her late seventies now, so Aunt Sheryl just been doin' all she can lately ta help G-Ma live her last days happily in da home my…our pops bought her in '88."

He paused. "G-Ma really got worse, tho', when my pops … damn, my fault. I'm still not used ta sayin' *our* yet." He then shrugged. "Anyways, G-Ma got worse when our pops died. It was already hard fo' her ta deal wit Unc Tyrell getting' locked up wit seven years, but she really fell off when pops died. She got so sick she couldn't even go to his funeral."

"Damn," was all Devon could utter.

"I know that'chu been hella bizzy, but maybe it'll be a good idea if ya stopped by an' seen her. It would make her day ta see you fo' da first time. She already knows about ya."

"I'll make sho' I make plans ta visit her soon," Devon promised.

After a brief moment, Bizzy asked, "Did ya go visit pops' grave? Ya' know last week made a year since he passed, rite?"

How could I forget the day a child-molesting, cold-blooded bastard was murdered, Devon thought. "Yeah, I know when his anniversary is. An' I stopped by his grave that day," she lied.

"You must've left befo' me, or showed up after me, becuz I didn't see ya there."

"I fa'got what time I went ta see him. I just know that was kinda a sad day fo' me."

"Yeah, me too." He inhaled deeply before exhaling. "I just wish pops didn't disown ya just becuz you ain't look like him. It's fucked up, but I believe if Pops knew that his daughter would grow up ta be an extraordinary, cool female, he woulda never did what he did. I also believe he just panicked when you were born,

48

becuz he was young and wasn't ready ta be a father of two." He shook his head ashamedly.

"He prolly was nowhere near bein' da man I grew up lovin' back then. The man I knew was quick ta give an' he gave da best advice, so I really believe if he was alive an' could do it all ova again, wit da knowledge he had befo' he passed, not claiming you as his seed woulda neva crossed his mind. An' I bet that'chu an' him would …" He stopped talking after seeing the sad, yet angry, look on his little sister's face. "What's wrong, sis?"

With a frown on her face, and a mouth like she had just finished eating a dirty gym sock, she answered, "I hate talkin' about … Demetrius … becuz he —"

"Say no mo', sis," he added, cutting her off. "I know what'chu 'bout to say, an' I totally understand."

Nigga, you don't know me, let alone understand what's really going on, she thought.

"Okay," Maggie said, popping out of thin air with a tray containing two plates and two OJs in the palm of one hand, "here's your breakfast." She placed the food on the table. "Would you two care for anything else, sugar?"

Devon regained her composure before she glanced at Bizzy, then collectedly replied, "No ma'am, not rite now. If we do, I'll call fo' ya, Miss Maggie."

"Well, you know I'm here for you, baby," Ms. Maggie said merrily before walking away.

"That's one nice white woman," Bizzy declared.

Devon only nodded in agreement and they then began to eat in silence.

Almost ten minutes later, Bizzy's plate possessed only the bone from the steak, while Devon's plate of food was barely touched.

"Aahhh, that was on point," Bizzy proclaimed after wiping his mouth with a napkin and throwing it on his plate. While looking at Devon's plate, he asked, "Why you ain't eat? You must be like me, if ya don't burn, ya don't have much of a appetite."

49

"Sumthin' like that. I really wasn't that hungry from da get-go," she claimed as her stomach growled a little.

Shifting the mood, he said, "In a few weeks, hopefully, I should be gettin' pops' bizness back on track. I think I told ya 'bout da furniture stores that pops owned befo' he died, rite?"

"Yeah, I rememba ya said sumtin' 'bout it befo.'"

"Well, I have to meet wit a few people first ta see if what I have in mind can get off da ground wit da lil' resources I have." He paused to burp. "'Scuse me. Anywayz, I plan on movin' from Orlando to West Palm Beach soon."

"Is that rite?" Devon said with a raised brow.

"Yeah." He leaned forward in the seat. "See, I really wanna try ta pick up where pops left off. I plan on changin' up a few things tho', like da name he had fo' da stores an' da type of furniture that he sold. But I'm keepin' da same goal in mind that he had."

"An' what goal was that?"

"To be da best at whateva he chose to do. So, since he was sellin' furniture befo' he died, I'ma be da best furniture salesman that he aimed ta be."

Hmph, this nigga is just as crazy as Demetrius, Devon thought disgustedly. *So, the saying is true: like father, like son.*

When Devon ultimately alleged that she had to get to StudioX to check up on some things, they prepared to part ways. Bizzy readily paid the bill for the food and Devon left the thirty-dollar tip for Ms. Maggie. They finally exited Denny's together, said their goodbyes, and made way for their cars.

As they both stood outside of their cars, which happened to be separated by another vehicle, Bizzy loudly said, "Yo', Devon!"

"Wassup, Biz?" she replied while opening her door.

"If er'thang works out how I want it, I'm gonna need ya help wit a few thangs, since I know that'cha plugged in 'round here. Bet?"

"When da time come, I'll see what I can do."

After she responded, Bizzy opened his door and began to climb into his whip. Then, jumping back out of his car, he yelled, "Yo', Dee!"

Frozen halfway in, halfway out of her car, she answered, "Wassup now, Biz?"

With a grave look on his face, he said, "You may not care as much becuz you ain't know him very well, but I ain't never givin' up."

Perplexed, she asked, "Givin' up doin' what?"

"Lookin' fo' da nigga that off'd my... our pops." He paused. "I know that'chu said da streets ain't said nuttin' 'bout him da last time I seen ya, an' you ain't say that'chu heard anything today, but still keep an ear out there. This yo' town, sis, so as soon as ya hear anything ... I mean *anythang*, you lemme know an' I'll put a handle on that, okay? Becuz da police damn sho' not tryna find out who killed our pops."

Devon only nodded her head, and they finally went their separate ways.

51

Chapter Five

March 17, 2010 8:15 pm

Orlando, FL

Precisely twelve hours after eating breakfast with his sister, Bizzy was currently in O-Town, a three-and-a-half-hour drive north from West Palm Beach, ready to talk business with Chad.

Upon arriving in the central Florida city around noon, however, he chose to kill time by hanging out for a few hours with his youngest son, five-year-old BJ, at his BM's place in Beirut, an uncivil, bloodthirsty project on the city's west side. He wasn't too fond of Beirut, nor was he too fond of his immature, ghettofied BM, LaShawn. Yet, he made sure that he spent as much quality time as possible with his little man, no matter what the circumstances.

Bizzy truly loved spending time with Byron Jr., as well as with his nine-year-old son, Bilal, in Tallahassee. But he was beginning to worry lately that he wasn't spending enough time with the both of them together, especially since the start of his relentless paper chase a year ago. He wished both BJ and Bilal could live with him in his three-bed, three-bath, two-story house on the southside of O-Town.

Bizzy hated that BJ had to grow up in such a terrible environment by reason of LaShawn's naivete, while Bilal lived well-off with his self-reliant thirty-three-year-old BM, Makelia. And another reason he wanted his boys together was so they could begin to grow up together, rather than them just seeing one another on their birthdays, Thanksgiving or Christmas.

Bizzy realized he was unintentionally doing to his boys what his father knowingly did to him, which was making them grow up with a father that was only around occasionally. He desperately strived to come up with a viable plan so that he could raise his sons together in the near future. There was no doubt he was going to be there for his sons whenever they needed him, which was exactly why he was now in the process of planning a quick come up before calling it quits. *In three years tops, I'll have both of my little soldiers with me under one roof,* he reasoned with himself, *if everything falls in place.*

After spending a good eight hours joyriding and playing with his son, Bizzy stood outside of LaShawn's front door saying goodbye to a saddened BJ. Once he promised BJ he would be back soon, he started to leave to go meet up with Chad on the other side of the city at his house.

Then suddenly, he stopped in his tracks, turned around, and did something he hadn't done in almost two years. He said more than twenty words to LaShawn.

"You still ain't tryna move an' live rent-free in my house on da southside in order ta get my son outta this fucked up hood that'chu lived in all yo' damn life, huh?"

LaShawn, who was now twenty-two with no job and a total of three kids by three different men, unbelievably answered, "Uh-uh, nigga. Like I told you da last time ya asked me, I ain't movin way out there wit them racist-ass white folks." She sucked her teeth. "An' besides, if I move way out there, how Kesha an nem gon' come see me? Becuz I sho' ain't 'bout ta spend my money that'chu give me on gas drivin' twenty, thirty minutes back an' forth, droppin' them off an' pickin' them up." She sucked her teeth again but rolled her eyes, too, this time. "An', on top of that, DCF will take my WIC away if I move outta here now. I need my WIC fo' …"

"See, that's exactly why I don't talk to yo' dumb ass." Bizzy bent down and gave his pouting son dap again before walking away. "If I knew what I know now, back when I was twenty-two, I never woulda fucked yo' young ass bare back becuz yo' ass soooo fuckin' stupid. You actually stuck on livin' in da hood fo' da rest of yo' maggot-ass life," he shouted as he opened his car door. "See, Bizzy, how you letta phat ass an' cute face entrap you wit a bird-brain-bitch fo' da next thirteen years!"

53

"Oh, no you just didn't! Byron, who you callin' a bitch, *Bitch?"* she screamed.

Bizzy never heard her, for he was half-way down the street by then.

Exactly twenty-three minutes later, Bizzy arrived at the home he rarely lived in. He pulled his Cadillac into the driveway of his three-hundred-thousand-dollar, two-story white house located in the Kissimmee Lakes gated community and parked. However, his car was not the only car parked in his spacious driveway. Along with his 'Lac, there was Chad's 2010 Mercedes-Benz S63 AMG and four other unknown vehicles ahead of his.

I know damn well I didn't make a mistake and tell Chad we were throwing a party, he thought, displeased as he climbed out of his Caddy with caution, *because we don't have time to kick back, it's time to get stacks!*

"What's happ'nin', Cuzzo?" Chad said as he hopped out of his Benz.

"Who cars are these?" Bizzy humorlessly asked, walking in Chad's direction, and gesturing towards the unknown cars in his driveway.

As the occupants of the unfamiliar vehicles began to emerge, Chad declared, "Oh … this here is da infantry that's gonna help get RBF on da streets poppin' again."

The titan that stepped out of the elevated Chevy Silverado 2500 was none other than Solo. Stanley "Solo" Simpson was not a hustler, he was Demetrius' personal bodyguard prior to his death. The six-eight, three-hundred-and-thirty-pound Solo was originally a bouncer at a few of South Florida's notable clubs. His last place of employment was StudioX, before being hired by Demetrius. Although he had only worked for Demetrius close to two years, there was no uncertainty that he was staunch and nowhere near being spineless.

His dedication was in fact proven when he took a bullet in his left shoulder during the successful jacking of Demetrius' last load of cocaine, which was the fatal blow in causing RBF to go belly up. And, out of ten other security guards protecting the load that night, he was the only one to kill a perpetrator and to flee the scene. He was now present not only because Chad called and asked him if he was down with keeping Demetrius' organization alive, but he was also simply there for two things. Solo needed the money for child support and alimony, and he needed to find out who had the balls to take his boss' life on his watch.

Climbing out of a hundred-and-twenty-thousand-dollar white Corvette ZR1, wearing all-white Louis Vuitton from hat to shoes, was JuneBug. Dayvan "Bug" Stubbford was Chad's childhood friend while growing up in Orlando. When they both were eighteen, Chad left the city to attend Bethune-Cookman College in Daytona Beach, while Bug stayed in O-Town and was taken under the wing of Chad's father, Bubba. Upon entering the hustle game as a rookie, he did little odd jobs for Bubba to learn the basics before Bubba gave him a few ounces of soft to sell.

He obediently followed Bubba's strict instructions, such as leaving the block-hustling to petty pushers and, within one year, he was officially a birdman. He hustled for nine years thereafter, stopping only when Bubba, his sole supplier, got locked up. He then chilled and lived off the money he had saved until Chad called on him to join Demetrius' last movement.

Unable to say no to drug money, because he loved living the lavish lifestyle of a dope boy, he shot out to Nashville and opened up shop. His shop closed when Demetrius, a man he never met, was murdered. It had been a year now since he pushed a pack, and he was in attendance now because Chad had presented him with a chance to hustle again, which was something he felt he was destined to do.

The last two super-clean, fully-loaded old schools in the driveway, a '87 Oldsmobile Cutlass and a '84 Pontiac Grand Prix, belonged to the Princes of Death, aka The Clean-Up Crew. The Clean-up Crew were Demetrius' four-member hit squad/disposal team. The four pestilent pals, all in their mid-forties, and only known to the world by their individual street names, were masters of the three D's: Distress, Destruction and Death.

Skinny-O, who was dark-complected, tall and muscular, was the brains of the order. The short and stocky guy, Beetle, was the enforcer and the disposal expert, as well as the jokester. The brawns and pugilist virtuoso was the Mark Henry look-alike, Bruiser. And the most demented, cutthroat and treacherous of the group was also the one that seemed shy, innocent and wimpy, and his contradictory name was Mouse. They were all present years before RBF was a figment in Demetrius' head. And now that Demetrius was gone, Chad didn't get a chance to ask whether or not they were willing to help when he called Skinny-O. According to Skinny-O, they were simply waiting patiently for anybody to take the initiative to try to bring RBF back to its glory, so they could return to torturing and killing the opposition, which was the one thing they all felt they were born to do.

Bizzy quickly acknowledged each man as if they were immediate family, then he quickly escorted them inside of his home before his nosey neighbors began to suspect anything. *I never had the police called on me since I've lived here,* he said to himself as he gathered the gangster bunch in his living room, *and I'm trying to keep it that way.*

After the diverse group of men had settled down, Bizzy proceeded to the kitchen to grab some drinks, preferably beers, if he had some. Gone only two minutes tops, with a twelve-pack of ice-cold Heinekens in hand, he returned to find everybody, except Solo and Mouse, laughing out loud.

"Oh shit, Cuzzo!" Chad said while holding his chest, "I can't … I can't breathe, 'cuz this nigga got me laughin' so hard."

Placing the case of beers on the coffee table, Bizzy asked, "What happened?"

While gesturing in Solo's direction, Bug said, "Maaannnn, that big-ass nigga can flip da script from superman ta super soft."

"Fuck you, featherweight-ass nigga!" Solo barked from the edge of his seat and with his face balled up in anger.

Turning his attention from Solo to Bizzy, Bug continued, "Maaannnn, when I first saw that nigga hop out da truck, I just stared at him cuz he a BIG BOY. But da mo' I stared, da mo' familiar he began to look. Once we got in here, that's when I rememba'd seein' his cryin' ass on da *Maury* show 'bout two months ago."

Bizzy surprisedly looked at Solo, who was ice-grilling the one-hundred-sixty-five-pound JuneBug.

"Yeah," Bug continued while gold-grilling Solo, "he was on there wit two broads. One chick, I think her name was Star or some shit like that, claimed he was her baby's daddy. Da bitch put on a show, cussin' him out an' comparin' her daughter picture ta his, just like da rest of da bitches do."

"Hold on, my nigga," Bizzy interposed. "What'chu doin' watchin' *Maury* in da first place? When do a *real* nigga have time ta watch that dumb shit? Becuz if ya gettin' real money, then ya don't got time fo' bullshit. An' if ya got time fo' bullshit, then ya ain't gettin' real money!"

"First … I like *Maury*. It teaches me not ta get caught up wit a foot-draggin' bitch like some stupid-ass niggas." He nodded pointedly in Solo's direction. "Secondly, a real nigga TiVo that shit, so I watch it at nite wheneva I got 'me' time. Anywayz, back to *this* clown-ass nigga. After da bitch said she was a thousand percent sho' he was da daddy, this Green Mile-lookin' nigga come marchin' out da back holdin' wifey hand. Out da gate, he cuss da bitch out in his John Coffee voice, an' wife do too. Eventually, Maury gets tired of da back an' forth shit talkin' an' says it's time ta read da results. Maaannnn, when Maury said that, this nigga looked spooked."

Bug made a face that resembled a slave's face caught by "massa" doing something he had no business. "Maaannnn, when Maury announced that he *was* da father, wifey started beatin' his ass while he chased da otha bitch backstage. Once in the back, he go Incredible Hulk by throwin' chairs, punchin' holes in walls, an' some mo' shit. Then, guess what?"

"What?" a clearly entertained Bizzy said with a half-smile on his face.

"Maaannnn, this pie-ass nigga break down boo-hoo cryin' on his knees when wifey said she was divorcin' him. When she gave him back his rang, da nigga went Hollywood by rollin' all ova da floor, cryin' a fuckin' river. Maaaannnn, when he finally got his big doofus-ass up, shakin' like he saw a ghost, his soft ass grabbed Maury an' cried on his shoulder while beggin' an' apologizin' ta wifey, but she wasn't havin' it. An' just befo' commercial break, wifey jumped up an' literally slapped snot outta his ass befo' confessin' ta fuckin' his cousin on da low anywayz. This nigga's lip quivered..." Bug made his bottom lip tremble like a terrified toddler, "...an' he started cryin' even harder on Maury's shoulder like a broad, befo' da commercial."

Bizzy looked at Solo. "Big Dawg, say it ain't so?"

Solo looked down at his left hand, which no longer possessed a wedding ring. When he looked back up, he had tears of anger in his eyes.

"See, he 'bout ta start cryin' again," Bug proclaimed.

While everybody burst into laughter again, except for Solo and Mouse, Solo rose up slowly out of his seat and began to approach JuneBug.

"Chill out, Big Dawg," Bizzy said, blocking Solo's path to JuneBug. "Ain't nuttin' finna pop off in here. Besides, you put ya'self in that situation by goin' on that dumb-ass show. Now niggas all around da world laughin' at'cha. Not just us. So, sit down, calm down an' let's talk money."

The discourse began with Bizzy asking the collective whether they had any previous dealings, or knowledge of any kind, with pills. Although their yes and no answers were insignificant to him, he just wanted to know for his own reason. He then informed the group that he specifically wanted to hustle opiate pills.

After a little flak from Chad and Bug only, Bizzy began to explain why he opted to hustle pills rather than coke. Now, he had plans on buying a couple hundred bricks to appease both Chad and

Bug, but he felt RBF was too hot to sell strictly cocaine, especially after the debacle that Demetrius faced just days before his murder. And that was precisely why he was changing lanes and sending RBF down a different avenue, an avenue less traveled by a black criminal organization.

Being a frequent club hopper and excursionist over the last couple years, Bizzy knew firsthand that pills were a hot commodity near college and university campuses at rave parties, gay bars, strip clubs, and hotel resorts. Seeing that pills were a different means to come up, he bought a few hundred pills, mainly oxycodone and ecstasy, from different undependable suppliers, and began selling them during the last six months throughout the cities that he visited in Florida. However, of all the pills, he noticed that there was a huge demand for Roxycodone, a cheap addictive opiate.

Finally, after almost two months, he found someone to reliably supply him with the pills. His pill plug was a white boy named Rusty in Vero Beach, FL. He met Rusty in the parking lot of the 45th Street Flea Market in West Palm Beach by chance. Rusty was boosting stripper outfits in the parking lot, when Bizzy approached the white boy in hopes of hooking him up with Devon. Upon learning that Devon was Rusty's main buyer, the convo eventually progressed from strippers to pills, thus forming an alliance between the two.

After Rusty told him that Roxy 30s were indeed the go-to pills, Bizzy purchased twelve hundred Roxys at eight dollars per pill, and sold each pill for fifteen, twice last month so far. And during their most recent transaction, Rusty extended to him a proposal to consider: if he was interested in selling not just Roxys, but all types of pills that the fiends crave in the streets.

Although he wasn't ready to accept Rusty's proposal at that time, due to his little experience with pills, he was now ready to expand due to the formation of RBF again. Therefore, with the one-point-three million dollars that Kelly left him in the bowling alley locker and the half-million dollars of his own money that he was willing to invest, he was ready to kick the new operation off by purchasing as many pills that he could, along with the necessities needed to be successful. However, since it was only Bug, Chad and him that were going to hustle, what he really needed now was to obtain two or three more reliable, trustworthy men. The extra men were essential in his plans of taking over the pill market from Central Florida down to Miami before eventually venturing into North Florida and beyond. But he needed more help doing so.

Aside from the Clean-Up Crew, the others agreed to bring some recruits to the table to be considered to help the new venture.

Once that was done, Bizzy briefly mentioned revamping the dogfighting and gambling businesses in due time. Then, he moved on to a more dire matter, which was more in the field for the Clean-Up Crew to handle.

"It's a known fact," Bizzy started, "that them Triple S niggaz jacked my pops. They out there ballin' an' flossin' rite now off of my pops' coke." He frowned. "My pops was feared in Palm Beach an', becuz he was feared, he became a legend. Them faggot-ass Triple S niggaz shittin' on my pops' legacy, as well as RBF's. I'm movin' ta Palm Beach soon ta take control ova all illegal activities that goes down in da streets my pops owned fo' so long. This a new generation an' Palm Beach is gonna be da headquarters fo' this come-up."

He looked directly at Skinny-O. "Skinny-O, I need ya to snatch them niggaz asses off da streets. I want'chu ta rob an' kill 'em till Triple S has their own cemetery. Bet?"

With an appreciative smile, Skinny-O responded, "It's my pleasure ta do just that … an' mo'. I'm just glad we finally have a reason ta start doin' what we do best again."

"I was startin' to feel … normal … chillen all day wit my naggin' bitch an' bad ass kids," Beetle proclaimed before sighing. "It's been a loooong time since I killed a man. I can't wait to get my hands on one of them lil' fuckers. I recently had a dream, an' in that dream I learned a new way to torture a man. See, you cut a man around da waist, pull da skin up over his head, tie a knot an' watch him suffocate."

Everybody had faces of disgust, except for the Clean-Up Crew, of course.

"Cuzzo, I told ya these muthafuckas belong in a fuckin' insane asylum," Chad declared. "Where da fuck did Demetrius find these niggaz?"

"Maaannnn, I'ma be da first ta say that I'm glad they on my team," Bug stated, "becuz I'm feelin' a lil' sorry fo' Triple S when they run across these deranged muthafuckas."

"I feel ya on that," Bizzy agreed before standing up. "Now that we're somewhat on one accord an' this is da birth of a new movement, I'm officially deadin' da RBF title." He paused to check out everybody's expressions. "RockBottom Family is obsolete now. We startin' from da bottom of da barrel an' from da bottom of da south. An' soon, we'll overpower Florida, we'll overpower da entire south an' we'll overpower whoeva till we reach da top! It's time ta let these niggas know... startin' wit Triple S... that *we*, Da Bottom Boyz, are after what's rightfully ours!"

Damn, this nigga has the same confidence, passion and dreams his father had, Chad thought as the same tingling sensation Demetrius usually caused after speaking over-whelmed his body. *I just pray he doesn't have the same shortcomings that his father had, also.*

Chapter Six

April 29, 2010 2:35 am

Wellington, FL

"Ooohhh, baby," Miracle squealed in pleasure, "that shit … feels … soooo good."

Both Devon and Rhapsody mightily sucked and licked Miracle's pussy as she swayed her hips back and forth, grinding her erect clit on their splendid tongues. As their hungry mouths ransacked her love cavern in search of her delectable sauce, her body twisted and turned this way and that way under their ministrations. Then, after a series of pants and moans, she let out a hoarse cry of unbridled passion, only causing Devon and Rhapsody both to bury their tongues deeper inside of her. Finally, Miracle's pussy lips seized their tongues as she grabbed both of their heads between her shapely thighs and shoved them into her wetness.

"Oh, God! Don't – don't – don't…stop… I'm cummin'!" Miracle climatically screamed, drowning the heads between her legs with her sweet juices. With her back arched up from the bed, her body trembled.

As "the most powerful orgasm she'd ever experienced" subsided, she emitted low moans of pleasure with every quiver, and released her firm grip on Devon and Rhapsody's heads.

Surfacing with a face totally drenched, and somewhat out of breath, Devon said, "Damn, I was so far up there, I coulda swore I seen an egg."

"You crazy, Daddy," Rhapsody giddily said before leaning over Miracle's body to clean cum off Devon's face with her thick tongue. Once she was done, she said, "Now, I want'chu ta fuck me in da ass, Daddy."

While winking at Miracle, who was still experiencing post-climatic quivers, Devon said, "Beg fo' da dick, bitch."

Rhapsody promptly climbed over Miracle to mount Devon. As soon as she was straddled upon Devon's lap, she began to gyrate her pussy against Devon's pelvis while pushing, pulling and squeezing her large breasts and lolling her head back.

"Daddy, I'm beggin' you ta please fuck me in my ass," she cooed, twiddling and elongating her large nipples now.

Extremely hot and aroused by Rhapsody's erotic display, while grabbing a handful of cotton-soft ass, Devon replied, "Bitch, tell me you want me ta bust open ya bunker."

"Daddy, I need da bunker buster," Rhapsody demanded hastily before hissing and moving her body like a snake as she continued to fondle her melons with her eyes closed and head dangling back. "I'm 'bout ta explode now, Daddy, just knowin' wha'chu gonna do ta me...ooohhhh, yes. Daddy, please fuck my juicy ass."

"I'ma bust that ass up, bitch," Devon declared. "Miracle, grab Big Boy." She winked again. "This bitch in a world of trouble."

Miracle slowly rolled off the bed. With warm juice running from her well-licked twat down the inner side of her dark chocolate thighs, she ambled over to the dresser, opened a drawer full of sex toys and removed a strap-on dildo. Instead of giving it to Devon, though, she commenced to put on the six-inch long, three and a half-inch diameter device herself. "Let me be the one to tear her ass up this time," she asserted, making her way back to the bed.

With a peculiar smile and raised brow, Devon watched Miracle climb back on the bed and said, "Do ya' know wha'chu doin'?"

Seeing the look of bliss diminish from Rhapsody's face, Miracle said, "All I'm tryin' to do is...spice it up, get outta our typical routine tonite, thas'all." She faced Devon. "It's always you that uses the strap-on. I wanna switch it up. So, once I do her, she can do me ... that's if she doesn't have a problem wit that." She then faced Rhapsody. "Because I don't."

"Okay," Devon eventually said as she gazed up at Rhapsody, who was somewhat scowling but still grinding. "You down fo' sum DP?"

After glancing over at Miracle, Rhapsody looked down at Devon. "Daddy, my body is *built* fo' fuckin'. Do as you please, cuz I can handle *whateva*." She glanced back at Miracle. "Can you?"

Sensing the competitive tension in the air, Devon gently pushed Rhapsody to the side. "Look, we gonna flip it up *an'* we finna continue ta have fun, ai'ight?" Climbing out of bed, the five-eight, hundred and forty-five pound, golden-brown complected Devon walked over to the open dresser drawer and removed a second strap-on dildo. Once she attached the average-sized contraption around her naked twenty-seven-inch waist, she climbed back on the king-size bed. "Since Rhapsody wanna get her ass plugged, she gonna ride this dick while you, Miracle, dog her from da back."

With that said and done, everyone assumed their fucking positions. And from there on, the tension in the air was replaced with an intimate woman-y fragrance, and they satisfied each other until they fell asleep nestled together.

April 29, 2010 11:39 am

Palm Beach Gardens, FL

It was nine in the morning when Devon arose after approximately five hours of restful sleep. She prepared for the day ahead by washing up and primping herself, before finally departing from the house in her stock, low-key 2010 Lincoln MKS.

Although she normally dropped in to StudioX every morning before leisurely cruising the streets, she decided to first pay RahRah an unexpected and overdue visit.

Since she didn't know if RahRah had a place of his own yet, she stopped at a few places on the periphery of downtown West Palm Beach that he was known to frequent, like Quinterria's crib. She searched and asked around for him, but nobody was able to tell her where he was or where he might be.

Unsuccessful at locating RahRah, Devon drove to the Palm Beach Gardens Mall to do a little shopping now, rather than later this evening, as previously planned. *I hope I can come across a killer 'fit to rock with these yellow, blue and gray Jordan XIII's I just copped*, she thought, while entering the grand, bi-level mall.

During the next hour or so, she entered and exited various stores, like Lacoste and Ralph Lauren, without purchasing a single item. Because she was unable to find anything that matched her Jordan's, or anything else that interested her, she began to scout the suburban mall for talent, potential money-makers for the club that had either an Ivy League-education appearance or a runway-model body. She employed enough strippers that had a GED aspect to them or a buffet-line build.

"Yo, Dee!"

Devon stopped and turned to locate the familiar voice. A second or two later, she spotted RahRah. He was fresh to death, standing in the middle of the mall with his boys, Bumper and Skat, at a kiosk that sold custom made t-shirts. She approached. "Wassup, my niggaz?" she said before giving each of them some dap. "What y'all up ta…besides no good?"

RahRah sighed. "We just getting' a few *R.I.P.* shirts made fo' da homies that passed this week."

"Damn…shit is unbelievable." Devon shook her head. "It's crazy how so many niggaz from da hood are turnin' up dead or missin' all of a sudden. Sumthin' up becuz, durin' da last two weeks or so, it's like … ten niggaz from 'round da way got hit up."

"Seven," Bumper chimed in, "an' two of my bros still missin'."

65

"Dawg, it's almost like that killin' spree that happened in 2004," Devon said, recalling the year when eleven people, both male and female, were killed in less than a week in downtown West Palm Beach, which caused the murder rate to continuously rise, until decreasing in 2008. "Do y'all have a clue who killed da homies? If y'all do, then I'm willin'—"

"What? What'chu think, we pussy or sumthin'?" Bumper said rather loudly, causing some shoppers to look at him oddly and with a measure of alarm. Known for waving his hands and jerking his body when he was aggravated, gesturing fiercely, he continued, "I am not da one, Dee, an' you an' da whole 'hood know this, so..." He lowered his voice a bit. "So, if *I* knew who it wuz that killed my bros...you betta fuckin' believe they entire family *an'* they 'hood would be goin' in da dirt as we speak. But, since we dunno who it is exactly, we ... Put it this way, Durt, I'm offin' eh-ver-ree-body that looked at me wrong ... came out dey mouth wrong 'bout me an' da clique ... anythang! An' that goes fo' da past, present an' future."

"We ain't bullshittin'," Skat added. "We gotta few niggaz from Da Raw last nite, an' ya can put da bank on it when I say they havin' closed caskets."

"It's da beginnin' of World War III," Rah said. "An' er'body who ain't Triple S is on da opposite end of da fiyah."

Once the four dozen t-shirts bearing the pictures and names of Mug, Wayne, Keno and Quince were done, all four of them exited the mall together.

Standing outside in the blazing ninety-five-degree weather, with only a welcome breeze blowing by every now and then, Devon said, "Ai'ight, I'm headin' ta my club ta oversee a few thangs." She turned towards RahRah. "You wanna slide wit me? Or do ya got some otha shit ta handle wit them?"

"Ummm..." RahRah glanced at Bumper. "Naw, I can't slide wit'cha. I gotta...my bad, we gotta take care of some shit our-selves today. I'll hit'cha up later tho'."

"Cool, an' if ya have time tonite, swing by StudioX. I got Gucci, Roxy Reynolds and a few otha celebs comin' through. It's gonna be off da chain." He paused you catch his breath. "AnI can give ya da bread I owe ya fo'..."

"I'm fifty-four. You keep it," Rah said rather bluntly. "An' I'll see 'bout slidin' thru StudioX

"Ai'ight." Devon felt heartbroken by Rah's attitude towards her. "Y'all boyz be safe out there."

They all gave each other dap and Devon went her way, while RahRah, Bumper and Skat went theirs.

It's good to see RahRah is finally on his feet, Devon thought in admiration of RahRah's million-dollar street-nigga appearance as she reached her vehicle, *but it hurts to know that it was Bumper and Skat to put him on rather than me, and that may be why he don't want the money I owe him.*

BOC BOC BOC BOC BOC

Without reluctance, the people in the parking lot scattered wildly and screamed hysterically as the shots rang out.

Devon, on the other hand, took cover behind her car until the shots ceased. The sound of tires screeching was heard before she slowly lifted her head just enough to see what was going down. The first thing that came into her view was a burgundy '96 Impala SS flying through the parking lot, trailing behind a silver Benz S550. And hanging out of the passenger window of the Benz, she saw...

*POW POW POW POW POW POW POW *

Immediately, Devon ducked down again once the passenger hanging out of the Benz window began busting at the pursuing Impala. *Is that Bumper's Benz?* she wondered before trembling a little, *because I swear the nigga hanging out the window looked like RahRah.*

In spite of the fact that she wasn't a hundred percent sure if it was actually RahRah she saw, she snapped out of her state of shock, jumped into her Lincoln and proceeded to follow the high-speed shoot out. She was no more than thirty seconds behind the

67

action when she turned onto PGA Boulevard and tried calling RahRah's phone. But she immediately received a message saying the caller was unavailable.

She was within a quarter mile of the chase when it moved from PGA Boulevard to I -95 South. Once on I-95, she was able to run down the swerving cars ahead due to the proficient powerplant in her Lincoln MKS. When she came to be just seven car lengths away, she then realized two things. One, it was indeed Bumper's Benz and two, not only was the Impala following the Benz, but there was also a new-school Pontiac G8 in the mix as well.

Instead of the typical twenty-minute drive from the Palm Beach Gardens Mall to downtown West Palm Beach, it took an incredible eight minutes to reach the bowels of the hood from the mall.

In the heart of downtown now, Devon somehow lost sight of all the cars while zigzagging through traffic. Frantically, she rode up and down known streets, looking for any indication that would lead her in the right direction. After about four agonizing minutes, she spotted the parked Benz in an alley. Without caution, she sped up to the Benz and noticed both front tires were flat, the windshield was smashed, steam was billowing from the hood, and the entire car was riddled with bullet holes. She finally hopped out of her car in a panic and sprinted up to the Benz to find it abandoned and speckled with blood.

Tires screeching

Responding to the screeching tires, Devon looked up and saw the burgundy Impala rushing down the alley towards her. And just as she was turning to flee, a hail of fully automatic gunfire suddenly commenced. *Fuck, I didn't plan on going out like this*, she thought as she fell to the ground with her body instantly going numb. *I just hope the Almighty God is waiting for me at the pearly gates with my mother.*

Flame

Chapter Seven

April 29, 2010 10:17 pm

West Palm Beach, FL

Uncertain. On this moderately warm, fair night, Bizzy was uncertain how Devon would react to his business proposition. However, if he was presented the chance to fully explain his proposal, he had a great feeling that it would be difficult for her to decline his offer once she saw the impressive numbers that would put a few extra commas in her pockets ... daily. Still, it surely was a toss-up, he felt. *Hell, either she's going to accept or reject,* he thought as he entered StudioX, *I'm just trying to keep this new move in the family, that's all.*

After a week of contemplating on whether he ought to call Devon ahead of time to let her know he would be at StudioX tonight to speak with her, he unexpectedly showed up in hopes of surprising his sister for the very first time. Apathetically, he sat and watched the strippers dance on stage and walk ostentatiously around soliciting from the bar until his sister showed her face. While waiting, he felt obligated to order a Grey Goose mixed with Nuvo.

And as he sat and sipped on his concoction, suddenly, he was confidently approached by a fine, mocha-complexioned female. She wore a white blouse held in place by thin straps around her neck and across her back, with snug blue jeans that gladly displayed voluptuous thighs and mouth-watering ass cheeks. Indeed, it was an ass so phat, he'd clearly seen it from the front!

Standing in front of him but off to one side, the female then placed a newly manicured hand on his broad shoulder, leaned in towards him and said into his ear, "Are you enjoyin' yourself?"

With his mouth merely inches away from her kissable, soft neck, he euphorically whiffed the fruity, invigorating fragrance she wore before replying. "I wasn't till you walked up," he said into her ear as he placed a hand on her fleshy hip. "So, since ya did me a favor by turnin' my nite from so-so ta betta by blessin' me wit'cha presence, can I buy ya a drink?"

She giggled sexily. "I would gladly accept your offer, but …"

"But what?"

"But … I really don't like bein' too tipsy while I'm on the clock."

"You work here?" he curiously asked.

"I sure do."

He leaned away from her and gingerly admired the beauty from head to toe. *As a matter of fact, I've seen this girl before, but where*? he wondered as he tried to recall her from his great memory. *It'll hit me soon where I've seen her before.* "Are you a waitress? A bartender? Or are ya 'bout to go in da back an' get dressed fo' ya shift?"

"Oh … you think I'm …" she giggled again. "No, I'm not a waitress or a bartender. And no, I'm not a stripper … anymore."

"Hmmm, that's too bad that'chu gave up da … pole," he winked, "becuz I woulda definitely made it rain so much money in here on *you* tonite that'chu woulda needed a life preserver from me tryna drown ya wit bills." He then smiled at her. "You … you da baddest here, hands down!"

"Drown me in money, huh?" she said before smiling back. "You ballin' like that?"

"Baby, if ya only knew who ya wuz talkin' to." He paused. "Altho' I'm pretty sho we met sumwhere befo', becuz I neva fa'get a…" he quickly glanced down at her rotund ass, "…pretty face like yours, but it's neva too late ta get ta know me."

With a grin on her face, she simply nodded her head, for she was somewhat impressed and intrigued by the good-looking, well-groomed young black man that she too, vaguely recalled meeting somewhere. Where they'd met, she had no idea at the moment.

"So, what exactly do ya do up in here?" he questioned. "Since you are not a waitress, bartender or stripper …" he frowned "… you must be a DJ or a spokesmodel fo' da club."

71

She giggled sexily again. "Well, this club that you're now enjoyin' yourself in is actually managed and owned in part by yours truly." She struck a pose. "My name is Miracle and—"

"Hold on, hold on," he interposed. "So, you mean to tell me you an' my lil' sis own this spot?"

"Your sister?" Miracle said perplexedly before stepping away from Bizzy and staring at him. "Boy, you're on them pills, huh? Devon cannot be your sister because for one, I've never seen you and two, she never talked about you. Devon only has one brother and it sure in the hell ain't you!"

"Hmph, how you're talkin', ya gotta be my sista's old lady." He looked her up and down again before licking his lips. "No wonda she ain't tell me 'bout you, let alone tell you 'bout me, becuz you... Mmm mmm mmm." He then shook his head. "Anywayz, where my sis at? I came here ta surprise her. Plus, I need ta holla at her 'bout a few thangs."

After briefly explaining to Bizzy that Devon's *real* brother made a brief and unusual call earlier, informing her that Devon would arrive before midnight after handling some unfinished business, Miracle proceeded to grill him about declaring to be Devon's *other* brother. She then attentively listened to every word that came out of Bizzy's mouth, and the more he revealed, the more agitated she became. *I'm really not too upset learning that Devon has lied to me,* she thought as Bizzy was concluding the story by explaining to her the new promising relationship he had been building with Devon recently. *I'm upset that from now on, I'm going to have doubts about whatever Devon tells me until this is straightened out.*

Nothing was said after Bizzy finished speaking. A few seconds into the silence, Miracle suddenly gasped upon realizing that she somehow disregarded the most crucial fact of Bizzy's entire story until now. It was actually Devon, not a cousin as she claimed, who witnessed the death of her mother and was raped by her biological father, whom she just recently murdered.

"Helllooooo?"

"Huh?" Miracle dazedly said, snapping out of the zone that she was in.

"Baby, you straight?" Bizzy inquired with concern. "Becuz you look like you wuz just on anotha planet. Talkin' 'bout me, *you* da one actin' like ya on dem pills."

Forcing a fake smile onto her face, she said, "I'm sorry. It's just that you said somethin' that caused my mind to wander."

"What I say?" he asked with an enticing grin.

"Hmmm…I can't remember what it wuz, now. I just know that, whatever it wuz you said, my mind ran with it."

"Well," he said, "since ya can't —"

"Damn, Miracle!" Shan shrieked, popping out of thin air. "Girl, you have got ta introduce me to this … fine-ass nigga rite here." Shan then leaned over and whispered into Miracle's ear. "He look like he got money, too. An' I ain't talkin' 'bout no ballin'-on-da-block money, eitha. I'm talkin' mo' like ballin'-wit-Kobe-an'-LeBron money, girl."

Once Bizzy and Shan were formally introduced, Miracle slowly withdrew from their powwow to contemplate the lies Devon had told her. Heedlessly, time flew by as she thought. And while occasionally listening in on the insipid conversation that Bizzy and Shan were engaged in, the disappointed feeling that she had toward Devon ultimately transitioned to a feeling of sympathy for her better half.

Putting myself in Devon's shoes, I guess I can understand why she did what she did, she thought as she observed fake-ass Shan all up in Bizzy's face, which seemed to convey more familiarity than before. Nevertheless, Miracle was still mad that Devon didn't trust her enough to share about the tragedy she experienced as a child.

"Well, I gotta hit da road," Bizzy suddenly insisted. "I gotta make a move befo' I call it a nite." He then turned and faced Miracle. "Tell my sis to hit me up when she can, okay? I need ta holla at her on a get-money play."

"I'll tell her ta call you," Miracle simply said.

"Oohhh, can I call you, too?" Shan asked, stepping in front of Miracle.

"Ummm ..." Looking past Shan, he noticed Miracle covertly shaking her head no. "I-I-I ... how 'bout givin' me yo' numba?"

Shan frowned. "You're not goin' to call me, are ya?"

"Yeah, I will."

After plugging the digits in Bizzy's phone, Shan said, "Now, don't have me waitin' too long to hear from you again."

"I won't, trust me." He winked. "Y'all have a good nite. I'm gone."

Both Miracle and Shan said goodbye.

The lovely warm air, along with the twinkling stars, impressed an exhilarating feeling upon Bizzy as he exited the club. Stepping just a few feet from the entrance, he stopped and took a second to embrace the phenomenal night. *Man, I'm going to take it in early before something or somebody ruins this good night I'm having,* he said to himself as he started to walk towards his car, *because a beautiful night like this always ends fucked up when I stay out too late.*

Phone rings

He shook his head disappointedly. "I spoke too soon," he said to no one in particular. He removed his smartphone from his Evisu jeans and looked at the caller ID. Not recognizing the number, he had intentions of letting the call go to voicemail. But being that it was midnight, and it could be an emergency, he answered. "Who dis?"

*****

Meanwhile, in StudioX's jampacked parking lot, a dark-tinted 2003 Mercury Marauder was parked near the entrance, and inside the rather conspicuous vehicle were two federal agents. One agent was a Caucasian named Trevor "Dino" Zimmerman and the other was a black man named Justin "Raw Deal" Holmes.

"We've got action," Dino blurted out. "Eyes on target."

74

"Where?" Raw Deal questioned.

"See the tall black guy talking on the phone?" Dino said, pointing out Bizzy.

"Yup."

"That's the one I told you that I saw in Palm Beach Gardens at the marina, talking to Kelly Kronkite after I followed Kelly there."

"Who is he?"

"He's the son of Demetrius Woodson. Heard of him?"

"Who hasn't heard of the notorious Kilo." Raw Deal paused. "Do you think this guy is trying to keep his no-good father's businesses and organization alive?"

"I don't know. But we will find out … sooner or later. And until our C.I. contacts us with good news, we just have to tail him for a while to see where he goes, who he meets. Since the beginning of this investigation a few years ago, I've only encountered this guy once or twice with Demetrius. So, I didn't think he was much involved with RBF … until he met with Kelly."

"Do you think he has anything to do with the increase in murders in the area?" Raw Deal asked.

Dino looked over at his rookie partner. "If he is anything close to his callous ass father, not only does he have something to do with it, he's the reason there's soon to be a raging war in the streets, just like the one his father started in the eighties."

"We cannot allow that."

"No, we cannot," Dino agreed, "which is why we have to get him off the streets as soon as possible. This investigation has been going on too long as it is. It's time to rid the streets of these damn RBF guys for good!"

Phone alert tone

Agent Holmes' phone alerted him to the text message he just received. After reading the message, he said, "And our C.I. just made contact with our target."

"Perfect," Dino replied with a smile. "It's only a matter of time now."

Chapter Eight

June 11, 2010 3:08 pm

West Palm Beach, FL

Just imagine living in a hood where roughly ninety percent of households made less than fifteen thousand a year, where the best legit job was considered working as a manager at McDonald's. Where a majority of students were projected to drop out of school before the tenth grade, where it was extremely difficult to do something positive, but oh-so-easy to do something negative.

Simply visualize growing up in a single-parent home, mainly because the other parent was either dead or incarcerated, with a handful of siblings, in a run-down two-bedroom residence in the middle of a city chock full of drug addicts, thugs, prostitutes, killers and crooked, biased police.

Just picture giving a hundred percent in order to escape the frequent gunshots that rang out every day, to escape the obscene sights and sounds that became fixtures of normality, to escape the secure grasp that those grim streets had on your reality. Simply envision doing everything possible to overcome defeat, only ending the pursuit of a better life due to a lack of love, support, resources and funds, then finally declaring to get out of the wicked hood by any means necessary.

So, just imagine that rather than slaving all day over the fryer at a fast-food restaurant that will barely make ends meet, picking up a pack to sell on the block, or toting a pistol to rob anything moving was an easier way to get the ball rolling on living the so-called American Dream.

But it wasn't.

Living well below the poverty line while scrambling to be wealthy by doing what's right is a Catch-22, which is exactly how "they" designed it to be, placing us in a lose-lose situation, Bizzy pondered as he drove back down to West Palm Beach from Vero

Beach after talking business with the pill man, Rusty. *The only two kinds of people to emerge from growing up in such a hostile hood are the ones lucky enough to escape the mayhem early and the unfortunate ones that become statistics,* Bizzy continued his thoughts.

"Man, I absolutely will not let my lil' man become a statistic," he said to himself, gripping the steering wheel of his Lexus LS460 tightly as he thought about the lives of poverty-stricken African-Americans, as well as his son's living conditions in Orlando. "I might just have to kidnap my lil' man." He paused momentarily. "Or betta yet, I'll kill that dumb-ass bitch, LaShawn. Then he'll be wit me … fo' good."

The lonely, yet reflective hour and forty-five-minute trip was nearly over now. Reaching West Palm Beach's city limits in the next five minutes, which was also the place of his new residence, he switched his train of thought from the disadvantages of being raised in turbulent environs to the launch of his new pill business. He also went over the two-hour long conversation he'd had with Rusty that would make selling pills very lucrative for Da Bottom Boyz.

Not particularly ashamed about being a novice to this trade, Rusty readily broke down everything he needed to know to get his new idea, a pill dispensary network, up and running. The knowledge he obtained was extremely helpful. He wouldn't allow himself to be strung along by anybody and would only follow through on deals that were most profitable for him. *Business without a path to profit isn't business, it's a hobby,* he thought as his smart phone began to ring.

Since his smartphone and his Lexus' infotainment system were linked together, the navigation screen on the dashboard displayed the ID of the caller. After pressing a button on the steering wheel, he said, "Talk to me, bruh."

"What's happ'nin', Cuzzo?" Chad replied quite monotonously through the sound system.

It had been close to a month since Bizzy talked to his cousin. He knew the lack of communication was only because of him being occupied with trying to get his plans formulated and the business ready for overpowering the streets. "Just tryna put da finishin' touches on some B.I."

"Fa sho'." Chad paused briefly. "Yo, we need ta cross paths real soon. I gotta holla at'cha 'bout sum thangs, ai'ight?"

"I'ma be at da crib in ... twenty minutes. You can slide thru now, cuz I'm chillen fo' da rest of da day... hopefully."

"Bet. Well ... I need directions ta ya crib becuz I'm halfway between Orlando an' Palm Beach now."

"You gotta navi system, don't'cha?"

Chad laughed. "Cuzzo, I got so many upgrades an' gadgets in this muthafucka that I feel like... George Jetson. Ain't nuttin' factory in *or* on my bitch."

Bizzy then promptly provided Chad with his home address before ending the call with a simple press of a button on his steering wheel.

Bizzy's newly purchased home was in beautiful suburban West Palm Beach, in an area known as Bear Lakes. Bear Lakes, one of the majority white sections in the county, consisted of numerous deluxe apartment complexes and multiple luxurious neighborhoods with homes that range from a quarter-million to three million. Selecting this locale to reside in was a superb choice because Bear Lakes was a ten- to fifteen-minute, light traffic commute from downtown West Palm Beach. As such, Bizzy was capable of observing the pill trade that was prevalent throughout the county, while assembling the right pieces for total domination, from a safe serene environment. *Living on the outskirts of my main objective is somewhat like being on the outside looking in*, he thought as he entered his moderately decorated home.

About an hour and a half after conversing over the phone, Chad was outside Bizzy's residence. Before his cousin had the chance to knock on his door, Bizzy expeditiously answered the door for his first visitor. After a short salutation, he led Chad through the completely furnished first floor until they entered into a cozy private room located near the back of the house. Finally, he asked Chad if he preferred anything, like a specific drink, before they began their two-man conference.

"I'm good," Chad replied, declining the offer of hospitality prior to settling onto a plush davenport. "Cuzzo, I coulda found this place without da navi since ya pops ain't live too far from here," he added.

Sitting down on an identical large, upholstered sofa adjacent to Chad, Bizzy bluntly responded, "So, what's new?"

Seeing that Bizzy didn't want to indulge in a pointless conversation, Chad straightforwardly replied, "That nigga Blaze got outta da feds three months ago an'…"

"Blaze? That name sounds familiar."

"His real name is Roger Wright an' he used ta work fo' Demetrius."

Forty-one-year-old Roger "Blaze" Wright was arrested by the feds during the first week of June 2007 with Demetrius, Tyrell, Bubba and Obie. Out of the eleven co-conspirators simultaneously apprehended at that time, two of them immediately agreed to cooperate with the government; Roger was one of the two. He and Demetrius had grown up together and had been doing business for nearly two decades. Roger was the only person in the upper echelon of RBF that was of no relation to Demetrius, that was included in RBF's private affairs, so he knew information that could cripple RBF and incarcerate anybody that knew of Demetrius' nefarious activities.

However, with the help of Matthew O'Hare, Demetrius' hotshot lawyer, who was able to discover the other co-operating co-conspirator was being coerced by the two lead agents on the case to give false testimony. Roger's "possibly coached" testimony was discredited by the judge presiding over Demetrius' trial, and Demetrius was acquitted on all counts and set free while he and the others remained imprisoned.

"Befo' we kick this new movement off," Chad said further, "I think it's best we find this nigga first an' take care of him becuz I don't wanna be out here doin' dirt while ... put it like this, I'm already lookin' fo' this hot boy befo' he try ta take us down. I believe he'll fuck wit us if he find out that'chu took over yo' pops operation, 'specially since he ain't succeed with tryna dismantle RBF a few years ago."

With nostrils flared, Bizzy said, "Now I rememba that name. That nigga Blaze called me 'bout two months ago, talkin' 'bout he wanna meet up. I been busy so I never set nuttin' up. But I got his info in my phone. I'll hit him up ta see where he at wit it. Till then, don't trip. We'll merk that nigga if da time comes fo' that.

"Rite now, howeva, we got our hands full in da streets wit these Triple S niggaz, 'specially after Solo's boy, Eddie G, failed ta put that nigga Bumper in da dirt. Now Eddie G claim that Bumper is ducked off hidin' sumwhere an' can't be found, an' this war in da streets is makin' da turf hot, to da point where nobody is focused on chasin' money." He took a breather. "I undastand why ya worried 'bout Blaze, but we gotta put a handle on these Triple S niggaz first an' foremost, so we can start makin' money off these pills."

"Cuzzo, tell me again why you tryna push pills instead of bricks," Chad said, changing the subject. "Powda has taught me an' an entire generation of niggas da metric system, which is da only reason why I'm good wit numbers."

Taking a few seconds to gather himself, Bizzy finally replied, "Let's keep it real wit each otha. You an' I both know that sellin' weed, coke, heroin, pills, *whateva*, is fucked up becuz niggaz ain't stickin' to da G-code like da OGz in da eighties an' early nineties. Niggaz out here now tellin' fo' no damn reason, an' us real niggaz nowadays doin' nuttin' to make these rats shut up. So, by sayin' that, da way I wanna sell pills deals wit less street niggaz than we would if we sold weed, coke an' heroin. Now I ain't sayin' that these pussy-ass crackas are some thorough muthafuckas, but I feel like Da Bottom Boyz can getta betta run wit da pills, an' make a decent profit befo' we pull out."

Bizzy then went on to tell Chad the come-up story about the Benjamin brothers, two white boys that lived in California. According to his new buddy Rusty, who heard about the brothers through the grapevine, the Benjamin brothers got into the pill business by first selling illegal steroid pills over the internet. After making a large sum of money from that illicit scheme, the brothers opened their first lawfully begotten pain clinic in 2008. They then linked up with a drug wholesale company named Acticon Pharm that supplied them with a million opiate pills for their clinic.

They eventually opened three additional pain clinics and staffed them with a total of thirteen doctors that saw as many as five hundred people a day. The doctors were paid per patient and netted as much as a hundred and fifty grand a month. Their "patients" were mainly drug dealers, runners and addicts with no legitimate need for the addictive pills. So, to help justify the pill prescriptions, the brothers had a friend that worked at an MRI company and they used the company's mobile MRI unit, which they parked and did business behind various clubs to issue phony test results. Therefore, the legit clinics gave out bonafide prescriptions.

From 2008 to now, a two-year span, the rumor was that the brothers peddled over twenty million pills out of their four clinics, generating so much money daily that employees toted cash away in garbage bags before stashing it in Swiss bank accounts.

Observing the intrigued look upon Chad's face after ending the story about the Benjamin brothers' lucrative pill mill network, Bizzy said, "Altho' these white boyz are supposedly runnin' da pill game in Cali without havin' ta sell a single pill outside of their clinics, I plan on usin' that same scheme on this side. Rusty claims he can get da pills from that same Acticon Pharm company, if I have da money to open up my own pain clinic wit a small staff an' a couple doctors first."

81

"How y' know sumbody ain't runnin' that game in Florida already, Cuzzo?"

"Rusty is lookin' into that —"

"You trust this white boy?" Chad inquired, cutting Bizzy off. "How y' know this shit 'bout these Benjamin crackas ain't nuttin' but a way ta get us fucked up? If it's as easy as ya white boy say it is, why he ain't tryna do it himself wit crackas he know?"

"Like I said earlier ... don't trip. Lemme quarterback this shit. Besides, Rusty won't know 'bout anybody in da clique, 'cept fo'me. He's my responsibility. Once I feel like he'll threaten *my* freedom, you bets believe that I'll turn his white ass into Casper." He grinned. "Bitin' this hand that feeds ya is not only an expensive dinner, it's a last meal."

Only after Bizzy felt he somewhat convinced Chad to have faith in his decision making, did he commence to break down the numbers so that Chad could start becoming knowledgeable about pills. Based upon the little knowledge he acquired from his stint of selling pills, the street value for the highly addictive painkillers varied, depending on the pill itself. Although there were a few users that bought a single pill at a time, most users purchased pills in packs, ranging from ten to fifty pills, while most low-level dealers bought no more than a hundred and eighty pills. The more pills purchased, the cheaper per pill in the pack.

And out of all the pills, Bizzy took heed how the best seller was the Roxycodone 30, or "blues," because, as explained to him, they were among the cheapest opiates. They had a cleaner high, compared to an Oxycontin 80, and they didn't have a time-release coating that required the user to scrape or wash off like an Oxy 80.

Being that he was in the early stages of forming the base for his elaborate scheme, he would just have to rely on Rusty to get him at least three boxes of pills at eighty-four hundred per box, with each box containing one hundred pills in twelve bottles, or twelve hundred total to sell at the clubs for now. While he was locating a vacant store in a nice plaza, two doctors willing to get paid just for their signatures, and waiting for Rusty to obtain the boxes of pills, along with the information on whether or not someone was utilizing the Benjamin brothers' scheme in South Florida, he had to formulate another complicated plot that would make his road to riches much easier.

He personally felt he had no choice but to place the current plan at the top of his agenda, to eradicate his adversaries, Triple S. *It's impossible for two kings to sit down when there's only one throne*, Bizzy reasoned as he and Chad sat in silence. *I must put all my available time and resources into this war in order for me to be victorious and move forward with my pill mill.*

"I gotta end this shit quick, fast an' in a hurry."

"Huh?" Chad asked, confused.

Snapping back to reality, Bizzy simply said, "If ya want sumthin' done rite, you gotta do it ya'self."

Chapter Nine

June 13, 2010 6:38 am

Beach, FL

Disarray.

Compromised.

From the freshly sewn seams, things were unraveling. It was onset, too soon.

The dark cloud had materialized, positioning itself over Devon's life yet again. For little over a year, her future was progressing for the better. Thinking this "new" life she had claimed would usher her to serenity, however, was indeed nonsensical, for it was once said by someone wise that all good things must come to an end. *Damn, can I ever beat the odds*? she wondered while completely disregarding her surroundings. *Lord, why must I continue to undergo trials and tribulations after all that I've endured already?*

"... the police so long to get here? Devon, are you a hundred percent sure the alarm ..." *Pause.* "Dee? Helllloooooo!"

Beyond agitated with the recent events that had passed, Devon was jolted from her train of thought, and irately said, "What da fuck do ya want? Dammit!"

"Oh, hell no! Uh-uh ... you will not talk to me like that!" Miracle retorted, matching her significant other's attitude after showing nothing but compassion. "I'm not the enemy, Devon, so do not come at me as if I am!"

Nonchalantly, Devon sucked her teeth before leaning forward in the high-back leather office chair and loudly snorting a thick, long line of coke off the birchwood desktop.

Then silence.

"See ... that's bullshit," Miracle frustratingly said as she stood up from her desk, "I've been the true definition of a 'ride-or-die' bitch, and this is the thanks I get? This how you treat me after five

---

years? I'm a hundred and you know it! But you… you've kept me in the dark, lyin' to me through omission from the moment we became committed. And once I discovered the *real* truth from your *real* brother, I still forgave you. I understood, so there was no need for you to explain. But *this* … bullshit attitude you got when I did *nothing*, I'm not havin' it." And just before exiting StudioX's main office, she added, "And it's obvious there's somethin' you're still not tellin' me. So since you don't trust me enough to tell me what's really goin' on, holla at me when you can do more than suck your fuckin' teeth!"

Door slams

With a clearly pissed off Miracle gone, that left Devon in the company of Rhapsody.

After several minutes of eerie silence, the quietness became uncomfortable and unbearable for Rhapsody. Seeing the fixed scowl on her lover's face, just staring at the now empty safe in the wall, gave her mixed emotions. She was afraid, sad and worried. She was at a rare crossroads, not knowing what could be done or said to help the situation. But she felt compelled to at least say something to show her undeniable support. This was one of those meaningful moments where she felt she must prove her love and loyalty was genuine, especially now that Miracle was out of the picture, at least for the time being.

Thought after thought, idea after idea, flooded Rhapsody's feeble mind, before finally feeling as if she knew the right thing to say. "Daddy?"

No response.

Rhapsody took a deep breath before forcing herself to say what was on her mind. "Daddy, I know that day them dudes shot ya changed everythang." She halted only because she attentively watched Devon's piercing eyes shift from the safe to her. Somewhat hesitant now as she plainly saw the anger in those generally serene eyes, she bravely continued, "Look at da bright side, Daddy, you're alive. Altho' ya had ta get a few stitches fo' a flesh wound in ya arm, you're alive! God is great!

"Anywayz, I gotta cousin that went overseas an' was shot while in Iraq. He's.... okay, but he came back home..." she sighed, "... different. He came back wit... ummm, what's it called?... Oh yeah, PTSD. What he experienced ova there changed him fo' da worse. He takin meds now an' goin' ta counselin'. So, I'm not sayin' you need meds, Daddy, but... but maybe ya should seek counselin'. If ya want, I'll call my cousin an'... "

"Get da fuck out my office, Keema."

Shocked, and frozen in fear, hot tears proceeded to form in Rhapsody's eyes.

Through clenched teeth, Devon said, "Bitch, don't make me repeat myself."

Rhapsody bolted out of the office with tears cascading down her face. Sadly, there was no way Rhapsody could've known that Devon's behavior after surviving the shooting was the least of the problems that Devon faced now.

Nevertheless, it was certainly true that the shooting had altered Devon. But she was confident she needn't worry, for RahRah, Bumper and Skat swore to handle the failed attempt on all their lives, STAT! *However, if there was no need to worry about that,* Devon thought, *it was unquestionably time to worry about "this."*

"This" was the recent burglary of StudioX, which occurred not even three hours ago. The least of Devon's worries was the thoroughly demolished, ransacked office. Neither was the stolen hundred and twenty-five thousand from the busted safe, nor Miracle's abrupt exit.

The shit did hit the fan mightily, however, the very moment that Devon realized her priceless video was among the loot stolen in the busted safe. That alone was cause to panic. With the break-in being extremely fresh, and with no clear evidence she could see that would lead to a sensible suspect, there wasn't much she could do except remain momentarily stunned at her inconceivable misfortune.

Past experience taught her that initial shock would subside, changing her inaction to action in order to pound the pavement for viable information. She must now take steady calculated steps, for her chaotic, compromised life possibly depended on it.

*****

Meanwhile, a sobbing and heaving Rhapsody ran unsteadily and carelessly from Devon's office to her Nissan Altima. And just when she thought matters couldn't get any worse, she saw a crisp piece of folded paper, flapping in the morning's light breeze, held firmly in place under her wiper blade. Usually, the outrage and anxiety after finding a note would soon fizzle out and give way to sad resignation.

This time, however, something felt profoundly different.

With her shift starting in about four hours, she'd only returned to StudioX approximately thirty minutes ago after Miracle informed her via text about the break-in. Therefore, this note was a clear indication that she was being stalked. Still, her reaction to finding the note was remarkably peculiar. She had no reaction, because she no longer gave a fuck!

Oblivious to her surroundings, she listlessly unfolded the note, read it and tore it up without reacting to the latest message. The wind would sweep it far away from her and her heartache.

As a deflated Rhapsody numbly entered her vehicle, the pair of eyes vigilantly watched her until she pulled out of the parking lot.

"It's almost ova, boo," the person said to no one in particular, repeating the exact words on the note before pursuing the Altima on his motorcycle. "Almost."

Chapter Ten

July 5, 2010 12:43 pm

Miami Beach, FL

Being the sole head man of any business had its perks as well its frustrations, and that was generally accepted in the world of business.

Even Bizzy experienced it.

However, the paltry "business" that Bizzy previously handled paled in comparison to what he presently had in the making. So far, all frustration, no perks. But it was too early to even think about aborting the mission.

Resurrecting a prestigious organization took relentless dedication and tenacity, and with the right help, Bizzy felt he could achieve his latest endeavor. Still, he had not the slightest idea about the condition of the road that lay ahead. And it would manifest to him the distinction between *understanding* and *knowing* soon.

The pressure Bizzy felt was immense and mounting. He couldn't quite picture what his father endured to become the street legend that he had been, from before the formation of the Rock-Bottom Family, until his premature death. He was jumping headfirst into shark-infested, unfamiliar waters. Now he understood why his father made endless attempts to steer him away from the grueling, cold-blooded society of the large-scale narcotics trade. *This is surely a man's game*, he concluded before shedding a single tear in remembrance of *the man* known in the streets as Kilo.

Bizzy undoubtedly missed his father dearly, thinking about him every day. His father may not have been an "American Dad" like Cliff Huxtable, but he learned a lot— both good and bad— from just watching him. Also, through the vast war stories that he'd heard, and the meager get-togethers that they'd shared, the lessons learned, and the knowledge gained had become clearer, more appropriate and extremely useful as he stepped further into the beast's belly. Yes, he was lacking criminal enterprise wisdom. But there was no more time to dwell on his inexperience. He would just have to learn as he progressed while exuding the poise of a well-rounded entrepreneur. And with today's particular meeting, Bizzy should learn if his façade and limited knowledge was formal enough to be in the company of the upper echelon in the game of drugs.

"Greetings, my friend," the man said after standing up from the park table to shake Bizzy's hand. "You must be Demetrius Junior. Wow, the resemblance." He smiled. "Excuse myself … I'm Adrian. Your father and I conducted a lot of business together before… before—"

"Yeah, I know," Bizzy interjected after the handshake.

"My condolences." After a moment of silence, Adrian suddenly stated, "Where's my manners? Please, sit." Once they were seated, he continued, "Thank you for accepting my invite. I wasn't sure you'd show since you don't know me. I'm glad you've come, however."

"Well, I'm here now. So what's this all about?" Bizzy sternly asked.

"This … This is a simple introductory meeting to feel each other out. There isn't too much for us to discuss now. Therefore, for a few minutes, we … chat. Because if you're anything like your father, I'm going to enjoy this brief conversation."

"Why is that?" Bizzy asked curiously as he adjusted himself in the seat across from Adrian. They were in a fairly busy park near North Miami's beach, and there was a chess game set up on the table.

"Because, my friend-in-the-making, I sense a lot of your father's business acumen in you, so I sense my accounts … yes, with an *s* … increasing tremendously real soon. I can feel it!" He glanced up as the sun hid behind a cloud. "I'd love to get a deal done with you today, but this isn't the appropriate time or place."

As the moderately warm breeze blew, Bizzy chuckled, then asked, "An' exactly how do ya' know that after dis *one* conversation, where we know nuttin' 'bout each otha, I'm willin' ta deal wit'chu?"

"Because … your father dealt with me for years … and *you're* here now," he answered sarcastically as if it was all so obvious. "Curiosity always gets the better of the cat." Adrian was an affluent, handsome Hispanic in his late thirties. Without much of a Spanish accent, he was the civil, chic version of Tony Montana. He surrounded himself with nothing but the finest money could buy, such as a custom-made wardrobe, brilliant jewelry, foreign-made cars, exotic women, and magnificent mansions. It was hard not to admire and envy his lavish lifestyle.

Being a flamboyant middleman for the biggest cocaine manufacturer in South America was both unsafe and unwise. But the umbrella of protection provided by his employer allowed him freedom to be a bit reckless. "Besides, I have something for you." A gust of wind blew open the top half of his unbuttoned dress shirt, exposing the fine curly hairs on his chest. "A package."

Man, I don't even know this Latin-lover-dressing-ass fool, Bizzy said to himself as he closely observed the man across from him in silence, *and he already talking about deals and packages, as if I'm settling for the first deal or accepting what he has to offer like a peon would do.*

After almost two minutes of no talking, with only the blowing wind and the hustle and bustle of Miami's street life providing background noise, Bizzy said, "I knew this meetin' was gonna drop sumthin' heavy." He leaned forward in his seat. "An' I knew you'd have sum package, or sumthin', fo' me today, which is da only reason why I accepted when ya people called me unexpectedly.

"How ya got my phone numba in da first place is beyond me … so that tells me tha'cha know all about me. Hell, ya may even know what I did, what I do an' what I'm tryna do. I know all this

90

becuz, altho' I haven't dealt wit many men of yo' caliber personal-ly, I've seen plenty of gangsta movies."

The serious look on Adrian's face gradually turned into a smile. "Hahaha … gangsta movies? You claim to know all of what you know *now* because of gangsta movies? Hahaha … You're giving too much credit to *Scarface, The Godfather* and *Boyz 'n the Hood* when you grew up in the shadow of a real, well-respected gangsta."

"True, my pops was da star in his gangsta movie. Howeva, he did his best ta keep me outta da game, ta keep me humble an' innocent. *But* I still know this da part of da movie you cut da bullshit an' get down ta bizness."

"Business like men … like with your father, I assume?" he replied quickly, disregarding Bizzy's juvenile remark.

"Not really. Bizness like men, of course …but bizness wit Bizzy an' Da Bottom Boyz."

"Da Bottom Boyz?" Adrian began to fiddle with the black king chess piece. "I-I-I cannot… recall any Bottom Boyz. Are they out of state? Are …" With a look of shock on his face, he blurted out, "Are you *already* trying to go regional with your pill mill?"

"No, I'm definitely not ready ta go regional. I'm steady gain-in' ground in PBC. An' no, Da Bottom Boyz ain't outta state. Da Bottom Boyz are RBF reborn. New name, new strategy —"

"With new problems," Adrian interposed. "Yes Mr. Bizzy, I'm well aware, thanks to your revelation, that it's *you* that's been going to war with Triple S … with your Bottom Boyz … causing the murder rate to increase recently in the downtown West Palm Beach area. I'm aware of what Triple S has done, so is this war about … revenge, is it?"

Trying to keep his composure, Bizzy calmly said, "It's only about da money. It will always be about da money."

"How is it *only* about the money when you cannot keep your feelings in check? This street war you've begun *may* be over prime drug territory and neutralizing the opposition, but I sense that your motive is revenge."

Swallowing the lump in his throat, Bizzy responded, "I'm in it fo' da money. That's all."

"But it costs money, a lot of money, to go to war with the likes of them. They have plenty of money, dope, guns and goons at their disposal. And they're only getting stronger, no matter how many of them you kill. If you're not going for the shepherd, the sheep won't scatter. So, before you make any real money, you'll lose all that you have now—money, family, friends—trying to fight this war *if* you're not killed in it yourself." He paused briefly. "Do you play chess?"

"No."

"Well, my friend, if you played chess then you'd know that every piece and every move is critical to you winning the game. You'd know to sacrifice only when necessary, mainly when it's beneficial for you. Chess is a strategic game, and you need patience and foresight. You cannot act off instincts alone in the game of chess, nor in this game we play."

After some thought and trying to figure out how to say what he felt without being overly offensive, Bizzy nonchalantly said, "It's kill or be killed in da game *I* play. An' da game of chess is fo' nerds, not G'z."

Adrian sighed after shaking his head in disappointment. "My friend, no more gangsta movies for you. You have a lot to learn about this game in *my* world, and you possess too much potential to waste it on this petty war that you'll surely lose since you're not going for the head. Once again, I understand that your father's stolen drugs are involved ..." he sighed again. "I'll tell you what... besides the package I already have for you, I have something personal to offer. Only because I like you, and I admired your father, may the Virgin Mary bless his soul."

Bizzy then observed Adrian retrieve a rather bulky manilla envelope that was tucked beside him in his seat. "What's that?"

"Well, to put it plainly, it's something you're not going to like, but you'll be glad to have it." He slid the package past the chess set on the table. "Now, I don't know the contents of the envelope.

It's none of my business. But I must warn you, I was informed it's pretty… breathtaking."

Bizzy stared at the package that sat on the edge of the table. He was confused. Here he was, a thriving young black man, sitting in a park with a prominent Hispanic, with a large suspicious looking manilla envelope on the table between them. *Just like in the movies, this is either a set-up or bad news,* Bizzy told himself as he covertly scanned his surroundings. *What's in there, Mr. Cat?*

And then, just like two magnets, Bizzy's hand slowly gravitated towards the package. He cautiously pressed on it. Inside, he could feel papers and the outline of something hard and square, like a CD case. Once he presumed it was safe, he picked up the package. There were no visible markings on its outside that he could see.

"Okay," Adrian began while looking at his million-dollar Piaget. "just like war, it costs money… time, that is, my friend. I really wanted to talk to you about your booming pill business," he winked, "and get a deal done today, as I said earlier. But I'll contact you soon. And how soon depends on how you handle …" He gestured toward the package in Bizzy's hand before standing up. "So, someone will contact you when it's time. And remember, it's like you mentioned, it's always about the money. Life is short, death is promised. Farewell."

As Adrian straightened himself and commenced to walk off into the hot South Florida sun, Bizzy added, "What happened to da offer? Da personal one?"

Adrian stopped. With his back to Bizzy, he glanced over his shoulder and said, "Don't worry, my friend. You've accepted that offer already. Like I said, you have to treat this game like chess. Patience. Foresight. Checkmate." He winked, then he was gone with the wind, blending in with the pedestrian traffic.

*****

During the intervening time …
"Bingo!"

"What? You gotta eye on him?"

Ignoring his excited partner, Raw Deal continued to watch the target's every move. It was rather easy tracking their mark the past few weeks, although a majority of the surveillance was of him overseeing his relocation to West Palm Beach from Orlando. Their suspect was always on the go. Subsequently, Agent Dino and he had a difficult time discerning whether their target's destinations were legitimate errands or places to hold quick secret meetings. Rather than speculating too much, he and Dino decided to bide their time until the lowlife fucked up big time. *No, I'm not going to let another Woodson embarrass the federal government again so soon,* Raw Deal thought in the passenger seat of the Marauder as he witnessed the hoodlum finally reach his destination. "Well, look at the fleas that fell off Fluffy."

"Okay, stop with the bullshit, rookie," Dino finally snapped. "Just fuckin' tell me what's going on, for crying out loud. Damn you starting to act like a jerk now when you get the binoc—"

"Our man is presently meeting with Mendoza ... as in *the* Adrian Mendoza, the most flamboyant drug-dealing spic there is," Raw Deal said bluntly without breaking his focus on Bizzy and Adrian. "He's virtually untouchable."

"Now we're on to something." Dino proceeded to rub his hands together as if he were in a buffet line with all his favorite foods. "Do we call back up? Do you think it's going down now? Tell me, what's happening? What're they doing, for Christ's sake?"

"Hold your horses ... they just sat down after an awkward handshake. There's a chess game on the table. But I doubt they're meeting in public on this beautiful afternoon just to play chess." Silence. "Not much action, just talking ... talking ... more talking." More silence. "Still talking ... oooh, wait a second ...oh, still talking ... talking some more ... just tal—"

"Alright, fuckin' smart ass. I get it."

"You wanted to know what's going on. Now you're mad because I'm keeping you up-to-date?"

94

"I don't know what's gotten into you, rookie, but fuck you." Dino grimaced, then he snatched the binoculars from Raw Deal's face.

"Hey!" Raw Deal barked. "Don't be snatching shit out of my hands or mishandling the unit's shit like that! You break them, they'll take it out of your pension."

Staring through the binoculars now, Dino replied, "Like I said, fuck you ... and the government." He laughed. "Now, where's our boy? Point 'em out."

Once Raw Deal showed him where to look, Dino observed the duo in silence. Then, "I see some odd movement from Mendoza," he informed his partner. "It looks ... he just grabbed ... a manilla envelope and ... placed it on the table." He lowered the binoculars. "What do we do now?"

"I don't know." Raw Deal shrugged. "You're the senior investigator here, having twenty-one years' experience doing this."

"Yeah, I know what I'd do, but I need you to start leading, to start applying your own tried and true methods now, to form your own conclusions. We've been partners for two years now. You're intelligent, attentive and brave, but you're scared to unleash your full potential. One day, you'll be senior investigator with a rookie beside you and going through the same. Until then, we must trust each other's decisions. It's time you start making the calls like when you worked for WPBPD. Just don't get me killed before I retire, that's all I ask." He laughed and watched his partner grin as well. "So..."

Raw Deal inhaled deeply before exhaling slowly. "It's been a while, but I... I-I guess we keep watching. Maybe something will happen that forces our hand."

"Good. And until then, we just watch and take notes, continue to build up our case, because nabbing Mendoza would be a *huge* bust for our unit, especially for you, if you're the arresting officer. But I doubt we'll be able to take him down for anything major, since he doesn't touch drugs. His time will come and when it does, it's curtains for him."

95

"What about our boy?"

"Again, what do you think?"

"Hmmm, I think he's in way over his head. He's a puppy playing with big dogs. So, all we do with him is watch his untrained ass until he shits where he lays."

Smiling at Raw Deal's analogy, Dino nodded in approval. "Good … good job." He then put the binoculars back to his face. "Oh, no!"

"What happened?" a startled Raw Deal asked.

"Mendoza has vanished, leaving our boy at the table by himself with the envelope." He scanned left, then right. "Yeah, Mendoza is gone."

"Hmph, that was a *rookie* mistake." Raw Deal chuckled. "Did he open the package at least? I wonder what's inside."

"Well, we may never find out because he's leaving now. And since this guy is an impeccable driver, I doubt he'll give us reason to have a local cop pull him over." He sighed. "So I guess we just continue to tail him until we have something promising for the grand jury. I can feel it, though. We're about to catch a big break."

As Dino put away the binoculars and started the car, Raw Deal said, "I'm going to call the C.I. Blaze, and tell him he needs to hurry up and get us something useful on this guy before it's too late."

"Yeah, the sooner the better."

They pulled away from the curb in pursuit of their target.

Flame

Chapter Eleven

September 11, 2010 10:21 pm

West Palm Beach, FL

Digging for information.

Unknowingly, two shadows busied themselves the past two months searching for generally the same answer: Who done it? That was the million-dollar question. And it just so happened that one shadow offered a one-million-dollar reward for an answer to that question, while the other remained incognito.

However, upon learning there was a reward being offered, "Incognito" began to worry, because it was only a matter of time before the truth came to light. "Incognito" no longer cared about "who done it," it would then become all about "what to do next?"

The plot thickened and Devon seethed. She tried her best to find out who broke into StudioX without being too aggressive or too inquisitive. She just put the word out in the street and left it at that, hoping that her street cred would lead someone to tell her something, anything. But as days passed with the streets saying nothing, she was starting to feel a little at ease, she was starting to no longer care. She prayed there was no cause to worry.

But Devon knew her luck.

Then, *WHAM!*

As expected, life slapped the shit out of her yet again.

Two weeks ago, club promoter DJ Kato released the fourth edition of his *Thugz & Gangstaz* DVD, causing Devon's world to flip upside down after it was released. Usually, the DVD simply showed the daily life in the streets of PBC, from niggas on the block hustling and gangbanging, to car shows and festivals to interviews with certain street niggas.

Devon wasn't interested in watching volume four, because after watching all of volume one and parts of volume two, she felt she'd watched them all. But when word got to her that volume four contained scenes from the graphic murder of the street legend Kilo, she felt giddy, her cat was out of the bag.

Then, as she presumed, shortly after the release of *T&G 4*, word on the street and social media was there was a cool M for anybody that knew who killed Kilo, or who leaked the tape. The matter became dangerous fast once she learned DJ Kato was in critical condition after being shot a week ago. She knew her brother Bizzy was busy hunting for information, which was him unknowingly hunting for her.

Prior to the release of *T&G 4*, Devon had a gut feeling something was off about Bizzy the past few months. For starters, she hadn't spoken to him since the end of May. That was strange to her, because they'd been in touch at least weekly once they were reunited. She naively believed he was mad with her after she turned down his proposal, which was to give him free reign to sell pills in her club. If he would've asked her a year ago, she would've accepted, but she was out of the game and all the way legit now.

After that brief get-together at Denny's, there was no further communication between them. She figured he'd get over it, cool down and hit her back sooner or later, but he never did. She even took the initiative a month ago to call him numerous times, but he never answered. And since he never attempted to call her after the release of the DVD with their father's murder, she was certain now that she had to tread light and be careful when she travelled. "Trusty .380, you saved me once," Devon said to herself as she drove around solo, "I pray you'll save me again."

Phone rings

Seeing the name pop up on her phone for the third time in forty-five minutes caused Devon to suck her teeth for the third time. Finally, she decided to answer the call. "What, Keema? Rite now ain't da time ta be playin' games, so what'cha want befo' I hang up … Bitch, you gotta be smokin'! Ya must don't think I know ya on them pills bad, an' ya blowin' all ya bread on 'em. But ya got me fucked up if ya think I'ma give ya some mo' money. I done already gave ya ass 'bout three stacks in da last two months or so. How ya gonna pay me back when ya ass ain't been ta work in ova a month?

"Keema, miss me wit those tears. An' ya dunno what I *really* got goin' on in my life rite now. But ya need ta tighten up, fa' real. So I ain't givin' ya nuttin'. As a matter ah fact, don't bring ya ass back ta work or ta da crib till ya kick that habit. Da last time I saw ya I almost got sick 'cuz of how much weight ya lost. I mean what I say, too, Keema. Ya hear me? ... Holla!"

Devon ended the call in a fouler mood than she was before. She decided to head to StudioX, since her club was the only place she could truly focus her mind, thinking of new concepts for her business, rather than thinking about running out of town for her safety once again.

What's more, StudioX was the only place that Devon saw Miracle nowadays. Miracle was still mad at her, spending most days and nights at her mom's house with Kamani, but she was devoted to her duties at the club. *I have to make things right with my one and only before it's too late,* Devon thought, *because the years of love between us has been forgotten in the hatred of a minute.*

*****

Meanwhile, in a motel in Lantana, Florida

"... what'chu doin', Daddy?" Rhapsody said rather sadly after Devon finally answered. "... I-I-I called ta see if ya would lemme borrow some mo' money... I know, an' I'ma pay ya back, Daddy, I promise ... I'm just tryna get myself togetha, Daddy. I'm sorry, but ya ain't gotta crazy nigga stalkin' ya like I do..."

crying ...

"Yeah, Daddy, I hear ya."

Rhapsody was completely depleted, for she finally burnt the last bridge. After her poverty-stricken mother gave her money twice before cutting her off, Devon was her last hope. Devon

100

unknowingly supplied for her pill habit for the last few months, so it was somewhat a shock to her that Devon now knew about her addiction.

Once she hung up the phone in the one-day overdue Super 8 Motel room, Rhapsody laid back on the bed and started to reflect on her young life. She couldn't believe how she went from a life of happiness, with plenty of money to blow to a life of sorrow, and dead broke, in a matter of seven months. Well, she knew the disturbing notes she used to find here and there were the main cause of her depression, but it had been nearly three months since she last found one. Still, that didn't stop her from stressing over the possibility that her stalker would pop back up and continue to harass her. And those never-ending thoughts drove her crazy.

With tears still in her eyes, Rhapsody reluctantly picked up the motel phone again and proceeded to dial the spider's number that came along and introduced her to the pill she came to love.

"Who this?" the spider answered.

"Hey, Bug. This Rhapsody."

"Oh, what's good, boo? Where ya at?"

"In da motel still." She sniffled. "Umm … are ya still good?"

"Of course. You gon' slide thru, wit'cha fine ass?" JuneBug laughed a little.

Rhapsody giggled a bit too. "Boy, you shot out. But yeah, I'ma slide thru." She paused again, thinking about how her gas tank was nearly on *E*.

"What's wrong, boo?" he asked, picking up that something was amiss in her tone. "Talk ta me, I talk back."

She sighed. "Ummm … I dunno how you'll feel about this, but … I-I ain't got no money. I'm broke. But I'll pay ya back as soon—"

"No problem, boo," he cut her off. "I'm pretty sho we can work sumthin' out, one way or da otha, feel me? But I'm at my dawg crib rite now. Can ya slide thru ova here? I'm in Bear Lakes. Y' know where that at?"

"It's in West Palm Beach, rite?"

101

"Yeah. A lil out west, tho."

"Okay. I'm on my way now. I'll be there in 'bout … thirty to forty minutes, okay?"

"Bet. I can't wait ta see ya fine chocolate ass eitha. Holla."

Rhapsody had officially met JuneBug in StudioX almost three months ago. That night, she was at the bar getting her drink on, once her shift on the pole had ended. With so much on her mind at that time, due to her hectic life snowballing out of control, she didn't want to be bothered. Yet, she frequently had to politely decline the advances and offerings of drinks from the endless line of horny men that approached her. She would only take so much, for she wanted to at least drink one drink in peace.

Then, yet another man approached her and set her off, causing her to snap on the unlucky fella, and that unfortunate man was JuneBug. Rather than snapping back at her, JuneBug simply smiled, which was a reaction that caught her totally off guard. That gold-grilled smile did something to her, something she hadn't experienced in a long time. She apologized to him before they aptly became acquainted and sparked up a conversation, thus giving her that moment of peace she wanted, also.

That convo they engaged in became so deep that she became deeply intrigued by the good-looking, rather intelligent and polite JuneBug. Ultimately, she would learn before they departed from each other's company that he had the means to help ease the pain he clearly saw she was enduring, with a little pill—Roxycodone.

JuneBug hooked Rhapsody up with a few pills for free that night, therefore hooking her on pills to this day. Nonetheless, she never attempted to "hook up" with him since it was strictly business, although they partook in some playful flirting here and there. She was still madly in love with her Devon.

But her love for pills was slowly overshadowing that love and obscuring her better judgment.

Rhapsody drove extremely slow to the address JuneBug had provided her, praying the whole trip there that she wouldn't run out of gas. Upon her safe arrival, she was met in the driveway by her dealer. She then noticed that he wasn't alone either. With him were two other men, and one of those men she instantly recognized, it wasn't only how big and tall the man was that made him recognizable, she knew him personally from the time that he used to work as a bouncer at StudioX.

"Damn, boo, did ya get lost or sumthin'?" JuneBug asked after he opened her soon-to-be repo'd Altima's door. "It took ya an hour to get here."

"Naw, I ain't get lost. I had ta … make a quick stop first," she lied.

"Ai'ight. Well, c'mon in da house fo' a second. I was so caught up out here, choppin it up wit my boyz, I fa'got you were on da way. I'll get'chu sumthin' ta drink while we in there."

As she looked back and forth between JuneBug and the six-foot-eight giant leaning against one of the cars in the driveway ahead of her, she casually said, "Ummm … naw, I'm good. I'll wait rite here. Besides, I gotta hit da road soon. I gotta … stop by my mama house."

Once again, sensing something was off, JuneBug said, "What's really good? I know ya ain't scared of my dawgz. They not gonna bite, if that's what'cha worried …"

"Damn, cake man! Tell ya friend ta get out da car!" Chad hollered before he and the giant laughed. "We don't bite!"

Smiling, JuneBug said, "See, I told ya they won't bite." He winked. Then, he grabbed her hand and attempted to pull her gently out of the car. "C'mon, I'll protect you."

She tried to resist a little to let him know she wasn't in the mood to exit her car. But his relentlessness caused her to eventually give up. "Well, we gotta make it quick, okay? I gotta leave in five minutes. No longer than that, okay?"

As the five-two Rhapsody trailed closely behind JuneBug up the driveway towards the others, she kept her head low with hopes the giant wouldn't recognize her. However, she knew it was going to be impossible for the giant and the other man to not stare at her, because of what she was wearing. Although she had lost close to thirty pounds and a few inches off her once forty-four-inch hips, the pink lace blouse and pink miniskirt with the white thigh-high boots was a bit extravagant for the occasion. *I knew I should've kept my damn jogging pants and big T-shirt on, she cursed herself as they drew closer to the others, this is what I get for putting on something seductive in order to get some fucking pills and gas money with no problems.*

"Goddamn Bug, that's how ya doin' it? Shawty lookin' good enuff ..."

"Hey, hey, watch what'chu say 'round my lady friend," June-Bug said somewhat seriously to his childhood friend.

"My bad, bruh. It's all grizzy. I'm just complimentin' ya ... lady friend ... on how good she lookin'!" Chad then turned his full attention to Rhapsody. "Hope I ain't offend ya, miss... " he stalled, waiting for her to give her name.

"Rhapsody," she mumbled. Then, she quickly said, "Can we hurry up Bug, please. I need ..."

"Rhapsody?" the giant finally spoke upon recognizing the name. "Yo', Rhapsody, it's me, Solo. You don't rememba me?"

Her heart began to beat fast, and she felt as if she were going to have an anxiety attack. However, she kept her composure as best as she could. Then, with a fake expression on her face as if she were unsure who he was, she stammered while looking up at him, "Solo?... Ummm... I can't rememba ... "

"Stop playin', Rhap. How many otha big niggaz my size ya know? It's only been ... hmmm, 'bout two years since I last saw ya. I used ta work at StudioX as a bouncer fo' ya boy... I mean, ya girl, Devon. Star is my baby mama, an' I know ya rememba her."

Still playing the clueless part in hopes of getting out of the situation sooner rather than later, she replied, "Of course, I know Star. But I still dunno who you are."

"You gotta be kiddin'," Solo said frustratedly, as both June-Bug and Chad looked on bewilderedly. After a brief moment, he then blurted out, "I got it! I bet'cha rememba that day when you an'... what's her name? ... Miracle! Yeah, you an' Miracle gotta ride home in my boss' silver Benz one day. Y'all had a flat tire an' it was rainin'. Remember?"

Seeing that there was no easy way out of the situation, she finally shrieked, "Yeah, yeah, I rememba now. Solo, Star's baby daddy. Duh. How can I forget. You were also on da *Maury* show wit her. Yeah, I rememba now. How are you? How's Star? How's da baby?"

Hating that the *Maury* show was mentioned, Solo coldly said, "Er'body good … just fine."

"Well, it was nice seein' ya again." She then turned to June-Bug. "I really need ta go. Can we make this move now, please?"

"Ai'ight," he said as he proceeded to lead her away and into the house.

Once inside the decked out mini-mansion, Rhapsody's eyes got big as dinner plates. "Damn, whose house is this? This place is super nice."

"It's my homie crib. He outta town rite now. Me an' my boyz house-sittin' fo' him till he get back. But never mind all that, you thirsty?"

"No."

"Okay, follow me, Miss I'm-in-a-hurry." He laughed.

"Boy, stop. I am in a hurry." She playfully punched him in the arm before following him up a set of stairs. Once on the second floor, she followed him into one of the bedrooms. "Oh my God, this room is huge!"

"An' this ain't even da master bedroom. This just a guest room."

Taking in the décor of the spacious room, she muttered, "Humph, I wish I was a permanent guest here."

An impish grin appeared on JuneBug's mug, then he said, "We can make that arrangement. Well, at least until my dawg gets back from outta town." He got quiet briefly. "By da way, why ya livin' in a motel? Fo' da last few days, you been callin' me from motels. Is ya cell phone off? An' I know ya fine ass ain't home-less. So what's good, boo? What'chu got goin' on? If I can help in any way, I will. I know ya heard it ain't trickin' if ya got it, an' I got it." He hit her with that irresistible smile that he knew fucked her up.

Not wanting to show any signs of shame on her face, she said with a fake smile, "I'm good. My phone broke an' I just ain't have da time ta get it fixed. An' I got into it wit my... wit my people an' decided ta hole up in a motel fo' a while. Y' know, to getta break from da drama. But I'm good. Seriously."

"Hmph, I don't believe none of that, but ... okay." He then went over to the elaborate mahogany dresser, opened a drawer and retrieved a big bottle full of blue pills. "So, what'chu need, boo?"

Although she had used X pills quite often while at work, and recreationally with Devon and Miracle at home, the first opiate Rhapsody ever tried without a prescription from a doctor was an Oxycontin 80. She had gotten the pill from Jazzy, who was also a stripper at StudioX, after she had complained about back pain before her shift started. The pain disappeared completely shortly after ingesting the pill, but the high she'd experienced was unpleasant and she never attempted to take another one again, no matter what pain she had.

The next time she took an opiate however, was that fateful night she had met JuneBug. Again, she was in pain, but a different type of pain. Still, the different opiate he had given her gave her a more pleasant high and the pill was a Roxycodone 30. After she took the five free pills he had given her in two days, she began to purchase the Roxy 30s from him daily, one pill at a time at fifteen per pill.

But as she and JuneBug conducted more business and her addiction got worse, she had reached the point where she was currently buying a pack of ten Blues for a hundred dollars every two days.

"Like I said earlier, I don't have any money so, I guess ..."

"Baby girl, miss me wit that bullshit," he contended. "Do I look like I'm pressed fo' money? So, do ya want'cha usual?"

"Ummm... I guess..."

"Maaannn, here! 'Cuz you trippin' rite now. You gonna learn I'm no simp." He then popped open the bottle's top, grabbed her hand and dumped two dozen or more pills into her palm. "There, that should hold ya fo' a while, at least till ya get on ya feet, boo. I undastand er'body hits a ruff patch from time ta time."

Standing there, not knowing what to really say, Rhapsody finally said, "I'll make sho I pay ya back, okay? I promise, Bug."

He shook his head in disbelief. "Damn, ya still don't get it, huh? I don't want'cha money. Here..." He went into his pocket and gave her a wad of bills. "...I don't care 'bout this shit. After getting ta know ya, I stopped wantin' ya money."

Confused, she said, "I don't undastand this."

Without saying another word, he grabbed Rhapsody by her waist and pulled her close for a kiss.

Somewhat taken aback, she dropped the pills and the bills in her hands, spilling it all over the plush carpet underneath them. At first, she tried to resist but after a second, she melted right into his warm embrace and went along with it.

Feeling she was game, JuneBug then guided her towards the California King-size bed. He stopped kissing her and said, "Since ya in a hurry, we gonna make this quick." Once again, that smile. "Now turn around an' lemme give ya a taste of what'chu can have in da near future ... that's *if ya* want it."

Breathing erratically, Rhapsody spun around without being told twice. She wasn't wearing any panties, giving him easy access. She laid the top half of her body on the bed and kept her phat, juicy ass tooted out. When she felt his strong hands grasp her waist, her breath got caught in her throat. Upon entering her honeypot bareback, she took a quick intake of breath before slowly exhaling, relishing the feeling of his long, thick meat missile.

After her walls adjusted to his size, she then began to rock back on her heels, meeting his every thrust. And before she knew it, she had cum hard—harder than she had in a very long time— even harder than when she was with Devon lately. *It's been so*

107

long since I had some real dick, this quickie was the best I've had in years, she thought with tears in her eyes as she remembered the last man she had been with before now. *And I'm sorry, Devon, but I just realized you never truly loved me.*

*****

Simultaneously, in the driveway outside the house ...

"Dawg, I'm tellin' ya, sumthin' ain't rite wit that bitch," Solo explained. "Ain't no way she ain't rememba me. That bitch hidin' sumthin,' or she up ta no good. Trust me. My intuitions are usually on point."

Chad played with the hairs of his goatee before he said, "Well, if Bug up there doin' what we think he doin', then we'll have da homie investigate that bitch. An' hopefully, she'll slip up an' fuck herself."

"Yeah, an' I know exactly what ta tell him ta ask her. I know this ratchet bitch foul. I can feel it." Solo was amped up.

"As they say, what is done in da dark must come ta light," Chad stated. "Now c'mon, let's go inside. I think my favorite show is on rite now. An' hopefully they replay da episode I been dyin' ta see."

"What show is that?" Solo asked with a raised brow.

Making sure there was quite some distance between him and Solo, Chad said, "*Maury*, nigga!"

Flame

Chapter Twelve

September 12, 2010 11:08 am

Mobile, AL

Conflict.

Not only was there an ongoing conflict in the streets of West Palm Beach between Da Bottom Boyz and Triple S, there was an ongoing conflict in Bizzy's head between what and what not to do about certain situations revealed to him the day he opened Adrian's package. That one package had flipped his world upside down.

Prior to opening that wretched package, the one thing that was a nonstop annoyance for him was warring with Triple S over control of the streets of downtown West Palm Beach and the surrounding areas. The contents of that package had nothing to do with that conflict but, with the help of Adrian and his soldiers, the war was now the least of Bizzy's worries.

Triple S was no longer a major element on his agenda. His blueprint of regulating the drug traffic in WPB was now achievable, allowing him to make all the money he desired in the area. However, with so much bloodshed in the streets during the last two months, it wasn't wise for him to immediately go through with his plans, thus causing him to hit the drawing board once more.

Now, the problems he was forced to deal with, whether he wanted to or not, were ones that he wished were nonexistent. With all his plans finally lining up, he didn't have the time to deal with these new problems.

The first matter that was beyond mind-boggling in the package was the paperwork revealing that his incarcerated Uncle Tyrell, was in cahoots with the known rat, Blaze. One of Adrian's many associates learned that the eighty-eight months Tyrell was doing in Lewisburg Penitentiary had gotten the best of him, leading him to call on Blaze for assistance. For an unknown amount of money, Blaze agreed to help his former RockBottom Family member get his sentence reduced drastically by way of Rule 35, and Tyrell agreed to Blaze's monetary payment.

The only condition Tyrell had was that he wouldn't snitch on a person of color, and Blaze immediately knew who the sacrificial white lamb would be to help spring Tyrell from the hellish penitentiary: Kelly Kronkite. However, before their plan got off the ground, Tyrell miraculously survived a brutal stabbing and was shipped to USP Terre Haute, a "drop-down yard," while Blaze mysteriously vanished off the face of the earth.

Although the news of his uncle becoming a rat, and almost being killed because of the choice he made, bothered him heavily, Bizzy had no choice but to charge it to the game with that disturbing news. He ultimately chose to wash his hands of his uncle, for it was really his only choice if he wanted to continue to play the game he was chest deep in. And the good news of Blaze's disappearance meant he didn't have to worry about dealing with him on his own later.

The second subject of concern that he had to address in the package was a bit surprising but not unbelievable. The astonishing disclosure was that two federal agents by the names of Trevor Zimmerman (he vaguely remembered Kelly Kronkite mentioning him) and Justin Holmes were hot on his trail. According to the information contained in the package, the two agents had yet to find any concrete evidence to send his case to the grand jury, but they were anticipating him to slip up any day now. There were also pictures of the two agents, along with the Mercury Marauder they routinely drove, and Bizzy could vaguely remember seeing that Marauder a few times as he ran errands.

Thanks to that information on the agents, Bizzy got a head start. As pre-planned, in the case of an emergency, he wrote a letter and mailed it to Chad's baby momma's crib in Orlando, because he feared his phone had been tapped. The letter explained to Chad that there was to be a sudden change of plans and that he was heading out of state to see if the pill clinic plan could be continued.

He ended up fleeing to Mobile, AL, hooking up with an old friend he knew from his days of running in Tallahassee. While in Mobile, he kept his head in the game by researching the area to see if it was a good place to open his first clinic, far away from the surveilling eyes of agents Dino and Raw Deal.

After a couple of stressful weeks of scouting and researching, he discovered Mobile would be the perfect place to set up shop. So, via another letter, he informed Chad that he would be staying in Mobile permanently to oversee the successful opening of the first clinic, while he, JuneBug and Solo stayed off the radar until it cooled off in WPB. He promised to keep them up-to-date and supplied with everything they needed, because the money they would make when the time was right would help open more clinics in the future. He also said they could live in his house until his return.

And lastly, the final matter in that package, a DVD, was something that made him throw up. The video of his father being sodomized and killed caused him to go ballistic, destroying his master bedroom in his new house. He had cried and sulked for three days nonstop, without sleeping, eating or communicating with the outside world. He was ... fucked up. And for some reason, he was mad at Adrian for putting that accursed DVD in that package.

But, on the fourth day, as he laid his funky ass on the floor of his trashed bedroom, he swore he was going crazy when he heard his father's voice clearly say to him, *"While we are free to choose our actions, we are not free to choose the consequences of our actions. We're only promised to die, son. And for men like us, you'll have no clue as to how you're going to die. Life is like a dollar bill, you can spend it any way you want, but you can only spend it once. So, know that as we speak, you're dying right now.*

"Therefore, live every second of your life to the fullest, pushing it to the limit as you carve your own path in life. Don't ... I

112

repeat, do not let temporary feelings lead to permanent decisions. I love you, Byron. You can do anything, but not everything. The pain you feel today will be the strength you feel tomorrow. Now go get it and let nothing stop you from achieving your goals and dreams. Love the life you live, live the life you love. And, most importantly, blood doesn't wash away blood."

After that pep talk from his father's spirit, Bizzy got up, cleaned up his room as best he could, washed his ass and put on some fresh clothes, then he set out to do what he had to do. And that was when he wrote the letter to Chad, hit up his old friend and hit the road without anybody's knowledge.

However, before he made the decision to fade to black and run to Mobile, he partially ignored his father's spirit and instructed the Clean-Up Crew to kill the person that produced the *T&G4* DVD and to put a million-dollar reward out for any information that would lead to the identity of the person on the DVD that killed his father and tarnished his legacy. Bizzy got those orders to Skinny-O via pay phone at a rest stop on his way to Mobile.

After he gave his Cadillac CTS-V to his BM LaShawn, and his Lexus LS460 to his other BM Makelia, Bizzy drove his newly acquired, yet ordinary 2009 Chevy Impala down Highway 45 in the Prichard area this morning, heading to a small shopping plaza. His mission for the day was to check out an empty storefront listed for sale, with the hopes of buying the vacant space and turning it into his first pain clinic.

Although it was less populated and lacked the infrastructure of downtown West Palm Beach, Prichard still reminded one of a little of WPB's urban core, because it was majority black and rundown. *Opening a clinic here in the rather poor northern section of the Mobile metropolitan area shouldn't raise many suspicions, he thought as he turned into the plaza that contained a Briar's grocery store. This area is most definitely the spot to get my operation up and running because it's already primed for business, being in the middle of addict utopia.*

113

Pulling up to the unoccupied store with the homemade "FOR SALE" sign in the window, Bizzy suddenly thought about his sister, Devon. Devon was a matter that wasn't included in the package, but one he'd be forced to deal with at a later time. After spending the last sixteen months getting to know each other, he felt bad that he had to up and leave her without an explanation. And since he destroyed his old phone, she had no way to contact him.

In fact, he wanted to reach out to her, but was unsure whether or not the feds had her phones tapped because of him. Whether or not he could fully trust her was another question. *When the time is right, I'll reach out to you, little sis, he said to himself as he pulled out his new cellphone, for which only two people had the number, and proceeded to call the number in the window. And when the time is right, sis, I'm hoping I can trust you and persuade you to get some of this money with me, so we can keep it in the family.*

September 12, 2010 12:37 pm

West Palm Beach, FL

Fist slams on desk
"I don't give a rat's ass how you lost him! Just find him before the both of you are investigating back-alley dealers! Do you understand? Now get out of my office and find him – like tomorrow!"

Both agents, Dino and Raw Deal exited their commander's office, furious after being chewed out over losing contact with Byron Woodson two months ago. And to make matters even worse, their commander knew their C.I. disappeared as well, after being unable to contact him since that day of surveillance on Byron and Adrian Mendoza in the park down in Miami.

Their investigation not only lost ground, the ground also fell out from underneath it. The only people they had intel on after

Byron and Roger Wright went missing were the peons Chad, JuneBug and Solo. And the phone taps and surveillance done on them the last month and a half had revealed nothing substantial or incriminating. It was as if Byron Woodson just walked off the face of the earth, and their careers weren't too far from following the same path.

The veteran, Dino, was taking Bizzy's disappearance the hardest. He had earned his nickname as a rookie after his superiors observed how relentless and energetic he was once he was on a bad guy's trail, just like how the hyper cartoon pet from *The Flintstones* always found his owners no matter where they hid. He never once lost a bad guy during his twenty-one years in law enforcement until now, and it was eating him up. *When I find you, Woodson, you'll wish that you never ran,* he thought as he walked adjacent to Raw Deal, *because I'm going to kill you myself.*

The rookie Raw Deal was feeling similarly about Bizzy's vanishing act, too. While working for the city of West Palm Beach Police Department, the streets had given him the moniker Raw Deal because he never gave a bad guy a fair chance. He did whatever was necessary to get his guy, even if that meant planting drugs or guns on a suspect during an arrest. Ninety-five percent of all his arrests resulted in a conviction, with his convicts receiving no less than ten years in prison.

The DEA in the area took notice of his outstanding work for years before deciding the eleven-year vet was worthy of wearing their badge. And since he had a tenacious work ethic like Dino, the department paired the two together. So, just like Dino, losing Bizzy was extremely bothersome to him. "Once I locate whatever rock you're hiding under, Bizzy, you'll pray you hid on a different planet rock," he said softly to himself as he strolled next to Dino, "because I'm going to use that same rock you're hiding under to squash you."

Once in the Marauder, with Dino behind the wheel, Raw Deal said, "It's time to grab the bastards living in Woodson's house by their fuckin' ankles and shake some info out of them. Those fuckers have to know where their boy is at. Why else are they squatting in his house? They don't seem like the perfect house-sitters to me, with all the girls coming and going from the place."

"Well, let's round up a crew and throw a house party of our own at their expense," Dino said with a scowl on his face and gripping the steering wheel tightly.

"Yeah, let's do just that. We'll invite ourselves over tonight. What do you say?"

Cranking up the car, Dino replied, "I say I'll bring the beer for the after party." Then he sped off.

Flame

Chapter Thirteen

September 14, 2010 8:59 am

Jupiter, FL

Outgunned, outnumbered.

The tables had turned severely, making it a laughing matter no more.

While Triple S had enjoyed slaughtering the niggas Eddie G had scraped together from wherever he could find them since the beginning of May, the last wave of niggas Eddie G had brought through downtown WPB a month ago were ... different. Rather than jumping out randomly on Triple S known hangouts, just to get ambushed in the process, the latest niggas with Eddie G moved with precision, like trained assassins.

In a matter of eight days, Eddie G and his upgraded hit squad killed ten Triple S members, hospitalized a dozen more and closed down five of their most profitable trap houses, effectively putting Bumper, Skat and RahRah on the run from their stronghold with their mentally, physically and emotionally weakened group of comrades. The few remaining Triple S members were now spread out and spread thin, all over PBC, waiting for Bumper and Skat to figure out what to do next.

Pacing back and forth in the fourth hotel in ten days, Skat furiously said, "I *still* can't believe pussy-ass Eddie G got us lookin' pie as fuck! Ain't no way we 'posed ta be jumpin' from spot ta spot like hop-scotch. Nigga, we da real-life Boogey Men, makin' niggas sweat an' scared ta close their eyes ta sleep! Nigga, we da Tony Montanas in da hood!"

"Wit all da bread an' dope we still got, why don't we just buy us some killas?" RahRah stated as he sat at the table and rolled the third dirty blunt in forty-five minutes. "It's obvious that's what Eddie G did. I dunno where he found them niggas that almost wiped us out, but I'm pretty sho we can do da same fo' da rite price."

The suite in the Ramada Inn was comfortably spacious and moderately cool, yet it felt overly crowded and extremely hot to Bumper. "Durt, we ain't rockin' like that!" he railed at Rah. "I'm not lettin' no-bah-dee take our glory. Whoeva them niggas is wit Eddie G will go 'bout their B.I. soon. An' when shit cool down, we'll come back at that scarred-face-ass nigga like *BeBe's Kids*!"

"Cuz we don't die, we multiply!" Skat declared as he continued to pace.

Silence consumed the room for a moment before RahRah said, "Ya' know today our boy Pedro posed ta be goin' in da ground. Y'all wanna pay our respects like how we did wit da othas?"

Bumper looked at his iced-out Breitling, then he said, "Yeah we can do that." He sighed. "Durt, it's beyond fucked up that we can't even go ta our own homies' funerals an' pay our proper respects."

Although Bumper, Skat and RahRah were cautious about showing their faces in public because of Eddie G's new crusade, they still paid their respects to the homies that lost their lives recently by simply driving by the cemetery as the funeral was in process. It was the least that they could do without putting their lives in danger. Still, in doing so, they collectively felt like cowards. Nevertheless, they swore that when their enemies had their day to be buried, they would make it rain bullets, no matter what the weather forecast was to be that day.

On their way to Pedro's funeral, in a borrowed Toyota Camry, they swung by a gas station in suburban WPB for Dutches and a six-pack of Heinekens. Like they did for the others, they planned to celebrate Pedro's short life, remembering all the good times they'd shared with their fallen soldier. Once they witnessed their homie go in the ground, they would pop the tops on the Heineys and fire up a big blunt of boonk as they cruised PBC until they were almost too geeked up to make it back to the telly safely.

119

As RahRah heedfully dashed inside the Shell gas station to make the necessary purchases, Bumper parked at a gas pump nearest to the store with the car running. As Bumper and Skat waited, with their seats laid as far back as they could go, they both kept their eyes scanning their surroundings, looking in all directions by way of the side and rearview mirrors. This was how they currently had to maneuver whenever they left the hotel, watching everything that moved. They knew that slippers counted, so they were always looking out for their asses, as well as looking out for the asses of their enemies to fire up.

"What's takin' that nigga so long?" Skat complained from the passenger seat as he looked from here to there like a meerkat. "If he ain't back in ten seconds, we burnin' off without his ass!"

"You trippin, Durt. He only been in there 'bout ten seconds now."

"Well, he got ten mo' seconds befo' we puttin' this car in drive an' we … Whoa, Kemosabe, wait a minute." Skat then attempted to duck further into his seat.

Skat's reaction made Bumper duck and look around nervously. "What, Durt? What'chu see? Is it one-time?" Receiving no immediate answer from Skat caused him to put the car in drive.

"Naw, Bump. We good," Skat insisted as his eyes stayed locked on the object in the passenger side mirror. "But this nigga ain't, tho'."

"Who is it, Skat? Is it that nigga, Eddie G?" Bumper couldn't see anybody he recognized as he quickly scanned the vicinity. "What's crackin', Durt?"

While still ducked low in the seat, and with his eyes still locked on the side mirror, Skat reached blindly into the back seat and grabbed the MAC-11. "Aye, Bump, trust me on this one. Put da whip in drive, an' when I start …"

"They ain't have no Dutches," RahRah began as he climbed into the back seat, "so, I got some Swishers—"

"Nigga, shut up an' close da door," Skat demanded with his heart beating faster than usual because Rah spooked him. "An' get down!"

With eyes bigger than twenty-four-inch rims with the tires, Rah whispered from a ducked position, "What's good, nigga?" Then he realized the MAC-11 was no longer in the back seat.

"This fo' Obel," Skat said to no one in particular as he rolled down the passenger window and proceeded to climb out of it with the machine gun. "Flush it, bro!"

Tires screeching

September 14, 2010 10:48 am

West Palm Beach, FL

On the fifty-inch flatscreen television …

"We interrupt our program to bring you this breaking news story this morning. I'm Westley McCambridge, reporting for WTKB Channel 7. I'm here live at the Shell service station, located in suburban West Palm Beach.

"According to multiple eyewitnesses, around 9:45 this morning, machine gun shots were fired out of a new model Toyota Camry before it fled this grisly scene. At this time, it is unclear whether the person, or persons, in that Toyota Camry was targeting a specific victim. However, in a chain of events, the shooting sparked a fire at a gas pump, thus causing the entire Shell service station to explode. The explosion itself left six people dead and caused dozens of injuries, from minor scrapes and bruises to severe burns. The deceased have yet to be identified.

"As of now, authorities are also asking the public for any information that will lead to finding the suspected vehicle in this heinous crime. Once again, we apologize for interrupting our scheduled programming to bring you this breaking news. I'm Westley McCambridge, reporting live for WTKB Channel 7 News, and we'll bring you further details as they become … "

"Change that shit," JuneBug said as he relaxed in bed. "Nobody reports live all da murders that's been happ'nin' in downtown. They don't care 'bout that shit, but as soon as some shit happens in those uppity-ass crackas' section of town, they make a big deal. It's good fo' all them people involved, dead an' burnt ta a crisp. Ain't nuttin' like fried white meat."

Lying on his chest, Rhapsody pinched him. "Bug, you so fuckin' mean! You're goin' ta hell fo' that." Ever since JuneBug put that good wood on her three days ago, she had yet to leave his side. She had been staying with him in the guest room that she loved so much. She was having the time of her life, getting high off pills for free, fucking good all day and night, and not having to go to work. He took care of her every need. She wasn't falling in love with him, but she sure was feeling the shit out of him.

"Ouch!" He laughed. "An' you say that like it's a bad thing. Goin' ta hell is where *all* da interestin' people gon' be. Heaven sounds borin'. It's gonna be loomin' down bottom, chillen wit old evil muthafuckas like … Napoleon an' Hitler, an' gangsta niggas like Bumpy Johnson an' Kilo."

Rhapsody suddenly tensed up after hearing the familiar name Kilo, the alias for West Palm Beach's own street legend whose murder she recently saw on the *Thugz & Gangstaz Volume 4* DVD. It was also the name of the person that she had a hand in helping to put on that DVD.

And JuneBug not only felt her reaction, he knew what it meant. *I guess there's no better time to ask those questions that Solo wanted me to ask her*, he thought as he kind of hoped that Rhapsody was official because he liked her a lot. "Lemme ask ya sumthin' real quick, Rhap … do y' know a broad named Beauti?"

Springing up off his chest and sitting up in the bed, without making eye contact, Rhapsody casually responded, "No."

"What about Demetrius, aka Kilo?"

Still no eye contact. "No… wh-what made ya ask me 'bout them?"

In the short time they had been chilling together, JuneBug sensed when she wasn't being honest. So, receiving the true answer to his questions, he then said, "I was just askin'." The mood had soured just that fast, and after a period of quietness, he added, "I wonda where Solo at? He called me 'bout an hour ago an' said he was 'bout five minutes away. He asked if we needed anythin' from da store befo' him, his BM an' their jit slid through ta chill fo' a while."

Slowly, Rhapsody laid back on JuneBug's chest, then said, "Him an' that crazy Star prolly got into a heated argument. Ever since they got back together after he got divorced, she been pushin' his buttons. That girl prolly shot off at da mouth an' said sumthin that caused him ta explode. I'm sho' that they're okay, tho', an' will be here shortly." She sighed. "So, what do ya wanna watch now?"

September 14, 2010 11:05 am

Deerfield Beach, FL

Once the last person entered the shoddy, inhumane motel and closed the door, RahRah finally spoke the first word. "What da fuck was that about, Skat?"

Skat calmly sat on the only bed in the room, with its stained covers and pissy smell. "That was 'bout revenge, lil' nigga. An' instead of it being served cold, it was served hot!"

Posted up by the window, peeking through a small opening in the curtain, Bumper said, "Durt, you my nigga an' I'ma ride wit'cha till da wheels fall off. *But*, we can't be swingin' like that, Jack. Not only do we have ta find anotha way back ta PBC, we gotta pray that those cameras at that Shell Station ain't pick up Rah's face."

"Oh shit! I ain't even think 'bout that!" RahRah then approached Skat aggressively, causing Skat to jump to his feet. Once in his grill, he said through clenched teeth, "On my daughter, if them folks get on my line cuz of ya stunt back there, I'ma—"

"You ain't gon' do nuttin', lil nigga," Skat cut him off, standing his ground. "Besides, when ya ride wit us, y' know anything liable ta happen at anytime. Rememba … from sunrise till SunSet! So, if them folks get on ya line, you better keep ya mouth shut. Now back back befo' dere's a problem!"

"Y'all boyz chill da fuck out," Bumper said without taking his eyes off their borrowed car in the parking lot. About ten seconds later, he said, "At least we don't have ta worry 'bout that no mo'."

The Toyota Camry, with the MAC-11 in the trunk, had just been stolen, all thanks to Bumper purposely leaving the driver's door ajar with the engine running. He knew the gimmick would work sooner rather than later, because the rundown motel where they rented a room with no identification—just cash—was in the poorest section of Deerfield Beach.

"Now da baser that rented da car fo' me gotta answer ta that, that's if those folks find an' link that car ta that Shell Station," Skat said before turning on the extra small TV.

"What if she, or he, tells on ya when Troll run down on them?" RahRah asked a bit nervously.

"Dawg, you not really built fo' this shit," Skat insisted as he stared menacingly into Rah's eyes. "But, if ya must know, that bitch only knows me by da name Matthew. An' I only dealt wit that bitch twice befo'. She dunno where I'm from or none of that shit. So we good, scary-ass nigga."

"Y'all niggas off da chain," Bumper insinuated as he finally sat in the rickety chair at the wobbly table. "But what was that all about, Durt? Why ya blow up that gas station like that? I'm just curious."

"Of course, ya rememba da big lick in Miami …"

"Ya talkin' 'bout da one where y'all hit fo' all that coke?" RahRah jumped in and asked, because he wasn't present that eventful day.

"What otha big lick in Miami have ya heard us talk 'bout, lil nigga? Now, don't cut me off again. But anywayz ... Er'body made it home that nite 'cept fo' my cousin, Obel. He da only nigga that got killed on our side that nite. I was close by when he took that fatal bullet. An' I rememba'd seein da big nigga that slumped my dawg, too. I neva fa'got buddy cuz I gotta good look at him.

"But anywayz ... just my lucky day today, I saw this nigga after almost two years. That nigga jumped outta that Chevy Silverado truck behind us at that Shell Station an' I almost shitted on myself. At first, I thought I was seein' shit, 'cuz I been havin' dreams 'bout that big nigga periodically ever since that nite. As he paid at da pump wit his gas card, an' I was sho' it was him, y'all know da rest."

"Well, if that's what happened, then today was a good day," Bumper said nonchalantly.

"R.I.P. Obel an' Pedro," RahRah said. "Now da homies can rest in peace."

Usually not the sentimental type, Skat had tears in his eyes.

"Yeah, rest in Thug'z Mansion, my Gz." A moment of silence. Then, suddenly, he blurted out, "Damn! Y'all left da Dutches, da Heinekens an' da dope in da car!"

125

Chapter Fourteen

September 15, 2010 11:56 pm

Wellington, FL

If it wasn't for bad luck, I wouldn't have no luck at all, Devon thought as she remembered Trick Daddy's "Thug Holiday" verse. *But if it wasn't for my .380, I would've been in Gangsta's Paradise a while ago.*

Arriving at her two hundred and sixty-five thousand-dollar, two-story home in the gated community Spinnaker Cove, Devon walked inside alone, once again. Although she hadn't heard from Rhapsody in four days, which was the least of her concerns, her boo Miracle had stopped coming home period. Because of the strained relationship between her and Miracle's mother, StudioX was the only place she had the chance to convince Miracle that changes would be made pronto if she were to come back home.

She wasn't too proud to ply Miracle with gifts or to beg for her baby to return to the home she'd purchased solely for Miracle and her little man, Kamani. With all of her efforts being disregarded though, Devon totally understood Luther Vandross now when he sung about a house not being a home when the love of your life isn't present, turning Devon's spacious three-bedroom, three-bathroom house into a constricted space.

Consequently, what hurt and bothered Devon the most was not knowing exactly why her pains to win Miracle back had failed, because Miracle never explained why she had distanced herself in the first place.

Devon languidly strolled through the eerily quiet house to the refrigerator to get something to drink. After grabbing a bottle of water and closing the fridge, she was caught off guard by a single piece of paper on the counter. Closer inspection of that paper revealed it was a letter, and she noticed it was written in Miracle's handwriting. Miracle's letter instantly caused Devon's body temperature to rise and her palms to begin to sweat. She then reluctantly picked up the letter and read it.

Devon,

The last three months have been hell for me. I'm more than sure that they've been hell for you too, but for other reasons. I've tried to understand what you've been through in the past, and with what you're going through now, but you refuse to let me in. Ever since the first day we made love, I told myself that I would be loyal to you, that I'd love you unconditionally, through thick and thin. I have fulfilled my vows every day since, even to this day. I'll always love you. I'll always remain loyal to you.

However, I'll no longer allow you to treat me unfairly. I deserve the same treatment that I give to you, no matter what the situation is. I can't make you trust me, Devon. And that's what all this boils down to-TRUST! I've trusted you with my life and with my son's life! You've put our lives in danger once before by holding out information from me. I forgave you though, when I myself had to find out that you had a real brother, a brother that would kill us all if he learned what WE did to his father.

But being the loyal woman that I am, I knew I wasn't going to say nothing to cause any suspicions. As far as Rhapsody saying anything, I trusted YOU to handle her so, I put my life in your hands on that, too. But this last shit that I discovered without you telling me has took the cake. I can't believe that you actually taped the murder of your father. What were you thinking? Obviously, you weren't thinking about me or Kamani. Now that shit is out for the whole world to see. And now there's a MILLION-DOLLAR REWARD for the person's identity on that tape. Lucky for you, I love you to death and wouldn't sell you out like you've done me.

Unlucky for you, Rhapsody knows that's you in that tape AND knows that you don't truly love her. And because of that, I have to go. It was a very hard decision to come to, but I must go for my sake and my son's sake. Knowing the person that you are, you'll

127

understand. I'm truly sorry, Devon, but you've made this bed and now you must lay in it.

My house key is on the key holder. I won't be returning to pick up anything, and I won't be returning to work, either. I'm leaving town soon, as well. Hopefully, you can make things right for yourself so you can live a peaceful, happy life. As for me, I'll live peacefully, but I won't be happy, because I'll no longer have my better half in my life—you! I love you, Devona Herrera. Now you be safe and remain strong and I'll try to do the same.

GOD BLESS, ITALY (I'll truly always love you)

Love,
Marie
P.S. Kamani says goodbye

Tears stained the letter.

For the first time in years, Devon felt alone. She ultimately felt like taking her .380 that she trusted more than anybody in the world and putting a slug through her now broken heart. She felt like … *nothing!* There wasn't a single word that could explain how she truly felt at that moment.

But in the end, Devon knew she was a *failure*, to both Miracle and Kamani.

Devon numbly dropped the letter, letting it float to the kitchen floor, before she walked zombie-like a few feet and collapsed into a heap. Balled up in a fetal position, she bawled like a baby. With nobody to hear her, or to soothe her pain, she remained in that spot on the floor, not caring how long she stayed there, not caring if she died. And before she realized it, she had cried herself to sleep.

Phone rings

Devon's cell phone startled her awake. With her body aching, and a splitting headache, she lazily dug into her pocket. According to the time on her phone, she had been out for over three hours. Although the ringtone wasn't Miracle's and she didn't recognize the number, she prayed it was her baby calling with a change of heart. "Hello," she answered groggily.

"What's up, Dee? This RahRah."

Devon only sighed.

"Yo', Devon? You there? Hello?"

"Yeah."

"You ai'ight, Dee? You don't sound too good."

"I'm … I'm good. Wh-what do ya want, Rah? Now ain't a good time. I gotta head …"

"I need ya, lil sis. I'm in a jam. I've been stuck in Broward wit Bumper and Skat fo' a few days now, an' we need a ride home."

"Y'all can't call nobody else? Like I said, now ain't a good time."

RahRah then sadly said, "I dunno 'bout them, but I can't call nobody else. You're all I got, Dee. Da only nigga I can count on when I'm fucked up. Ya da only person I trust."

Hearing that word *trust* stirred up Devon. And with that said, not wanting to let the only other person she cared for in her life to be left hanging out in the cold when they needed her, she said, "Where in Broward y'all at?"

Chapter Fifteen

September 16, 2010 9:13 pm

West Palm Beach, FL

It was a family matter now, because it was personal now.

In times like this, calling upon the Clean-Up Crew would've been the most obvious choice, since extracting information from a victim was their field of expertise. Hell, the Clean-Up Crew would make most innocent victims confess to things they never heard or saw. But the upcoming task wasn't a job for the savage crew, although savagery would be required to get the job done.

The planned hit job would be carried out by Bizzy himself, along with Chad. Although neither Bizzy nor Chad preferred to get their hands dirty, when the opportunity did present itself, they didn't hesitate to answer the call for blood, like the sons of gangstas they were. And since it had been quite a while since either one of them had to get blood on their hands, they were definitely going to enjoy killing their hapless, ignorant victim. It didn't matter to them that it was a female that would face their brutality.

Chad could tell that JuneBug didn't really want to expose Rhapsody for the blatant lies that she had told him. However, upon learning that Solo and his family were blown to smithereens in that Shell gas station explosion, JuneBug felt compelled to tell Chad what he had suspected about Rhapsody. Once JuneBug came clean about his suspicions, and Chad relayed that info to Bizzy via a coded letter to Bizzy's BM in Tallahassee, Bizzy responded by returning to PBC, STAT!

And although Bizzy had acquired both the store front and the necessary staff to open his first pain clinic, this obligation was, mentally and emotionally, a top priority that he must attend to for him to move forward with his plans in Mobile. *Trying to forget about a beef with someone you hate is like trying to remember someone you never knew,* Bizzy reminded himself of one of the many quotes his father told him over the years.

Slowly climbing out of the rental car, exhausted from the approximately twelve-hour drive, Bizzy bluntly said as he dapped up Chad and JuneBug, "This is all work, no play. I'm in an' out. So where this bitch at?"

"I tried ta get her ta stay," JuneBug started, "but she swore that she had ta go take care of some B.I. in Wellington real quick. She left 'bout a hour ago. I just called her ten minutes ago an' she said she'll be back befo' eleven."

Bizzy glanced at his G-Shock. "That's cool. We can't do it here anyway. It's best ya have her meet ya sumwhere that's not crowded tonite, like a park or sumthin'. Cuz if we try ta kill that bitch here, she liable ta scream, an' shit can get outta pocket. I don't need da neighbors in our bizness."

"That sounds like a plan," Chad said with a grin.

"C'mon, let's go inside," Bizzy then insisted. "I'm tired. At least I can get a lil rest befo' we off dis bitch. An' I hope y'all boyz ain't fuck up my place. 'Cuz if y'all did ... Ya broke it, ya bought it."

Once everybody was situated in the living room, JuneBug eagerly asked, "So wassup? How's er'thang up in Mobile? I know ya done bagged a few of those thick-ass country hoes up there already."

Blowing out air in relaxation as he sunk into the sumptuous sofa, Bizzy said, "I really ain't have da time ta be fuckin' around. Since it's just me doin' all da foot work, I'm always on da go. I already got da office furnished, tho'. I also got two doctors an' a receptionist on da payroll. All dey waitin' on now is fo' me ta return, then it's time ta pull out da money counter." He then chuckled. "An' I did bag a few bitches. I had to, 'specially wit all da shit I'm dealin' wit mentally. I been takin' my frustrations out on dem hoes. Now most of dem hoes won't even hit me back 'cuz of da pressure game I put down. Them country boyz up there ain't hittin' dem chunky hoes rite, trust me."

131

"Maaannnn, when can we slide wit'chu up there?" JuneBug said. "I wanna fuck me a country bumpkin."

Bizzy laughed heartily with his dawgz, then said, "Not rite now. Y'all gotta hold da fort down, down here. This gon' be y'all operation ta run in West Palm in a lil while, while I got it all unda control up there. But don't worry, we all gon' eat." He took a quick breather, then he continued, "So, tell me what's good down here? Where da boy Solo at, by da way?"

Bizzy hadn't heard the news about Solo's fate, so Chad took the liberty to tell him the unfortunate news. "Solo is no longer wit us."

Puzzled, Bizzy asked, "What's that 'posed ta mean? What, he quit on us?"

"Naw ... he dead."

Damn near about to jump off the sofa, Bizzy yelled, "What? Ya gotta be shittin' me! How that happen on y'all watch?"

"Maannnn, we not fa'sho fa'sho, but we think dem Triple S niggas had sumthin' ta do wit it," JuneBug replied. "If it was dem, they ran down on him at da gas station an' they blowed da whole block up in da process. Him, his BM an' his jit dead."

The heartbreaking news left Bizzy mute. Learning of Solo's demise was weighing heavy on his heart. But the killing of Solo's BM and their kid almost compared to the feeling he had when he learned that his father was killed. *You and your family didn't die in vain, Solo,* thought Bizzy before vowing to put the final nail in SunSet Syndicate's coffin. *I put that on my life!*

The silence ended when Chad said, "An' one otha thing, Cuzzo. One-time ran up in here four nites ago."

I knew the front door looked different, Bizzy said to himself as he simply stared through Chad, waiting to hear what happened.

Chad swallowed the lump that had formed in his throat. "Yeah, they ran up in here, but they ain't find nuttin'. They took me, Bug, Solo an' da bitch, too, downtown ta da police ... "

"How they get da bitch?" Bizzy finally spoke.

Chad looked at JuneBug, passing him the mic.

132

"Da bitch been stayin' here wit me in da guest room."

Bizzy shook his head disappointedly. "Don't be a sucka fo' love, pot'nah. That shit'll get'cha killed. Just ask my pops. That's ya lesson fo' today. Now, Chad, continue."

"Yeah, like I wuz sayin', they took us down ta da station. An', of course, ya' know we ain't say shit. They mentioned you an' talked 'bout conspiracy. They then tried ta boo-game us wit bogus charges an' blasé-blasé. Even da bitch held her own, fo' real. So, after a few hours wit dem gettin' nowhere, they let us go." He paused. "Oh, I mentioned da lawyer, Matthew O'Hare, too, just like ya tole me to when we get in a jam. Once I tole them O'Hare represented all of us, I guess dat spooked 'em into lettin' us go."

Bizzy rubbed his chin after hearing Chad's account. He eventually said, "Yo, Bug. Go 'head an' call that bitch up. Get her ta meet ya ... I dunno ... let's say ... tell her ta meet ya at John Prince Park in Lake Worth at 11:30. I don't care wha'chu gotta tell her, just make sho she there on time." Once he finished speaking, he got up abruptly and exited the house. Moments later, he was pulling out of the driveway, heading only he knew where until 11:30 pm.

September 16, 2010 11:28pm

Lake Worth, FL

Phone rings
"Hello?"

"Bug, where ya at? I'm in this park like ya tole me ta be. This park is too big an' I ain't tryna get lost. It's too dark out here."

"If ya came in da way I tole ya, then just keep comin' straight. You'll see me waitin' outside my 'Vette."

"Okay. An' da surprise that'chu got fo' me better be good. I don't like surprises."

"Don't worry, boo. I guarantee you'll love what I got fo' ya. Have I disappointed ya yet?"

"No." She giggled cutely. "Oh, I think I see ya car up ahead now."

"Ai'ight, just keep comin' straight then. See ya in a sec."

"Okay."

Ending the call, JuneBug waited outside of his car like he said he would be, while both Bizzy and Chad laid off in the bushes less than ten yards away with silenced MP-5 machine guns. The plan this warm night was to light Rhapsody's car up before she knew what happened.

"I see sum headlights, Cuzzo," Chad reported to Bizzy.

"I see them, too," Bizzy replied. "An' rememba, empty da entire clip once dat bitch put da car in park. We gonna leave dis bitch so holey that Swiss cheese gon' be jealous."

After a slight chuckle, Chad seriously said, "This fo' Demetrius."

"Naw, this gangsta shit fo' Kilo." Rather than interrogate Rhapsody for any information that would lead him to his father's actual killer, Bizzy made the final decision to not play any games. He was sending a clear message with this hit. *I know you did it, and it's only a matter of time before you're next.*

As the headlights in the distance drew closer and brighter, they suddenly stopped approaching. Not even ten seconds later, the headlights cut off.

"What's da bitch doin'?" Chad asked what Bizzy had to be thinking, too. "Did she park in da wrong spot?"

Baffled, Bizzy had nothing to say. He just watched where the car was before the headlights cut off. Then, before he knew it, he heard something strangely familiar. "Is that a … motorcycle?"

The low vibrato humming of a motorcycle's engine could be heard coming from the direction where Rhapsody's car was supposed to be.

"What da fuck is goin' on? I know dis bitch ain't park her car just ta hop on a bike," Chad said a bit nervously.

Abruptly, the motorcycle's engine revved, startling the once quiet, warm night. And before JuneBug, Chad and Bizzy could properly react, the crotch rocket was upon them.

Sppppprrrrraat-tat-tat-tat-tat-tat-tat-tat-tat-tat-tat-tat-tat-tat

The sudden hail of bullets raining upon them left both Bizzy and Chad pinned down and unable to return fire. Endless rapid fire lit up the night, drowning out the motorcycle's engine and every other sound. Bullets shredded the bushes into confetti, ricocheted off the concrete like ping pong balls, tore through Bizzy's and Chad's stolen getaway car like wet tissue. And the rounds kept flying like a swarm of deadly African killer bees.

When the bullets finally ceased, the motorcycle could be heard once again, fading off into the night.

"Oh shit! I'm hit!" JuneBug hollered from the parking lot. "Yo, sumbody help! Help me!"

A slight burn could be felt on Bizzy's right shoulder. The tell-tale sign let him know he'd been hit as well. However, it felt more like a flesh wound than a direct hit.

"Yo, Chad, we gotta roll. Get up! Let's go befo' Troll roll through."

Silence.

"Bruh, let's go befo' one-time ..." Stopping mid-sentence, Bizzy sensed that something was wrong. He then shook Chad's body slightly. "Yo, Cuzzo, you straight?"

"Oh, God! Help me, please!" JuneBug continued to scream. "Yo, Bizzy! Chad! Help me!"

Ignoring JuneBug's cries for help, Bizzy tentatively moved to lift Chad's head, which was face down in the dirt. Although it was pitch black, his eyes had adjusted to the darkness, and he gasped in horror after seeing the huge gaping hole where Chad's forehead used to be.

"Sumbody ... help! Any ... Anybody ... help! Ple-please!" JuneBug continued to shout. But his cries were not as loud as they were a few seconds ago, signaling that he was losing his strength fast.

135

There was only one thing Bizzy could do from there - run! He unconsciously picked up his MP-5 and ran off, disappearing into the darkness of the park.

Flame

Chapter Sixteen

September 17, 2010 2:01 am

Lantana, FL

Godsent.

Or, perhaps, it was one of the devil's miracles.

Whatever it was, Rhapsody was thankful for it.

Rhapsody was so thankful that she sat extremely still and quiet as she drowsily stared at her savior, fearing that if she moved or spoke, he would vanish and never return. And just like her quiescent state, her hero simply sat opposite her in a similar state of inertia and looked fixedly at her with wide-open eyes. Ever since she regained full consciousness ten minutes ago, they were engaged in a fierce staring contest.

After gradually returning to a state of normalcy, tears began to form in Rhapsody's eyes. "So, it was..." she attempted to clear her throat "...you this whole time, wasn't it?" She finally said, her voice hoarse from dryness. "It wuz you leavin' me those god-awful notes that had me so stressed out, I turned ta pills ta help me cope. It wuz you, Javon, this whole time, wasn't it?"

With a nervous diamond-studded, platinum-toothed smile, the clearly alive JJ casually said, "I missed ya so much, Kiki."

No longer with dreads, sporting a Caesar fade instead, he almost looked the same. He was still oil black. But, areas of his dark skin were now scarred from badly healed, second-degree burns, exposing the pink tissue on mainly his arms and hands. Also, there was a small first-degree burnt patch of skin on the lower left side of his face and neck area. "An' I know ya missed me, too, rite?"

Rhapsody took a deep breath before exhaling. "Why? Why didn't ya just lemme know tha'chu were alive all this time? Why ... just why, Javon?" By then, most of her face was wet with tears.

"Look at me, Kiki," he sternly said. "Look at what he did ta me in da process of killin' my mama."

"Who are you talkin' 'bout?"

"That muthafucka Bizzy, that's who. You actin' like ya dunno who did this ta me an' killed my mama!"

Rhapsody would never forget JJ's mother, the sweet Miss Sadie. But she only vaguely remembered the name Bizzy. "Is that why ya showed up tonite after all this time? Fo' revenge?" Then it hit her like a bolt of lightning. "Hold up ... Please don't tell me tha'chu been stalkin' me an' usin' me as bait! If so, is that all I am to you?"

He replied, with no shame at all, "I had ta do what I had ta do. An', hopefully, I got my man tonite. An' if I didn't, then I gotta go back undaground till I do. I ain't stoppin' till I know that nigga Bizzy is dead an' stankin'."

Hearing that name again, she attempted to recall Bizzy from her memory bank. Once it finally came back to her, she said, "I rememba him now. Bizzy is ... I mean, he was ya homie that hustled wit'chu in Savannah. He did some time in da feds, too, rite?"

"Yeah, that's him."

"Well, I hate ta burst ya bubble, but I wasn't in that park ta meet no Bizzy. I haven't seen him in years. I was in da park ta meet ... ta meet my pill man named Bug. He had a surprise fo' me."

JJ laughed. "You're so naïve, Kiki. You're smart, but naïve. That nigga Bug..." he frowned, "...had a surprise fo' ya, ai'ight. Like I explained ta ya briefly in da car, after ya woke up delirious, I rescued you from being set up. Put two an' two togetha now, Kiki. Did Bug ever say sumthin' that caused a red flag ta go up in ya head? Whetha it was a while ago or recently?"

"Hmmm ..." she began to jog her memory. Nearly a minute passed before she said, "He did come out da blue an' ask me a question a few days ago that made me wonda why he asked." She recalled the day JuneBug asked her about knowing both Beauti and Demetrius.

"An' I quess ya gave him da wrong answer 'cuz he ain't believe ya. Regardless, thankfully, I found ya thru social media an' learned that'chu worked at StudioX. I been followin' ya fo' da last thirteen months, *after* I recovered from my burns, of course. When I followed ya ta that crib in Bear Lakes an' ya stayed over there, I quickly found out da house belonged ta Bizzy. What a coincidence. I then knew my luck had changed fo' da better an' it was only a matter of time befo' I caught Bizzy slippin'. Howeva, I didn't know if ya knew whose house it was, so I didn't jump to any conclusions.

"But while ducked off in a cut one night at da house, I overheard them niggas in da driveway say that Bizzy been outta town fo' a while, an' that's when I figured that'chu didn't know what was goin' on. Still tho,' I waited an' watched, keepin' an extra close eye on ya at that point. An,' thankfully, tonite, I felt sumthin' was off. After I followed ya from Bizzy's crib ta Wellington then ta that *closed* park..." he shook his head disappointedly, "...I knew sumthin' wasn't rite. Luckily, I'm always prepared an' ready ta act quick, 'cuz I never know when I'ma bump into that fuck nigga.

"An', by da way, I apologize fo' breakin' ya driver side window wit that rock befo' druggin' ya. I had ta find a way ta stop ya car ASAP 'cuz I wasn't sho' how far away ya were from their trap."

Rhapsody wrinkled her nose, still able to faintly smell the chloroform's ether-like odor, then said, "I-I guess I can't complain. What'chu did saved my life. So … thanks." A few awkward seconds passed by, then she added, "So, do ya think it's done now?"

"I'm pretty sho' I know why ya was almost killed tonite, an' I have a feelin' that'chu know why, too." He saw the guilt on Rhapsody's face before she lowered her head. "Whateva it was ya did, or know about … if I really know Bizzy, he woulda wanted ta be there ta kill ya himself. It's personal fo' him. So, I dunno who that was by the car, but I hit him up real good befo' sprayin' er'thang else around him fo' good measure. Now, there's only one way ta find out who got hit tonite an' that's by watchin' da news in da mornin'. If sumbody died at that park, we'll know exactly who it was."

"An' if it wasn't Bizzy?"

"Then, like I said earlier, I gotta continue my mission. An' since I can't use you as bait no mo, 'cuz it'll be too dangerous ta do so, ain't no tellin' how long it'll take befo' I get ta him. *But* I got one mo' thing I'm bankin' on ta help me get Bizzy."

"An' what's that?" Rhapsody curiously asked.

Knowing from past dealings that Rhapsody wasn't a squealer, JJ broke it down from the beginning for her. Just like he had found her on social media, he had tried to locate Bizzy the same way. Unfortunately, Bizzy was a ghost on the internet, so he had to find another route. Going back to Rhapsody's *FaceSpace* social media page, he began to scour through the pages of all her "friends," well over four thousand of them. Happening by chance, however, he found something peculiar without having to go through all those pages.

Starting from the names beginning with A's, JJ didn't have to go further than the D's before he landed on the name Devon, who he knew was Rhapsody's lover. While zealously scanning through Devon's page, he saw a post on her timeline that stood out to him, and it mentioned something about being reunited with a new brother. On a hunch, he decided to look further into that since he had nothing to lose if it turned out to be nothing.

Unable to breach the gated community where Devon lived with Miracle and Rhapsody, he chose to break into the next best thing that might give him a clue: StudioX. He got past the security system by gaining access through StudioX's roof. He then rummaged through Devon's office, looking for anything with Bizzy's name on it, either his government name or nickname. Not finding what he hoped for on or in Devon's desk, he eventually rummaged some more until he stumbled upon a safe. It took a while, but he was able to break into that safe, and he emptied its contents and bounced.

Once back in the hideaway he'd been living in since he found Rhapsody, only then did he realize there was an old VHS tape amongst the money and papers he took from the safe. Out of curiosity he played the tape, and that was when he discovered it was the actual murder of Bizzy's father, which was the jackpot he would not in a million years think he'd have in his hands. Then it hit him like a left hook from Iron Mike Tyson. *Why in the world did Rhapsody's lover have such a tape in her possession?* And that was when he also learned Rhapsody's life was possibly in danger.

After replaying certain parts of the tape a dozen times, JJ couldn't match Devon to the person in the tape. He wracked his brain trying to connect Devon and the tape to Bizzy. So, since his bait was Devon's girlfriend and he didn't want his assumptions to put Rhapsody's life in any real danger or to fuck up everything that he had planned, he resolved to mailing the tape to a scapegoat.

From the short time that he'd been in PBC, JJ had learned that DJ Kato had a selfish, insatiable desire for fame and was always looking for the latest raw and uncut street footage to put on his trending *Thugz & Gangstaz* DVD series. And just as he had hoped, DJ Kato delivered by putting Kilo's death on *T&G 4*. He then prayed the damning footage would draw Bizzy out of the dark. However, it only caused Bizzy to put out the outlandish million-dollar reward, which only aggravated him. Not to be deterred, though, he created a fake *FaceSpace* account to try to collect the reward, posting a message with the hashtag *KILORE-WARD*.

He was soon privately messaged by a "C.C." and told to meet up at an industrial park at a specific time to collect the reward money if the information led to the killer of Kilo. He had showed up early to the meeting place, but he observed it from a quarter mile away by using binoculars. He ultimately saw a lone person show up on time at that spot, and it wasn't Bizzy. Instead, the guy that showed up looked like the wrestler Mark Henry to him.

And that was where JJ was currently at with the situation, praying that somehow Bizzy would let his feelings get the best of him and make him come out of hiding so that revenge could finally be served for Miss Sadie's sake.

Carefully digesting everything that had been said, Rhapsody let her feelings get the best of her. Under different circumstances, or if it had been anybody else, she would have kept her mouth closed. But since this was the man that she had fallen in love with over two years ago and she never stopped loving him even after his "death," she felt obligated to help JJ any way possible. Besides, she owed him her life, and she had nowhere to go. *I need him more than ever now,* she thought as she stared into those eyes that weren't altered like some parts of his body, *and I know deep down inside that he truly loves me, unlike Devon.*

"Well, baby, I got some good news an' some better news," Rhapsody said before getting up and going over to sit in JJ's lap. And then she kissed him.

After their lips unlocked, JJ finally was able to say, "Hopefully, that's just a small token to show ya appreciation after all I had ta go through tonite in order ta save ya. Only if ya knew all da troubles I had ta go through just ta get'cha back ta my crib safely in *your* car. I felt like Tom Cruise in *Mission Impossible!*" he grinned. "Anywayz, what's this good news ya got fo' me?"

"I missed ya, too, Javon. That's da good news." She smiled. "I'm so glad that'cha alive. I'll never leave ya side again, an' I'll kick ya ass if ya leave me again!"

Smiling himself, he said, "I got'chu, baby. An' it's just like I said in one of my notes to ya, this is *my* body," he squeezed her tightly, "an' daddy got'chu, okay?"

"I believe ya, daddy."

"Ooohh, I like how ya say daddy." He laughed before kissing her neck. Then he said, "So what's da better news?"

She grabbed his face with both hands, stared deeply into his eyes, and seriously said, "I know exactly how ta get Bizzy ta come ta us."

143

"Fa' real? How?"

"Cuz da person that killed his father is gonna help us. That's how."

Flame

Chapter Seventeen

October 1, 2010 11:17 pm

Jacksonville, FL

Were it not for Devon, Bizzy would've wiped Palm Beach County from his memory. That one area had taken so much from him in his short twenty-seven years on this rock called Earth. Ascribing PBC to having a black cloud over it, he begrudgingly moved on with his life and moved forward with his plans. *I've made it this far unscathed for a reason, so there's no need to dwell in the past any longer*, he thought as he prepared to visit his aunt and grandmother for the first time in months. *I've got my mind made up and I'm going to live for me and my boys.*

Bizzy had just left Tally from seeing his oldest son, Bilal, before deciding to head to Jacksonville. He had gotten over his paranoia a bit and eventually bought a second prepaid cell phone that was strictly for his family to call. Even his bum-ass baby mama, LaShawn, had the number. The only person that didn't have his new number was Devon, and that was because of his fear of the PBC curse. But he swore he'd reach out to her soon ... somehow.

After knocking on the door, Bizzy's aunt answered. "Hey, Byron!" she said excitedly, with her happy-go-lucky self. "I'm so happy to see you. *God* is good. Come on in here and give your auntie a hug and kiss."

He promptly did as he was told. After entering the cool house and giving her a firm hug with a quick kiss on her cheek, he said, "Wassup, Aunt Sheryl? Where's G-Ma? How is she?"

Sheryl's mood swiftly changed. "Oh, Byron. I'm afraid that she ... she isn't doing too good, baby." She sighed. "With all the bad things that's been happening in our family in the last two years, it's taking a toll on her mind, body and soul. And battling that devil that's eating at her brain isn't making it any better."

146

"Is she home?" Bizzy inquired rather sorrowfully.

"Yes, she's in her room. She's so weak, though, Byron. She might not ... I don't think she'll be with us too much longer." She took a few seconds to gather her thoughts. "But, maybe, she'll cheer up once she sees her handsome grandson. Look at you, looking just like your lovely father." Her smile returned. "Come on."

Bizzy then followed Sheryl through the house his father paid for in full twenty-two years ago. Walking through the house was always like taking a walk in the past as he recalled living here briefly. The antique smell of the house, along with the family pictures and décor, had never changed, unless there was some small keepsake or new picture added.

Before stepping through Louise's doorway, Sheryl stopped, and said, "She's real sick, Byron, so don't be shocked by what you're about to see. She hasn't spoken much in the last few months. And the latest news of Tyrell being stabbed in prison and Chad passing has only made her more weak."

She would surely die if she ever saw the tape of her son's murder, Bizzy thought. *Hopefully, she'll never see that atrocious footage.* "*Why* won't ya take her ta da hospital or a hospice if she's so bad?"

"My momma and Demetrius have a lot in common and being hard-headed and stubborn are just two things. She's adamant about spending her last days in the home her favorite son bought her. She doesn't even want nurses in her room, so I'm her sole caregiver. It's hard, Byron, but I'm honoring my momma's wishes. But the money Demetrius left us, along with the money you give us, most definitely makes it a whole lot easier. She has the best of the best equipment, medical supplies and medicines. And, because of that, she isn't suffering ... too much." She sighed again before leading Bizzy inside.

The sophisticated hospital-style bed surrounded by all the machines and hoses that were hooked up to Louise's body was nothing new to Bizzy. However, his grandmother's condition since

147

his last visit was beyond shocking, to say the least. *Damn, all the shit that the family has been through is really killing the matriarch of the family*, thought Bizzy as he struggled to look at his extremely frail grandmother, *she already looks like she's in a casket.*

As they carefully approached a sleeping Louise's bedside, Sheryl nodded at Bizzy, signaling to him to speak. "Grandma? Wake up, Grandma. It's Byron."

With the continuous low whir of the oxygen machine and the faint beep of the heart monitor, Bizzy's deep voice caused Louise's eyes to slowly flutter open. From a slightly reclined position, she then turned her head barely towards the familiar voice. A faint smile spread across her face as she stared into Bizzy's eyes, then she mumbled, "De... Deme... Demetrius?"

"No, Grandma. It's Byron, Demetrius' son."

"Oh ... I – I ... I haven't ... seen you in so ... so long, Demetrius. I ... I missed you, son."

Seeing that it was no use in trying to convince his clearly senile grandmother that he wasn't his father, Bizzy just went along with it. "An' I missed ya, too. How are ya doin', pretty lady?"

Louise swallowed, then mumbled, "Water." Sheryl readily placed a cup with a straw to her mouth. After a few savory and audible sips, she continued, "Demetrius ... please stop ... what you're doing, son. You're ... you're going to end up... dead just like your father. You were ... only ten years old when ... when George died in that ... in that gambling house. Please, son ... you have to ... take care of Byron. Don't ... don't leave him alone ... like how your father ... left you, okay? Demetrius ... you be a good son ... and do what ... do what your mother says." She smiled faintly again as she stared at Bizzy with dull eyes. "That's my... that's my good boy ... I love you, son." Then she closed her eyes.

Bizzy was crying when Sheryl touched his shoulder, startling him a bit. "She's tired, Byron," she said to him. "She hasn't spoken that much in months, so I know it exhausted her. Let's go back to the living room. There's something I need to tell you." She then grabbed Bizzy's hand.

Before Bizzy left Louise's side, however, he bent down and kissed her sunken-in cheek and lightly stroked her thin gray hair. Not knowing if this would be the last time seeing her alive, he whole-heartedly said, "I love you, Grandma Louise. Always an' forever. Thank you fo'… just thank you. An' I apologize fo' everything we put ya through."

Once in the living room, Sheryl tenderly wiped her nephew's tears from his face, just like she had done many years ago in this house after he fell and hurt himself. "She's going to be alright, Byron. Momma lived a good life, thanks to all the caring men in her life, especially your father. She isn't an evil person, been a *God*-fearing woman all her life. Momma was a schoolteacher for over thirty years, helping countless children and their parents any way she could.

"She has a great heart, so know that she'll be going to sit next to Jesus Christ our Savior when *God* calls her home. So don't cry tears of pain, cry tears of joy for her. And take heed to her message back there. Your father wasn't always there for you, so be there for your sons. Do that for her, okay? That'll make her happy when she smiles down on us from paradise. You hear me?"

Bizzy simply nodded as he sniffled. Once he composed himself a bit, he asked, "So what is it that'chu gotta tell me, Auntie?"

Uneasiness could be seen on Sheryl's face as they stood in the middle of the living room. "Just like my momma and my brother, you have that hard-headedness in you, too. But I want you to know that, whatever it is that you have going on, Byron, you need to give it up now. And you remember this, a leader takes people where they want to go, while a *great* leader takes people where they don't necessarily want to go but ought to be. Be the great leader, Byron, that I know you are, and instead of leading impressionable young people toward destruction and death, lead them to glorious things, like *God*, baby."

149

Reading between the lines, Bizzy asked, "Where is all this comin' from? What's wrong, Auntie?"

She shook her head with her eyes closed, then said, "About three or four days after your cousin Chad was killed, two federal agents stopped by the house. Their names were Zimmerman and Holmes. After they spoke with Chad's mother in Daytona, she gave them the address here, because they couldn't find you for questioning."

"What did they say? An' why didn't ya call da lawyer I told ya ta call when police come askin' questions?"

"I did tell them I was calling that O'Hare guy, but then they just told me it was best you contact them before you got into something you couldn't get yourself out of. Then, before they left, they mentioned something about you maybe being involved in some guy name Roger Wright's disappearance and you may know something about Chad's death. They also mentioned that a guy named ... I can't remember his real name but they said JuneBug ... yes, they said this JuneBug guy is in critical condition in the hospital and he mentioned the name Bizzy when he was found in the park where Chad was killed.

"So, I know you're not going to turn yourself in, Byron, and you don't have to worry about me telling on you. I may be a Christian, but I'll never turn on my family. Still, you need to give it up, Byron. Take all the money that you have and run, baby. Go away for a long, long time. Make them forget about you. Please. My momma and I will be just fine. But if something were to happen to you soon, it's going to surely kill my momma, and I know you don't want that. Consider quitting while you're ahead."

Bizzy would've considered taking his aunt Sheryl's advice under different circumstances. Only she didn't know the great lengths that he had gone to just to get his pain clinic open. Good niggas close to him had died and a lot of money had been spent in pursuit of his latest venture, so he had no plans of just giving it up to run away and hide. Besides, the grand opening of his clinic nearly two weeks ago was *very* lucrative.

In the twelve days that Bizzy had been back in Prichard after the botched hit that led to Chad's death, he successfully opened the seven-day-a-week clinic without an MRI mobile unit and started raking in the money. So much money, in fact, the potent cash flow kept his mind off all the bullshit that had recently occurred.

During the first two days of business, Bizzy's doctors only filled out a dozen prescriptions, with majority of those being legitimate diagnosis. However, the few addicts that did try their hands in those two days were underhandedly prescribed pills at eight dollars a pop, instead of five or less per pill with a legitimate diagnosis. Straight cash money, unless covered by insurance.

On the third day, the doctors had signed off on and dispensed an astounding forty inauthentic prescriptions, with the "scripts" ranging between a hundred to two hundred and forty pills, for a total of fifty-five thousand, seven hundred and sixty dollars. And since one "patient" could only receive nine hundred and sixty pills in thirty days, there were a few patients that used up their monthly scripts in less than a week.

By the end of the twelfth day, the clinic had made a whopping six hundred and sixteen thousand, all cash, running through nearly seventy-seven thousand different opiates. With Bizzy's pill connect, Rusty, now charging him five bucks per pill because he was purchasing over ten thousand of them, he pocketed about a hundred grand in those twelve days, after paying each doctor sixty thousand and the receptionist ten grand.

Therefore, in thirty days, at the rate the clinic was pulling in money, and at the rate he paid his "employees," he could at least profit two hundred fifty-three thousand - not including the deduction of the monthly rent, utilities and other small expenses. *I won't have to worry about opening any other clinics,* he thought as he looked into his aunt's sad eyes, *but there's absolutely no way I'm walking away from this pot of gold without squeezing a good year out of it before purchasing a mobile MRI unit to keep the heat off my ass.*

"I love you, Aunt Sheryl." He was ending the brief visit. He then hugged and kissed her. "I gotta go now. Gotta handle some stuff. Call me if ya need anything. An' don't talk ta da police no mo,' okay? Call Matthew O'Hare, ASAP. Please."

Sheryl just nodded and ruefully smiled.

Bizzy left the house more determined than ever to get the money up so he could raise both his sons together under his care, and more mindful of what his life choices were doing to his loved ones.

October 1, 2010 5:51 pm

Prichard, AL

During the roughly six-hour trip back to Mobile, Bizzy decided beyond dispute or doubt that he was indeed cutting all ties with Palm Beach County. That meant that the Clean-Up Crew were on their own - but he would pay them handsomely *if* they ever tracked down and killed his father's murderers. That also meant Devon had to be abandoned. *Now that I have no reason to look back, I can look forward to all this green I'm going to make*, he said to himself with a faint smile.

Before taking it in for the evening, Bizzy chose to pay his thriving business a quick visit.

"Hello, Mr. Woodson," the gorgeous twenty-two-year-old Caucasian receptionist greeted upon Bizzy's entrance of Prichard's Center For Pain. "Good to have you back. The doctor's just left a few minutes ago, and I was just closing up for the night."

"Stacey, what I told ya 'bout that Mr. Woodson stuff, huh?" Bizzy said with a smile, remembering the time after paying her ten grand. He had overhauled the beautiful redhead doggystyle in the back office right before closing a few days ago. "Call me Bizzy, okay?"

As Bizzy stood in front of her desk, Stacey blushed as she reminisced about being stroked long and deep by her handsome black boss, while surrounded by the money he had given her. "Okay... Bizzy." She giggled. Then, as if it had slipped her mind, she quickly looked over her shoulder, and said, "Oh, I forgot to mention there are two Spanish men in the back waiting for you. They look … important."

Waitin' fo' me?" he asked with a raised brow. "Are ya sho?"

Stacey simply nodded. "They're in exam room number two."

"How long have they been here?"

"Ummm … about two hours."

Sensing that something wasn't right about the situation, he asked, "Did they see one of da doctors already? Did they specifically ask fo' me? What did they say when they first came in?"

"No … yes … and after I told them you weren't here, and maybe you wouldn't be returning at all today, one of the men insisted on waiting until I closed up."

Bizzy nervously tapped on the desktop, trying to figure out what to do next. Eventually, he walked silently and cautiously toward the back. As he approached the examination room, located at the end of the lone hallway in the clinic, he removed the Glock 17 from his waist that he always carried nowadays, chambered a round and held it behind his leg out of view. The room's door was closed when he reached it, but he could faintly hear voices emanating from inside the room. Without knocking, he carefully opened the door a little until both men came into view. The men stopped talking in Spanish as he stood in the hallway accessing them to see if they were threats.

"Please, come in," one man respectably said in a gentle, smooth voice without the slightest indication of an accent. "We're no threat to you, so you can put up your weapon."

How did he know I had my weapon drawn? Bizzy wondered as he covertly placed the pistol in the back of his pants, praying they weren't lulling him into a false sense of security. Now at their mercy, he fully opened the door. While standing in the doorway,

153

in his peripheral view, he saw a visibly scared Stacey at the other end of the hallway. He gave her a "one minute" gesture before entering the room and leaving the door slightly ajar behind him. With the man who spoke sitting on the examination bed, and a big, burly man sitting on the doctor's rolling stool, he stood by the door and said, "Can I help you, gentlemen?"

"Yes, you can," the man spoke again. "But first, let me introduce myself. My name is Cesar Vargas DePalma. And this gentleman with me is my personal assistant. Now, I'm here merely to speak with you about an important matter, a matter that was left unsettled by your father, the late Demetrius."

After quickly looking over the black-clad "personal assistant" that sat quietly on the stool, Bizzy looked over the man who called himself Cesar. The man, whom he guessed was nearly sixty years old, was in great shape like himself, with skin that was perfectly tanned. He then observed how well-groomed Cesar was, rocking his salt-and-pepper hair cropped rather close on the sides with short curls on the top. He also admired the silk dress shirt, slacks and alligator boots that Cesar wore, all of it apparently made by artistic hands. He finally concluded that Cesar had to be *the* man his father dealt with overseas.

Trying to play it cool, Bizzy replied, "An' what matter is that?"

"First, let me compliment you on how nice this establishment is. My colleague, Adrian, informed me that you have so much of your father in you, so after I bribed a few higher-ups in America, I secretly traveled here from Peru to personally witness if what he told me was true. Now that I can see and sense you are proficient enough to handle a business corporation, I cannot wait until we're able to conduct business ourselves. But first, you have to settle your father's debt."

"My father's debt? What does my father owin' you have ta do wit me?"

Cesar sighed. "It has a lot to do with you, Byron ... do you mind if I call you Byron? Or do you prefer Bizzy?" He waited for an answer, but never received one. "Byron it is, then. Well, Byron, the sum of money your father owes me is significant. I would've counted it as a total loss if it weren't for your current prosperous dealings, so, since I know you have the capabilities, in addition to the perfect business, that will generate *millions* of dollars in an adequate amount of time, I have no choice but to have you settle your father's debt."

Curiously, Bizzy asked, "An' how much is this debt?"

"Forty-three million dollars."

Bizzy's stomach dropped to his toes, as well as his jaw, before he shrieked, "*Forty-three million dollars*? You're out of ya muthafuc—"

"Whoa. Hold your horses, cowboy," Cesar cut him off. Although he knew Bizzy would be visibly agitated once he heard the debt amount, he said, "You don't have to pay the whole forty-three million dollars, Byron, because it wasn't totally your fault. This is how I broke it down ... your father owing me that large amount of money is partly my fault because I trusted him with so much product on consignment.

"And since I was well-informed about your father having it bad for specific women, I had a feeling a woman would be his downfall. But I ignored my gut instinct." He shrugged. "The other person to blame in this is Adrian, for not keeping a close eye on Demetrius. When he saw Demetrius slipping, as you would say ... he should have immediately intervened and got him back on track or repossessed my drugs. Then, of course, blame most definitely must go on Demetrius. But, since he paid with his life ..."

He then cleared his throat. "And lastly, being that you're Demetrius' only child, you inherited his debt, unfortunately. Now, because there are four parties to blame, you only have to pay a quarter of his debt. That's only fair, right?"

"Ten million dollars," Bizzy griped, itching to grab his Glock and putting holes in both men.

"I know you want nothing more right now than to pull out your gun and shoot us both dead," Cesar said with a smirk. "Hell, I don't blame you. But it's only going to get you and that pretty receptionist of yours killed in the end by the men that have surrounded this building. Now, before, we go any further, if you don't mind, let me tell you a quick story about the Packard brothers," Cesar said, jumping to a different topic.

"There were three brothers, Alfred, Jefferson and Willis Packard. While all in their thirties, the eldest brother, Alfred, was a marketing genius, while Jefferson and Willis were notable scientists. In the late seventies, Alfred helped sell an unprecedented one million pills that helped people with sleeping problems. With the commissions he made, he and his brothers hit the lab, and they eventually created and patented a revolutionary drug in 1995 called Oxycontin.

"They then opened up a business called Dupree Pharma, and the marketer, Alfred, sold the pills in record numbers, convincing doctors at conventions throughout the U.S.A. that the powerful pain pill had a less than one percent chance of becoming addictive to their patients. The doctors bought Alfred's spiel about Oxycontin, as well as the other opiates that Jefferson and Willis soon created and patented and spread worldwide. And because of the Packards, the many patients in pain have become dependent on the so-called non-addictive pills, of which you're turning a *huge* profit."

"What does that story have ta do wit me?"

"Like I said, you're seeing money that's unheard of in the drug trade. Look at you," he waved his hands around, "you and a couple others have nice offices as fronts to sell pills somewhat legally, right in public view, tripling your profit. So, I figure, you shouldn't have a problem getting the *measly* ten million. In fact, if my calculations are correct, it should take you roughly two and a half years to pay that debt with what you have established now. Now, do you want to hear some good news?"

Not in the mood to play games at the moment, Bizzy gruffly said, "What?"

"I'm going to help you, my friend, settle this debt in a year ... *tops*." He laughed. "Yeah, I'm going to help you get two more clinics up and running. The second one will be opened in the next thirty days in a location of your choice. I'll pay for a hundred thousand pills, while you handle everything else. *Then*, once you get half of my money, I'll take it a step further and supply you with the pills for a third of the price you're getting them for now. How does that sound?"

"Where's da third location gonna be?" Bizzy didn't miss a beat.

Cesar looked at his henchman, and said, "See, I told you that he would be intelligent and attentive, just like his father." Turning his attention back to Bizzy, he continued, "Since Adrian decided to aid you in your little street war, without my consent, the third store will be opened in Palm Beach County. Those streets have been cleared of all your enemies and problems, so you'll get that third store open in ... let's say, the first week of January 2011. And Adrian will continue to aid you any way that you need him."

"Befo' I agree to anythang ..."

"You agree," the personal assistant finally spoke in his heavily accented English. "Or you die ... Now!"

Ignoring the man's threat, Bizzy, while staring at the hench-man, said, "As I was sayin,' befo' I agree to anythang." He looked at Cesar now. "I need ta know why ya gave my pops only a few days ta get'cha forty-three million when ya knew he was robbed fo' all that coke?"

"Well ... I had to put a little pressure on Demetrius." He paused. "If it does you any good, I never intended to kill your father, though. He was a great businessman, and I knew he'd find a way to scramble up at least half the money in a week or two. If he wouldn't have gotten half in two weeks, I would've had someone very close to him killed to motivate him to get my money. Overall, it was a business decision, nothing personal. You understand, right?"

157

For at least two minutes, Bizzy stood motionless and silent by the door, trying to understand. Then he abruptly said, "I accept your proposal. *But*, instead of a hundred thousand pills, make it *two* hundred thousand." He witnessed Cesar's facial expression change. "You want'cha money ASAP, rite?"

Cesar finally jumped down off the examination bed, walked over to Bizzy, and said, "Deal."

They concluded the meeting with a firm handshake.

Flame

Chapter Eighteen

October 9, 2010 8:21 pm

West Palm Beach, FL

Knock at door
Devon cringed.

Nowadays, disturbing the peace while she was in her sanctuary always caused her to react abnormally. Currently, the only constancy in her life was her work. She no longer had Miracle, Rhapsody, RahRah, or even Bizzy, to fill her days with time-consuming conversations and activities. Her days dragged along now, overstuffing her mind with fickle thoughts that kept her deeply depressed, and scared for her safety.

Knock at door
"Yo', Dee!"

The recognized voice put Devon at ease ... a bit. But she knew whatever it was her employee wanted had to be major, because she had informed all her staff to let her be while she was in her office, unless it was pressing.

"Dee, it's important!"

Devon, uptight, got up from her desk and undid the four newly placed locks on the door. "What's goin' on, Big Herb?" she said after opening the door just wide enough to see his Herculean physique.

"There's an old nigga out here lookin' fo' ya. He tall an' dark-skinned wit a bald head. I told him that'chu not meetin' wit nobody tonite, but he persistent 'bout talkin' wit'chu. He hangin' 'round da bar in da club, not acceptin' no dances, just waitin'."

Devon then walked back over to her desk with her immense bouncer in tow and pulled up the security camera feed. The two dozen state-of-the-art security cameras she had put in place following the break-in, covered every nook and cranny in and out of StudioX, even the interior of the bathrooms. Her life was on the

160

line so she wasn't taking any chances. On her computer screen, there were small boxes, with each one streaming live footage of a specific area. She then clicked on the small box that showed half of the club's bar in high definition.

"He on da otha end," Big Herb declared, then he pointed to the correct box for her to click on. Once the correct screen had popped up, he placed his sausage-like finger on the computer monitor directly below the person-of-interest's head, and added, "That's buddy rite there."

Because of the advanced camera's ability to clearly capture the unknown man's complete profile, Devon was quickly able to determine she had, by no means, ever seen the fellow before. However, she still monitored the man closely for a couple of minutes, noting over time that his behavior was methodic and rather off-beat for someone in a strip club. He held a drink in his hand that he never sipped, scanned his surroundings on end, and sure enough, he had declined all solicitations. *Either this dude is a paranoid, non-drinking homosexual,* she began to reason as she kept her eyes locked on the mysterious gentleman, *or he's on a mission.*

And the latter was her most valid deduction.

Devon's natural epinephrine then kicked into high gear. "Big Herb," she uttered, "go out there an' tell buddy I'm busy at da moment. Tell him, if what he has ta say is important, ta meet me in da parking lot at midnite, an' we can talk then."

Grasping that something was amiss, he declared sincerely, "Aye, Dee, I'll fuck his old ass up if need be. Gimme da green-light—"

"Naw, that ain't necessary," she cut in before pausing. "But I pray ya offer doesn't come back ta haunt me."

After Devon shot down his chance to crush the older gentleman, he said with a tinge of jadedness in his voice, "I got'chu, Dee."

Prior to Big Herb making his exit however, Devon insightfully decided to have him do one more favor for her. "Befo' ya go, Big

Herb," she called out then waited for him to turn around to face her. "After buddy leaves da building, an' ya make sho' he's gone, tell DJ Knotty Head ta announce that we closin' up early." She glanced at the clock on the computer's screen. "Tell him we closin' at ten. You come up wit some lame excuse as ta why, ai'ight? Then, once ya handle that, tell er'body that's workin' tonite that I'm havin' a mandatory meetin' in da restaurant area at 10:30, you got that?"

An ill-at-ease look overcame Big Herb's face. "Is er'thang grizzy, Dee? What's really goin' on?"

"I'll explain it all at 10:30, Herb. Now, please put a handle on it."

Saying no more, Big Herb spun his massive body on his heels and went about what was asked of him.

An oh-so awful two hours ticked away before the strippers, bouncers, bartenders, and all the other central employees, had gathered in the designated meeting place. The once frosty area had quickly turned into a toaster oven, thanks to the staffs' angst of having to attend the rare, odd meeting. Before long, the fifty or so employees had huddled up into small groups throughout the floor space, and their chatter grew louder and louder with speculation as to why this unexpected gathering was mandatory. And Devon's prolonged absence was only causing the situation to grow more tense by the millisecond.

"Ai'ight," Devon said as she emerged through the sliding door that separated the strip club and restaurant. Once all eyes landed on her and the chattering ceased, she resumed, "There's no easy way ta put this, so I'ma just give it ta y'all blood raw." She paused to take a quick breather. "I'm shuttin' shop down till furtha notice."

All but a few of the eyes in the room blazoned with astonishment. And a handful forced out a sharp audible gasp from the bombshell bulletin. As soon as the stark news settled in, the gang of employees, en masse, proceeded to bombard Devon with questions. Unable to make out a single word that was hurled her way, she began to shout and wave her arms in an attempt to silence the bedlam. It took her several seconds to grasp control over her disorderly, hot-blooded personnel.

Only once the high-strung swarm quieted down to one or two people still grumbling did she speak. "I know y'all gotta million an' one questions, but my only answer to them all is that I have some personal shit goin' on in my life rite now that I have ta handle. I can't fully focus on solvin' my issue while runnin' operations here. What I got goin' on is way mo' important than this."

"Where is Miracle?" the stripper Mystic blurted out. "Why can't she run da club while you handlin' your business? She ran things for you two years ago when you took a long vacation."

The mere mention of Miracle's name flooded Devon with a range of emotions. Yet, she kept her poise and replied, "Like I said, shop is closed. But don't trip 'bout findin' work cuz I made a couple calls an' er'body here, as well as da ones that's not, can carry on at any of da clubs from Palm Beach down to Dade till I handle my B.I. I had ta make sho' y'all were hella straight 'cuz I knew this would catch y'all off-guard. It was da least I could do since y'all have been loyal ta me." With nothing more to say, she shrugged nonchalantly, then disappeared through the same sliding door from which she came.

While sporting a new long wig and oversized sunglasses, Rhapsody posted up way in the back of the crowd that was now dissipating person by person. Although she hadn't been to work in more than two months, once Jazzy called her seeking information about why Devon was having an unforeseen meeting tonight, she made sure she would be in attendance incognito, nevertheless.

Unlike the others on hand there tonight to receive Devon's news, Rhapsody was only present to catch wind of as much vital information as possible. And the surprising news that she'd just heard let her know in a flash what Devon had in mind.

"Well, I'm on my way out now, girl," Rhapsody said. "Thanks fo' callin' me so I could be here personally to see what was goin' on."

"Rhap, since you and Devon livin' under da same roof, you obviously had to have known what was goin' down tonight," Jazzy began her rant in her squeaky voice, "because you don't seem fazed at all 'bout hearin' that fucked-up bullshit. How she just gon' close da club all of a sudden then have da nerve to tell us she set us up to work elsewhere?"

Gazing directly into the eyes of the person whom she truly considered a friend, she said, "I swear, I had no idea what Devon was gonna say tonite, Jazz. An,' just like you an' da othas, I'm in shock, too. Da only reason why I don't seem bothered by what was said is becuz I'm not da theatrical, fall-to-pieces type of bitch after receiving bad news. I've heard an' seen way worse in my life."

Jazzy shook her head disappointedly. "This is fucked up on so many levels, though. I got regulars that take damn good care of me and my kids. Now I got to go dance over there in da jerry-built Illusions 'cause I'm not travelin' out da county just to shake my ass." She sucked her teeth. "You and Miracle so damn lucky, livin' all high-and-mighty with Devon. Right now, I hate y'all hoes." She then shuffled off, leaving Rhapsody standing without saying goodbye.

Without a second thought, Rhapsody promptly, yet casually strolled off, moving to blend in with the herd that was exiting StudioX. Once outside, the clammy night's air smothered her. But she wouldn't break a sweat for she was feeling *Rhap*turous. She walked on air through the parking lot until she arrived at the passenger door of a low-key Toyota Corolla. Tucked away safely in the vehicle at last, she excitedly fixed her body in the seat to look toward the driver.

"You must uncovered sumthin' major cuz of that big goofy-ass smile on ya Cadbury-chocolate baby face," JJ asserted with an expression on his marred face that rivaled hers. "Don't keep me on edge now. What it do?"

Since she strongly felt that her sixth sense about Devon's intended plans were on the money, she was in a playful mood this minute. In a theatrical manner, she popped her tongue and rolled her neck, prior to speaking in hood-rat-twang. "You know I *luuuvs* you, rite?" she flamboyantly batted her eye lashes. "An' since I *luuuvs* you, I'm gonna *tell* ya that my *ex*," she rolled her eyes "is plannin' on skippin' town." Seeing that JJ was going to interrupt her, she quickly placed a finger to his lips.

"Lemme *finish*, Daddy. *Dang* ... *Anywayz*, da reason I *know* she gonna skip town, which you were going to ask me how I know all this," she winked, "is *becuz* she announced *tonite* that she shuttin' down *StudioX* so she can *focus* on handlin' a *personal* problem. She would *never* *c*lose da doors to her money-maker *unless* she was leavin' town fo' a while, or fo' *good*." She popped her tongue again while batting her eyelashes, thereby wrapping up her prediction.

To JJ, Rhapsody's news flash didn't quite blow him away. Admittedly, however, he would bet big stacks on her intuition being on point, for she had been Devon's companion for a long time and was well aware of Devon's tendencies. His one question at the moment was ... if their bait was conspiring to make a run for it, how was he going to get his hands on Bizzy?

"Da unpleasant look on ya face," Rhapsody began, "let's me know da gears are turnin' at full speed in ya head. I can almost see smoke comin' from ya ears. So, what's on that far-out mind of yours, daddy? Talk ta mama."

Although she had shattered his train of thought, he couldn't help but smile at her timely humor. "We gotta figga out a way ta make ya girl stay in town if she ..."

"See, I gotta be da long-lost daughter of Miss Cleo." She tee-hee'd, then launched into speaking in Jamaican patois. "Ya rude gurl is lewd but *shrewd*, yunno. Me learn a whole heap ah patois when me go inna dancehall club since a likkle gurl." She blew him a kiss. "Anywayz," she said in her normal sultry voice, "I sensed that'chu were just thinkin' 'bout a way to keep Devon from cuttin' an' runnin.' I got that covered. I know exactly how to keep that from happenin'. That's plan B."

"Plan B?"

"Why you soundin' so surprised?" she pouted before grandiosely crossing her arms over her hefty chest. "As if *I* can't go in depth wit my plottin.' As if *lil ole me* can't be so bold as to takin a crack at reelin' in Bizzy myself without consultin' wit'chu first. See, I'm fed up wit everybody thinkin' I'm some dumb bitch. Just becuz I'm trustin' an' I don't stand up fo' myself that much, I'm no pushover by no means. I'ma show you, Devon, an' everybody else that—"

"Whoa, Nellie!" he then cut her short before she hit the roof, both literally and figuratively. "Don't jump on me, bae. I ain't mockin' ya, puttin' ya down, beefin' wit'cha, none of that." He sighed. "Yeah, I-I admit I was surprised when I heard 'Plan B' at first. But it wasn't like how ya thought. I was beyond surprised ta learn that'chu had a Plan A. Once it registered in my head that'chu been plannin' without me, I was mo' like, Damn, my boss bitch playin' fo' keeps."

Bit by bit, her frown turned into a beaming smile. She then leaned over and gave him an appreciative kiss.

"That's my girl. An,' just so ya' know, I'll never handle ya like a black Kelly Bundy." He cracked himself up, causing Rhapsody to giggle also. After several seconds of hearty laughter, he slipped back to the moment, and in all seriousness, said, "Now, lemme hear every plan that'chu cooked up in that brilliant mind of yours."

As Rhapsody set forth with explaining what she had put in motion already and what she had in mind, JJ crunk up the car and proceeded to head home, soaking up every intricate detail that was revealed with a fiendish grin on his face.

Chapter Nineteen

October 10, 2010 9:37 am

Mobile, AL

The west side was the best side.

Or so they said.

In Bizzy's current position, that cliché was on the mark.

Located on Passover Road in West Mobile was the prominent community Kingston Pines. Nearly all of the population in the large neighborhood consisted of African-Americans, and they weren't your average Negroes, either. The black folks in this tasteful part of the city were financially stable, with the lion's share of households containing a happily married couple and their world-class children.

Although the only "grind" that Bizzy ever experienced firsthand involved several units of measure, his well-bred facade laid out the illusion that he belonged in the hub of the earnest blue-and white-collar residents. He was presently feeling like the Fresh Prince of West Mobile, blending in with no problem. It was rather refreshing knowing the neighbors would barely blink twice at him as long as he wasn't a nuisance. And with his eggs all in one basket, his townsmen would perceive him as nothing more than a wifeless workaholic.

In all honesty, Bizzy went overboard when he paid his comrade from Tally to sign the bill of sale and title for the modest, yet stylish home. The roughly quarter-million-dollar two-story half-brick, half-stucco house had a little over 2600 square feet of floor space, which was entirely too much house for one person. Summarily, the layout was two bedrooms and a bathroom on the ground floor. A library / study and a master bedroom—more like a chamber—with its own spacious bathroom on the second level. Furthermore, there was a fireplace that heated both floors through the living room and master bedroom.

168

And yet the key factor about purchasing the ducked-off crib was that it took him twenty minutes, more or less, to travel to his pain clinic in Prichard.

So, all in all, Bizzy couldn't have been happier with his latest arrangements. And he had nobody to thank but his Tallahassee homeboy, whose relocation to Mobile in 2005 turned out to be beneficial for Bizzy. He was grateful for his homie going to bat for him when he faced dire straits. That loyal homie of his, sad to say, was no longer around to witness his successful come-up, because signing for the house was in effect signing his death certificate. His unwed, childless friend simply vanished without a trace.

As luck would have it, I don't need Jermaine here to pay all the bills since the bank automatically performs those transactions, Bizzy said to himself as he lay in his boxer briefs in bed feeling triumphant about his present Machiavellian achievements, *and I can continue to deposit money into his account with a money order.*

Phone beeps

The beep signaled he had just received a text message. Though just about all the people who hit up his prepaid phone lately were calling from the Eastern time zone (he was in the Central zone now), it was still too early in the morning for him to be bothered. And since the few people that had his number knew that he rarely took leisure calls, especially before noon, the text message had to be of importance.

No longer flying high, instead feeling uptight now, he inhaled loudly through his nostrils before blowing a jet of air out of his mouth. Skepticism about the context of the awaiting message caused him to tentatively reach for his Samsung Galaxy on the nightstand, inch by tedious inch. After clutching the device and pulling up the message, he calmly glanced over it. He read the message at least five times because digesting the coded text was an uphill battle. *There's no way this shit is true*, he tried to convince himself as he sat up and negligently tossed the phone back on the nightstand. *Skinny-O is simply trying to make something out of nothing.*

As much as he would've liked to believe Skinny-O's discovery was off-the-wall, it still bothered him in a big way, that someone dared to attempt to cash in on his father's murder reward with what he prayed was an unreal assumption. The god-awful and cryptic message said that someone fingered his sibling as being indirectly linked to Demetrius' death.

Without warning, Bizzy erupted into gut-busting laughter. It was one of those dreamlike moments for him where the saying went, "Sometimes you have to laugh to keep from crying." His deranged cackling carried on for a few minutes until he felt a major migraine setting in. And with that, he slipped out of bed in a trance and began a desperate search for Tylenol, Advil, or any painkiller. *Even if I was to find something for this rising headache,* he said to himself between swallows of water directly from the bathroom sink's faucet, I'll *have to see about this bullshit concerning my sister no matter what, which will be a chronic headache until I get to the bottom of it.*

Before long, he chose to bear with the pounding in his head, because he knew prior to starting the search, there were no OTC medicines in the house. Every second counted now, so he had to get along with exploring the ridiculous idea that Devon was … "Ain't no way Devon coulda been involved wit *our* Pops gettin' merked," Bizzy tried to reassure himself even further by speaking aloud. He then splashed water on his face before returning to the bedroom. Sitting on the edge of the bed, he grabbed his phone, scrolled through his short contact list and thumbed Skinny-O's name. Upon Skinny-O answering, he said in short, "Don't make a move till I get there."

He ended the call.

October 10, 2010 11:14am

Riviera Beach, FL

"Marie!"

"Yes, ma'am?"

"When you finish up there with your father, come and help me cut these oxtail, please!"

"I'll be there in a second!" Looking at her father now, Miracle said, "Well, I'll come back once I'm finished, okay?"

"Go now, Marie," her Jamaican-Cuban father, Beres, instructed. "I can look after tings until your return. Besides, I got me sidekick to assist me. Isn't that so, Kamani?" He patted his grandson on the head lovingly.

"Yeah!" Kamani shrieked, fired up.

"Okay," Miracle said, looking down at her son now. "You know the rules. You be good and listen to what Pop Pop says, okay?"

Kamani repeatedly jumped up and down, indicating that he understood.

Miracle simply nodded with a smile. She then bent down to kiss him before obediently going to help her mother in the kitchen.

Work. That was the only thing that kept Miracle's mind from thinking incessantly about Devon and driving her plumb crazy. Since writing Devon that heartrending goodbye letter, and effectively stepping away from her role at the club, she passed her days by volunteering at her parents' restaurant, *Taste of Montego Bay*. Besides, working hard was deep-rooted in her otherwise fiery temperament. At some point in time, she and all seven of her U.S.-born siblings, had worked in their immigrant parent's restaurant, with her beginning at age nine after school. What's more, she wanted to spend as much time with her parents before she moved a few counties away.

"Come now, Marie," her Haitian mother, Michelle, said a bit breathlessly without looking up from what she was doing, "the ox tail not going to cut themself."

171

Once Miracle put on a smock and grabbed a butcher's knife and cutting board, they commenced to work silently side by side. About ten minutes into the task, Miracle broke the uncomfortable silence. "So, Mom … are you okay?"

Chopping nonstop without looking up, Michelle answered, "What do you mean, child?"

"I mean … since I've been workin' here daily for the last coupla weeks, I've noticed that you've been … a little out of breath. Is there somethin' you're not tellin' me?"

Still chopping, still not looking up either, she replied, "I'm okay, child. Just a little tired. That's all." Then, to put an immediate stop to the invasive questioning, she quickly changed the subject. "When are you going to go back to school, Marie? Now that you no longer work at that … at that *demon-filled* club and you left that *disgusting* … whatever you want to call …"

"*Her* name is Devona, Mom," Miracle straightened her in a respectful tone.

"Ugh!" Still not looking up, she brushed off Miracle's revisal with a wave of her knife-wielding hand. "Whatever. But you need to make good on your dream as little girl to go to college. You have money. So go, child, while you have your youth and smarts still."

It was true that a young Marie aspired to attend a big university out of state. Northwestern University in Evanston, IL, a suburb of Chicago, was her top choice because she had learned in fifth grade that the Windy City had more Blacks living there than in any other city in America. She had marveled at the likelihood of being around so many people that she resembled and could relate to. And since she wished to help people of color in need, she dreamt of studying to be a nurse, specifically a pediatric nurse. *My mom is absolutely right*, Miracle thought as the prospect of actually going to school began to weigh heavily on her. *I need … no, I must achieve something important and rewarding that can provide a better life for me and set an example for Kamani.*

"Marie!"

"Huh? What?" Miracle responded after being lost deep in her thoughts.

"What's wrong?"

Michelle was now looking at her wide-eyed with concern. "Are *you* okay, my child?"

She chuckled. "Yes, Mom, I'm fine. I was just …"

Phone rings

She finally heard it, which was more than likely what her mother was trying to direct her attention to.

With her hands covered in fat and meat trimmings from cutting the oxtails, she was unable to retrieve the phone stuffed in her jean's back pocket. And since she had no clue as to how long her phone was ringing, she dropped the butcher's knife and scurried over to the wash basin to rinse the offal off her hands. By the time Miracle could access her phone, however, it had stopped ringing. She then gingerly pressed a few icons on the touchscreen with her damp fingers and soon saw whose call she had missed, which triggered her to grimace. After seeing red for a few seconds, she forced herself to return the missed call.

"What do you—" she started to rant before the caller immediately cut her off. "What?" she hollered after listening closely to the hysterical caller rattle off the unsettling news.

"Is everyting irie back here?" Beres asked at once upon entering the kitchen with a confused-looking Kamani by his side.

Unbalanced and disoriented from what the caller proclaimed, Miracle had trouble pulling herself together. She knew what she had to do, but her body wasn't responding. She simply stood frozen in shock, her arms dangling by her sides, with the phone falling unnoticed from her hand.

"Marie, what is wrong?" both Beres and Michelle asked fearfully in sync, both approaching her swiftly, yet carefully.

Miracle cringed when her father grabbed her by the shoulders. His touch caused her to jump into action. She then proceeded to walk out of the building.

"Where you go, Marie?" inquired Beres.

173

Michelle asked, "What happened?"

Without breaking her stride or looking back, she answered, "I'll be right back. Please watch Kamani until I return."

And with that, she left the building, blindly heading toward imminent danger.

October 10, 2010 11:29 am

West Palm Beach, FL

In the intervening time, in Pleasant City ...

"Have y'all boyz ever thought about buyin' life insurance fo' y'all kid's sake?" RahRah posed the question to his homies.

"Life insurance?" Skat retorted as he continued to play *Call Of Duty* on Xbox. "What da fuck I look like givin' them crackas money fo' my life when I'm out'chea livin' ta die?"

"Yeah, Durt," Bumper jumped in while piloting his own soldier in the game, "that shit should be called *death* insurance fo' niggas like us. So, fo' once, I agree wit Skat. I'd ratha put my own bread up fo' my lil ones ta get when my time comes."

"See, that's da thing, who can y'all trust ta give y'all kids that bread when ya die?" Rah said, sitting in a second-rate recliner and browsing back and forth between the TV and Bumper and Skat, who were sitting on opposite ends of a sleazy couch. Their prolonged silence gave him his answer. "Exactly. Y'all niggas don't trust nobody that much. So buyin' eitha whole or term life insurance will make sho' y'all jits get paid ... wit no hassles ... when that day comes."

"Fuck that bullshit you talkin'! Besides, nigga, I'm immortal anywayz," Skat declared while operating the joystick effortlessly. "Ima' take care of my shorties till they eighteen, then they on their own. So, that goes back ta me sayin', I'm not makin' them crackas rich cuz I'm not finna ..."

"Die, nigga, die!" Bumper yelled as his soldier snuck up on Skat's fighter and gunned him down. "Ha-Ha! Betta hope that nigga got life insurance!" He then scooped up the pile of money on the cheap smoked-glass coffee table.

Skat threw the controller to the floor. "Man, I got distracted wit all this bullshit Rah talkin' 'bout." He turned to Bumper, and said, "Run that shit back, tar baby. Lemme win my cheese back. Double or nuttin'." Then, he turned to RahRah. "An' you, fake-ass David Banner, shut da fuck up wit all this political bullshit!"

"It ain't political, lil ignorant muthafucka. It's financial, Gary Coleman-lookin' ass boy."

If looks could kill, the way Skat eyed RahRah would make anybody without life insurance consider getting some ASAP.

These friendly wars of words were the new norm for the trio. Although the war in the streets was dying down, they had been self-quarantining for nearly two months at PopTart Tina's apartment in the city. They were MIA, only roaming the streets in the dead of night to offset cabin fever, and to fuck a bitch or three besides PopTart Tina. They were biding their time inside by mainly strategizing on when and how to take back the turf they had strong-armed from RBF. But, in between time, RahRah, a semi-conscientious politically interested ex-convict, and Skat, an alumnus of the Academy of Tragedy quite often squabbled. RahRah aimed to discuss civics and government when possible, while Skat went all in on speaking about bitches, bullets, Beamers and bankrolls all day.

And Bumper ... well, he usually straddled the fence, not caring about much nowadays except for keeping Triple S and his name gator (good) in the streets. Even so, he enjoyed watching his bros feud since he knew at the end of the day, they wouldn't go at each other's throats, literally.

"As long as I got y'all two clowns togetha, I neva have ta watch *Comedy Central* again, cuz watchin' y'all is *real* comedy. Y'all both flap y'all pussy-suckas 'bout some oddball shit." He smirked, then he looked directly at RahRah. "You wanna talk politics, Durt, then let's talk. Sooo ... you wanna talk 'bout how da recently passed Affordable Care Act, aka Obamacare, still

175

won't be affordable fo' people in da hood? Hmmm ... I got it, how 'bout da Deepwater Horizon Oil spill in da Gulf of Mexico an' how petrol prices gon' skyrocket now? Or ... let's see... do ya wanna debate 'bout what this financial reform bill that Obama recently signed is gon' do ta help our mommas? Huh? ... precisely." He nonchalantly turned to Skat.

"An' my pot'nah, my nigga if he don't get no bigga ... you wanna rap 'bout ... *again*... why fine-ass Rhianna let that lame Chris Brown beat on her? Or ... AHA! I gotta even betta one ... how much time ya think T.I. gon' get in da feds next week after getting' caught wit them beans in L.A. an' violatin' his probation? How much? ... Bingo."

Dripped with heavy sarcasm, Bumper's rhetorical questions left both Skat and RahRah tongue-tied at the moment.

Phone rings

Thankful for his ringing phone, RahRah couldn't answer it fast enough. "Who this?" he asked because he didn't take the time to look at the caller ID. "Who?" he asked again. But instead of identifying themselves, the caller forged ahead. "WHEN?" he shouted after getting an earful of unexpected news from the stranger.

"What da beat is, Durt?"

"Yeah, why ya over there yellin' like ya hit da lottery or sumthin,' nigga?"

Juiced up from what the unknown caller proclaimed, RahRah startled both Bumper and Skat when he jumped out of the recliner, shot over to the couch, reached behind it and fetched a Russian AK with a 100-round drum attached to it.

"Heigh-ho!" Skat exclaimed pirate-like. Not caring at all about RahRah grabbing his personal chopper, he added, "'Bout time we got some action." No question asked, he stood up on the couch, felt about behind it and snatched up an Israeli Uzi with a homemade reversible clip. "Voila. Now this is what I call Point an' Click. Just like a mouse on a computer, but you point and I click this muthafucka till it's empty. Now, point to where him, her or it at? It's wabbit huntin' time."

Detached from the sudden excitement, Bumper got up and stepped off towards PopTart Tina's bedroom.

Meanwhile, RahRah jetted out of the back of the apartment with Skat on his heels. Although it was the middle of the day, they sprinted down one of the many alleyways in the city headfirst with the high-powered weapons raring to go. Once they approached the end of the alley that ran into Beautiful Avenue, RahRah ducked off into some bushes in the nearest backyard and Skat did the same but on the opposite side of the alley. RahRah almost instantly started sweating bullets as he squatted in the bushes waiting for the moment to arrive while Skat eventually proceeded to giggle to himself in anticipation of the upcoming murder.

With a wide field of view, RahRah was able to see at least seventy-five yards of Beautiful Avenuein both directions. He knew exactly what to look for and, according to the tipoff he had gotten, his target should be in sight any minute now. Finger on the trigger, he looked over at a laughing Skat and shook his head, then he began to wonder where Bumper was at.

Finally, he saw it in his peripheral vision, a white 2009 Infiniti G37S. The closer the car approached his location, the more his nerves fired. *Something isn't right about this situation*, he suddenly began to think as his eyes widened as the rather familiar car closed in on his position, *this shit don't feel right.*

Fifty yards away.

Forty yards to go.

Thirty yards.

Twenty yards and closing.

On the other side of the alley, Skat kept his eyes trained on RahRah once the car came into view. Although he had not an inkling as to who the target was, he knew that by watching RahRah's every move he would receive some kind of sign as to when it was about to go down.

177

And Skat finally got what he was looking for when he noticed RahRah's eyes damn near pop out of their sockets the closer that car got. Already feeling like a hellish pitbull fighting his leash the moment this began, he impulsively jumped the gun. He leapt from his hiding spot, sprinted into the street, and let the killer bees fly, officially giving the city a big cup of Folger's this midday.

After emptying the Uzi's first clip, the car swerved around Skat and kept traveling down the street. As he masterfully reversed the clip and prepared to fire again, a black figure took shape next to him and began unloading .45 caliber bullets from a Thompson submachine gun into the back of the car as it lost speed.

Bumper officially crashed the party, making a grand entrance only the way he could.

RahRah, on the other hand, was nowhere in sight.

Not one to leave a scene until every slug in his possession flew at his intended target, Skat fired up his Uzi once more as he laughed like the Joker, while Bumper coolly handled his favored weapon. Once the luxury vehicle jumped the curb and hit a fire hydrant, and all magazines were spent, both Bumper and Skat took flight, not knowing or caring, in truth, where RahRah was.

Flame

Chapter Twenty

October 12, 2010 3:41 am

West Palm Beach, FL

"Byron," the vaguely familiar voice echoed far and wide in the unlit place. "Byyyyyronnnnnnn," the voice then sang.

"Wh-who-who are you?" asked a shaken Bizzy. "Where am I?"

"Awww, my baby boy. Tsk. tsk. Look at what your ruthless father turned you into. My poor, poor baby boy. What a shame."

"Ma-Mama, is that... you?"

"Yes, it is me, Byron. It is your mother, the once attractive, youthful, gullible woman that your father undervalued before ... KILLING ME!"

Those last words bellowed on and on, growing more thunderous and earsplitting each time it reverberated. It boomed so loud in the void, or wherever it was he was at, that he expected to lose his hearing any time now.

Without notice, and to his satisfaction, the echoing ended. There was all-out quietness for several seconds before she cried out, "You're a fucking murderer, Bizzy, just like your evil father, Kilo! And like father, like son... DEAD!"

Bizzy awoke totally outfitted, red-hot, and trembling like a dog shitting out a peach seed. He wildly dabbed at the sweat glazing his face before he began normalizing his swift and off-key breathing. Employing a trick that he had got down pat from his father, he minimized the anxiety attack he was experiencing, to a point where he was just about back to his usual self.

Once at ease, he eventually took in the indistinct backdrop in which he was confined. The unfamiliarity of the bedroom nearly caused a resurgence of the apprehension he'd just overcome, until he discovered he was in the coziness of his other house in Bear Lakes. In a relaxed way, he rolled out of the soaked sheets and went to the bathroom. *That was the first time I've ever had a bad dream about my mama,* he thought after cutting on the light and looking in the mirror and instantly seeing his father's reflection, *and I don't know what to exactly make of it, either.*

He sighed as he focused on the man he idolized in the mirror.

However, before he let his thoughts run too wild and get the best of him, he shook it off and commenced to get down to what brought him back to PBC. It was bad enough PBC made him out to be a liar, since he swore that he would never, ever, return, so he was strictly here to track down the truth about whether Devon had any connection to Demetrius' murder or not. Time was of the essence because the more time he spent down in PBC, a place he purely felt was under the evil eye, the more time he spent not designing ways to expand his pill mill project.

Then, he remembered.

It almost slipped his mind that Cesar, the Peruvian kingpin, ordered that he open a clinic in the accursed PBC in January 2011, which was three months away. So one mission suddenly turned into two for him, and he now had to search for a vacant store, on top of searching for why Devon had been implicated in his father's death. *Oh, what a wonderful life,* he thought as he proceeded to undress in preparation for a shower, *what have I gotten myself into?*

It took him no time at all to shower. It was imperative that he left the house right away. Not only was he in a rush to get busy handling the two ugly missions that he now had on his plate, but he was also in a rush to get out of the house that could very well be under surveillance. This was the first time he had been in the house since the night Chad had been killed. The one and only reason why he had returned to the house was because he flew to PBC last night, arriving about 11:30. And although he was using fake names when needed, he didn't want to check into a hotel. So, after catching a cab to Bear Lakes and being dropped off by the community pool, he cautiously walked to his house with plans of spending a few hours to rest up before leaving the house for good.

181

Once dressed, he called up Skinny-O and asked to be picked up by the community pool. Skinny-O, who suffered from sleep deprivation, had no problem with scooping him up before dawn. Besides, it was a must he consult face-to-face with the man that gathered the denouncing information about Devon.

When he was finally inside of the immaculate 1984 Pontiac Grand Prix, in order to kill two birds with one stone, he asked Skinny-O to assist him with tracking down a few choice locations that could hopefully, be turned into a pain clinic, while he also got to the bottom of Devon's uncertain involvement in Demetrius' demise.

"Now, run it by me how Devon's name got mixed-up in this shit," Bizzy said upfront.

"No problem, young blood," Skinny-O replied before starting from the top. From the moment Bizzy entrusted him with finding his childhood friend's killer, he had put forth maximum effort. After spending the last ninety-one days scouring the turf and monitoring FaceSpace constantly for the hashtag KILOREWARD, checking out all but a few bogus leads daily, he finally struck black gold three days ago. With mainly all the people creating phony accounts to post using the hashtag KILOREWARD, a direct message to "R.J.," the lone poster that day, resulted in him receiving a DM back that contained a password and URL for *DumpTruck.com*, an online storage website. The website prompted for the password that he had been given before he received a brief message and a link to a download. He had read the message first, and it simply provided dirt on a woman of interest. He read that Tamara "Beauti" Carter was the last known female acquaintance of Demetrius, and she worked at StudioX, and if she couldn't be found, Devon knew her whereabouts. Consequently, he clicked on the link, and the item that downloaded was a picture.

With one hand working the steering wheel, Skinny-O pulled out a first edition iPhone from the center console. As he pressed buttons, he said, "I dropped by StudioX da same day I got da info. After I learned from multiple strippers that nobody by da name of

Beauti, or Tamara Carter, worked there, I then tried meetin' up wit Devon. I asked one of da bouncers ta get Devon fo' me, an' he eventually came back an' told me ta return at midnite so me an' Devon could talk.

"But when I bust a quick block ta make it seem like I hauled ass, an' came rite back ta wait it out, I saw da club close early. Since I never crossed paths wit Devon, I didn't know if she left wit da crowd or what, but I do know she stood me up. I knew sumthin' wasn't rite at that point, an' that's when I hit'chu up." Finally finding what he was looking for in his phone, he handed it to Bizzy. "That's a picture of Beauti. I neva seen her, eitha."

One quick look at the photo was all it took for Bizzy to nearly drop the phone. He did, however, drop something in disbelief—his jaw.

October 12, 2010 10:43 am

Riviera Beach, FL

The only day that was sadder was the day her mother was killed and she herself nearly died after being viciously sexually assaulted. Although she came to comprehend what real pain was at the age of four, the pain she felt now was different, but it hurt all the same.

She had only been in Charlotte, North Carolina for two days, having run from the troubles that had unfolded in her hometown. Right after she had closed StudioX, she rushed home, threw some clothes in a few bags, cleaned out the hundred and forty-six thousand from her safe, jumped into her BMW X6 and skipped town, leaving everything of importance behind—her house, her club and Miracle—without thinking twice.

Her intention had been to start a new life in the Queen City, a city that she had picked randomly, and nobody would know her. However, her plan of settling down had been swiftly interrupted when she saw on her *FaceSpace* page's timeline that Miracle, her of-no-importance Miracle, had been shot and was currently on life support in a coma. Although her life was on the line, she threw caution to the wind in order to be by her former lover's side.

The same way she had gotten to North Carolina was the same way she left. After driving, more like speeding nearly fourteen straight hours, she pulled up at Saint Mary's Hospital. Then, right when she was going to leap from the car after barely shifting it into park, she realized that Miracle's family was more than likely by her side. And since it wasn't a state secret that Miracle's mother absolutely hated her for no good reason, she slouched back in her seat and started crying, which was something that she had done, on and off, the entire trip back to godforsaken PBC.

She wasn't crying now because she was scared of the potential quarrel between her and Michelle once she mustered up the strength to go see Miracle. She was crying because she had failed to do everything in her power to fix things between her and Miracle, to prevent something like this from happening in the first place.

She simply cried, because she knew with all her heart that it was her fault why Miracle had been shot. *Miracle was right when she wrote in that letter that I wasn't thinking about her or Kamani when I started all this,* she thought as she stared at the hospital through the car's windshield, *I most definitely put her and Kamani's lives in harm's way.*

Six minutes later, she was prepared to face the inevitable and prepared to bear the brunt of the blame. She exited her vehicle and immediately felt overloaded with invisible weight. Walking from her BMW to the entrance of the hospital was a struggle, because the realization of actually seeing her baby in a coma and clinging to life overwhelmed her with shock, anger, sadness, regret and panic.

Once at the nurse's station, she nervously and politely asked for Marie Maxwell's room number. The nurse then began to locate Miracle, typing away on a keyboard. The waiting caused her nerves to fray all the more. The longer it took the nurse to pull up Miracle's information, the more she felt as if she was too late.

"I'm sorry, sir, but there is no Marie Maxwell in our system," the chubby white nurse said in a courteous tone.

Taken aback, Devon fired back, "Are ya sho'? Are ya spellin' her name correctly? It's M-A-R-I-E ... M-A-X—"

"Yes, sir, I have tried multiple spellings and I'm positive she's—"

"You have gotta be mistaken!" Devon cut in, raising her voice in the process. "Where's ya supervisor? I need ta see ya supervisor, please!" When the nurse didn't budge, Devon began to smack the countertop. "Now, goddammit!"

"Sir, you need to calm down! Or I'll be forced to call security!"

Just when she was about to throw a massive fit, she realized everybody in the waiting room was staring at her. However, there was just one person in particular staring at her that stopped her from going hog-wild.

Penetrating Devon's soul with intense hatred in her eyes was Michelle.

"What are you doing here, ou vacabond? You have no business here. It is because of *you* my child has been shot down! And it is possible you had something to do with my brother-in-law, Virgil, being killed. So get out of here, ou puri!"

The accusation opened Devon up as if she had been sliced from throat to navel. Nevertheless, she had anticipated it, taking it on the chin like a champ and standing her ground. "Look, Mrs. Maxwell, I ain't come here ta fight wit'chu. I came ta see Marie, da woman I love mo' than life itself. I totally undastand that'chu don't like me fo' da fact that I'ma lesbian, but maybe you'd undastand if I told ya my life story. An' I undastand why ya blame me fo' what happened ta ya daughter. Hell, Mrs. Maxwell, I blame myself.

"As fo' ... Virgil? I dunno what'chu talkin' 'bout." Devon shrugged sympathetically. "But I'ma tell ya I was in North

185

Carolina when I heard da news 'bout Marie. An' I'ma tell ya loud an' clear that'chu ain't gon' stop me from seein' da woman we both love. I'm already late, Mrs. Maxwell, but I'll be here all day, *every day*, campin' out here if I must, till I see her. I ain't budgin', an' I ain't bluffin', eitha. I let her slip away once an' it won't ever happen again. So, there ya have it. I love Marie an' I'm stayin' here, whetha I see her or not. We're so close that she'll feel my presence anyways."

Lips quivering, with tears welling up in her now serene eyes, Michelle suddenly approached Devon and did something unexpected. Michelle hugged Devon and started to bawl on her shoulder. After her initial shock subsided, Devon embraced Michelle, and they cried in unison.

"I'm sorry, child," Michelle stated in between sobs. "I'm ... so ... sorry. I know ... how much Marie ... loves you. She loves you so much that ... before she go into a coma ... all she say was ... 'Is Devon okay? Is Devon okay?' Then, my grandson, Kamani ... all he say was, 'Where is Devon? I want to see Devon.' So, that let me know ... how much you mean ... to those I cherish dearly." She sniffled.

That surprising, yet refreshing, revelation shook Devon to the core. She was speechless.

Once Michelle recovered from her breakdown, she said, "I'm sorry for blaming you for Virgil's death. I-I'm just so upset, child." She sighed. "Now, the reason you can't find Marie is because she under a fake name. Since the authority arrested no one, they feel it was best to use a fake name for Marie. So, come now. Visiting hours are almost over."

Gaining admission to visit Marie was excruciatingly long for Devon. Although it took less than two minutes for the process to be completed, it seemed like two hours had passed by before Michelle and Devon reached the Critical Care Unit, otherwise known as the CCU, on the third floor. Beres, who was visibly distressed, was sitting in a small waiting area with some of Miracle's extended family members when Michelle and Devon crept up on them. When they finally saw her and Michelle moving toward them, the looks on their faces showed a range of emotions, with most of them indicating unhappiness.

And Devon knew exactly who those dejected looks were aimed at.

There was one person, however, overjoyed to see her.

"Dee!" Kamani yelled as he got down off the bench seat and sprinted toward Devon. He crashed into her, causing her to stumble backwards a bit, and squeezed her tightly. He then began to cry a river, soaking the middle of her Polo shirt with tears. "Where were you? Where have you been?" he demanded.

"I know, it's okay ta be upset wit me, lil man." Devon consoled Kamani while caressing him endearingly and trying to soothe him. "But I'm here now, that's all that matters. I got'chu, okay? An' I'm sorry I'm late. It won't happen again, I promise, okay?"

Devon's loving consolation of Kamani kept Miracle's family in line. Soon after she had calmed him down, Michelle introduced her to the family. Although she had encountered Michelle and a few of Miracle's siblings briefly beforehand, this moment was as if she had been adopted and was meeting her new family for the first time.

With the awkward introductions out of the way, Michelle pulled Devon to the side, and said, "If you didn't know, Marie was shot four times. She lost a lot of blood, De-Dee …"

"Devona. You can call me Devona, Mrs. Maxwell."

She smiled slightly. "She had two good surgeries already. Right now, the doctor don't know how many more surgery she may need. They are looking over her carefully. Still, if you know Marie like I do, she is strong, a fighter, and she will survive this."

"Yes, Mrs. Maxwell, she will. She's da strongest person I know."

"Okay then. Now, you have a few minutes left. I will let you see Marie alone, okay?" Michelle gestured with her hand to go ahead into the CCU ward. Seeing Devon's reluctance, she added, "Go, Devona. She will be happy to hear your voice."

The moment of truth had arrived. Her feet felt like she had on cement shoes and her heart beat faster than a hummingbird's wings, because the last person close to her she saw shot up was her brother, RahRah. Although she couldn't visit RahRah in the hospital at that time, because he had been charged with a crime that day, she had nightmares every blue moon—even to this day—about that tragic event. Now she was certain she would have to relive that unforgettable day again once she saw Miracle's condition for the first time.

Time to put my big boy boxers on, Devon pep talked herself just before entering the ward, *because if the shoe was on the other foot, Miracle would kill just to be by my side.* Then, inhaling deeply and exhaling slowly, she walked into the ward.

After stopping by a different nurse's station and requesting to see Miracle, she was escorted to her doorless room. Finally, she slid the sheer curtain to the side and slipped into the room.

Paralyzed.

Not Miracle.

Devon was paralyzed, frozen in place, from what she beheld. The sight of her angel left her so blown away that she couldn't cry even if she wanted to. She was totally vacant. Then, without being consciously aware of taking a step, she had materialized by Miracle's motionless body.

As she stood dormant by Miracle's side, silently lamenting, a thousand questions flooded her thoughts, with the main stumper being what was Miracle's reason for riding through war-torn Pleasant City? That question needed to be answered pronto, and she would find that answer one way or the other. *Whether this was my fault or not, you never deserved to be ambushed and nearly killed, because of me getting payback for what was done to me first,* Devon telepathically spoke to a heavily bandaged and bruised Miracle before gingerly petting her hand. *I apologize, Marie...*

"An' I swear," Devon then said aloud, "I'ma take care of who did this ta ya ... personally. Now I got mo' than one person ta deal wit." She gnashed her teeth. "I love ya, Marie."

Devon then gently stroked Miracle's bandaged, swollen face with the back of her hand before slipping off with her mind instantly dwelling on ways to get back at Bizzy. Her brother would soon meet the same fate by her hands as his father did.

And right when Devon slid the curtain closed behind her, Miracle's electroencephalograph or EEG, a machine that detected and recorded brain waves through electrodes in a cap that touched the skin of the scalp, now showed that her brain neurons were firing and changing the electrical activity in her brain. Although she was unable to open her eyes, move or speak, the EEG displayed that she was aware of Devon's voice, and aware of what Devon said she was going to do.

Chapter Twenty-one

October 16, 2010 2:27 pm

West Palm Beach, Fl

All A's are B; C is an A; therefore, C is B.
Logic: a highly formalized way of thinking and reasoning that involves using language as a precision tool. Aristotle was the first philosopher to explain the methods of logic, showing how two true statements that share one "term" can draw another true statement from the first two. This method is known as logical syllogism. Proven logic shows a formal relationship between statements.

As long as the first two statements are true, the sequence will always work. Even when you remove the content, the third statement remains true. Logic of this kind cannot be proven false. However, the usefulness of philosophy is filling in the terms, and determining the statements, that result in practical and significant conclusions.

Sure enough, Bizzy had two true statements that drew another true statement from the first two. Filling in the terms and determining the statements, however, wasn't too difficult for him, and the statements most definitely led to a valuable and valid conclusion. And his logical syllogism was: Beauti played a role in killing Demetrius; Devon was Beauti; therefore, Devon played a role in killing Demetrius.

After Skinny-O showed him the picture of Beauti, there was not a trace of doubt in his mind that Devon was indeed Beauti. Prior to seeing that picture, he had heard about a fine bitch named Beauti that had spent a lot of time with Demetrius just before his death. Not too long ago, he had thoroughly poked into every hole and looked under every rock in PBC during his witch hunt for Beauti, uncovering nothing at that time, and now he knew exactly why he had found squat. So, since Beauti was a "creation," and the "creator" was the last woman known to have been hanging around his father before vanishing, she had to have played a role, whether minor or major, in Demetrius' death. And because Devon was Beauti, the lying butch absolutely had her hand in their father's unseemly end.

The question he now constantly brooded over the last few days was … *Why?*

And over that same time period, he had been searching all around for Devon to get that answer. But, like a whacky magic trick, Devon simply disappeared, which further made his logical syllogism truer.

With other fish to fry though, he couldn't waste all of his time on that perplexing matter. He still had the headache of locating a store to open up a pain clinic because there was still the matter of settling his father's ten-million-dollar debt. So, while he handled finding a store, he had Beetle, Bruiser and Mouse from the Clean-Up Crew out there sniffing for Devon's whereabouts. And to motivate them to search diligently, the money from his now-on-sale house in Bear Lakes was the incentive.

Seeking revenge is natural; engaging in a vendetta involves seeking revenge, Bizzy contemplated his latest logical syllogism as he navigated through the streets of West Palm Beach, *therefore, engaging in a vendetta is natural.* Even though the logic was ethical, the content was not, but Bizzy didn't give a fuck.

This overcast afternoon, not giving a fuck was exactly how he was feeling. Ever since he left his Bear Lakes house for the last time, he had been staying over at Skinny-O's place. On top of living with the old psychotic bachelor, who he learned suffered from a mild case of OCD and insomnia, he had enlisted the brains of the Clean-up Crew as his personal bodyguard and chauffeur. Today, however, waking up with that familiar IDGAF attitude, he left Skinny-O behind with the rest of the Crew and drove around in Skinny-O's "undercover" car, a tinted Toyota Camry, looking for a vacated store and thinking about Devon. *Lord, if you hear me*, he began to silently pray, *let's make all this quick so I can get back to chilling. Amen.*

Then, *Hallelujah!*

The big block-lettered *FOR RENT* sign caught his eye in the shopping center to his right. Just as he was about to pass the entrance, he sharply swerved from the far lane into the plaza with the strong inclination that this store, in a popular part of the city, would become his future cash cow. He genuinely smiled for the first time in days. While parked in front of the abandoned store, he prepared to dial the number displayed on the sign.

Phone rings

"Damn, just my fucking luck," he said to himself before looking at who was calling at such a bad time.

"Wassup, Shan?" he answered, a bit agitated. He had met Shan in StudioX around six months ago, and it was a memorable first encounter. Because of Shan's snazziness that night, he easily remembered the caramel-skinned stunner when he had a bit of spare time and stumbled upon Shan's name in his phone not too long after they had met. Although he eventually destroyed his old phone with all of his contacts after fleeing PBC, other than his BMs' numbers and his Aunt Sheryl, he committed Shan's easy-to-remember number to his memory.

Now that he was presently back in town, his schedule had been too full and chaotic for them to hang out, and just like now the timing was always bad. Still, every conversation they had engaged in was remarkable, filled with laughs and toying with each other. With their calls being few and far between, he still really enjoyed chitchatting with Shan, and he really wanted to make future plans for them to link up.

"I'm sorry, but I can't talk rite now, boo. I'm busy. Lemme hit'cha back when ... What? ... Naw, I ain't wit no otha bitch. You buggin'." He chuckled. "Of course, I wanna see you. Da stars just ain't linin' up fo' us, that's all ... Oh, really? Make *me* see stars, huh? ... Tongue trick?" More chuckling. "I can't wait ta *feel* that. But, on da real, I'ma call ya back ... As soon as I'm done, crazy girl ... Holla."

That quick pretentious conversation caused Bizzy to both smile and shake his head in disbelief. *Women, the more mysterious of the two sexes,* he pondered as he began dialing the number listed on the sign, *and man will never find the key to unlocking the paranormal creatures.*

"Hello? Is this Joshua Landry from Landry Commercial Realty?" Bizzy asked gentlemanly. "Yes, my name is ... Craig ... Craig Hurley. How are you today?... Good, good. I'm fine, thanks for asking. Well, I'm calling to inquire about your rental property on Congress Avenue. Is it still available? ... Yes, please, I would like to take a look inside to see if it's spacious enough for what I have in mind ... Is that so? It was last used as a furniture store? ... Timeless Treasures Furniture? Hmmm, I don't recall ever hearing of it ... Yes, I can wait here until three o'clock ... I'll see you soon."

Unheard of.

What Bizzy had just learned about the last occupant of the store up for rent was surreal. The odds of what just took place had to be somewhere in the ballpark of one billion to one.

Chilling, too.

Just the thought of him coming upon one of his late father's furniture stores sent chills through his body. Although he knew Demetrius used the legit stores as a front to move coke from here throughout the South and East Coast, it was more than just a coincidence — it was amazingly spooky to be honest — that his plan for the store was in line with his father's vision for the same space. Now here he was, making his own plans to open up a legit pain clinic as a façade to push pills all over the county of Palm Beach from his father's old venue.

Of two minds now.

In retrospect, going forth with renting the space for his operation was beginning to look like a bad idea. Even though he swore by the saying, "Whatever will be, will be," he didn't want to tempt fate in this bizarre instance.

Then, up in the air.

Torn between whether to pursue renting this special locale or not, he eventually decided to flip a coin to determine the outcome of his dilemma. He grabbed a quarter from the loose change in the cup holder. "Well, here goes nuttin," he said to no one in particular. "Heads, I get da spot. Tails, I find sumwhere else." Finally, he flipped the coin in the air, caught it in one hand, and slapped it onto the back of the other.

Instead of dragging out the outcome, he quickly removed his hand, revealing ...

October 16, 2010 2:38 pm

Lantana, FL

"...Ai'ight, girl. Just keep me informed wit er'thang, okay? An' rememba, this is serious. Ya life is on da hook if he finds out who you really are ... I know, I know. Ya told me a thousand times befo' how ya owe me big time. An' I appreciate ya helpin' me wit this. *But*, ya still gotta be careful. Ya already tricked him into thinkin' that'chu someone ya really ain't. So, don't getta outta pocket by pressin' him, callin' too much, or actin' too funny ..." She laughed. "Girl, ya' know what funny I'm talkin' 'bout. Silly ass ... okay, take this serious now. An' make sho' ta call me ASAP when he finally decides ta hook up wit'chu in person, okay? ... Ai'ight. Be safe an' I'll holla at'chu later, Shan."

While South Florida's weather was beginning to cool down slightly, Devon's plot for exacting retribution was starting to heat up by a few degrees. All that she had devised in the past few days was strictly done in honor of Miracle, motivating her to work overtime in overdrive in pursuit of her man. And not only did she find a way to make use of Shan, who had limited knowledge of

194

what was really going down, she fell back on a proven rock-solid helper.

What was the most remarkable, however, was that Devon's reliable *girl*friend had introduced her to a highly unlikely asset that could expedite the plot of x-ing out Bizzy once they pooled their resources together.

No sooner had Devon walked out of the hospital after visiting Miracle did she dial Rhapsody's number. Although it had been well over a month since she last talked to Rhapsody, dangerous situations called for desperate measures, so reaching out to someone who she felt she could count on was a no-brainer. Besides, she had nowhere else to go because going back to the house in Wellington or staying a while with RahRah was out of the question.

When Rhapsody gladly welcomed Devon over to a house that she was currently living at in a neighborhood called Homes of Lawrence, aka Da HOL, Devon wasn't as surprised by the fact that Rhapsody was staying in an unfamiliar house as she was when she discovered that Rhapsody was actually living there with a … man. Instead of blowing out a candle in a burning building, however, she shrugged off Rhapsody's two-timing ways and zeroed in on what needed to be done.

Soon after Devon was abruptly introduced to JJ, Rhapsody's "friend," she somewhat recognized his name but couldn't immediately place where she heard it before. Then, after jogging her super-duper memory, she remembered that JJ was the same guy that Rhapsody had allegedly fell in love with and scampered off with to Georgia almost three years ago. She also recalled that JJ had been Bizzy's homeboy until Bizzy supposedly killed him and his mother. In the end, when JJ confirmed her recollection, and made it known that they shared a common enemy, she felt more optimistic about taking out Bizzy because the more man-power, and the more hatred towards a particular individual, the more likely they would hit their mark without any collateral damage.

195

All three of them immediately got to work, with JJ disclosing everything he had done to set a trap for Bizzy—except for him telling Devon that she was the bait—and Devon telling all that she knew about her now cut-off brother. Once everything to know about Bizzy was laid out in the open, the next step had been to figure out how to ambush their irrational and suspicious target. Then, after two days of deliberation, Devon had received a call and learned from the caller something that gave her an idea.

That caller had been Shan.

Shan had only called Devon to check in with her. During the middle of the call, Shan mentioned Bizzy and how they had been talking on and off for the last few months, thus giving Devon a possible avenue to blindside Bizzy. Thinking quick on her feet, Devon had decided to cash in on that favor that was owed to her by asking Shan to slyly lure Bizzy into meeting up somewhere for dinner, with the location to be a surprise. And Devon's excuse for not doing it herself was that she and Bizzy had a major disagreement, and the surprise dinner was her way of apologizing. Shan ultimately agreed to do the "small" favor for her sister from another mister.

Now it was just a waiting game, and time for a new look for Devon once more.

Chapter Twenty-two

October 17, 2010 4:52 pm

West Palm Beach, FL

"Durt, I can't wait ta drop da top on my seven-four an' beat down da block wit a bottle of Hen Dogg an' a Dutch filled wit some grade-A squeeze."

"And I can't wait to drop you two triflin'-ass niggas off! Y'all ain't shit!" the female driver replied to her passengers.

"Shut yo' baser-ass up! An' miss us wit that bullshit. We can't wait ta be dropped off eitha, then maybe you'll think about droppin' this raggedy, filthy muthafucka off da nearest cliff, becuz Grave Digga an' Big Foot won't jump ova this rusty bitch from fear of getting' tinnitus."

"Tetanus, Einstein."

"Ya' know what I meant, darkness."

"Oh, hell no. Don't be talkin' about my baby, Skat."

"Yo' baby? Ha, ha-ha! This old piece of shit mo' like yo' great-great-great grandfather. This rust bucket gotta fuckin' *tape deck*. What da fuck?"

Bumper and PopTart Tina couldn't help but to laugh at silly ass Skat.

"On my mama, I hate y'all niggas," PopTart Tina groused. "First, y'all got me transportin' y'all from eater to eater house as if fuckin' me ain't good enough fo' you two. Then, you got the nerve to be talkin' about my ride. Y'all niggas ain't shit!" Double Bag, that was another name for PopTart Tina, because a bag was surely needed for your dick as well as one for her head. She had the body of a goddess but the face of Godzilla. She was in her mid-forties, of average height and weight, with an ass like two volleyballs, titties like a pair of cantaloupes and enough baby fat to fill out her curves. Her facial flaws, however, were attributed to her love of PopTarts and crack cocaine, which led to her rotten teeth and

198

blotchy skin. It seemed like an overnight occurrence how she transitioned from an eyeful to an eyesore.

For about a year, Bumper and Skat, who had dope for days, used PopTart Tina's weak point to their advantage, plying her with all the dope she needed in return for her doing whatever they said, whenever they said it, no questions asked. And as of late, they used her more than ever, working on her last nerves in the process.

Now the three of them were cruising way earlier than usual in Tina's multicolored, corroded 1993 GMC Safari minivan, which had at least two years' worth of mylar Pop Tart wrappers strewn throughout the inside of the van. PopTart Tina, as she grew accustomed to doing, was shuttling Bumper and Skat around PBC to pacify their insatiable libido. She hated being used like a toilet, but she simply loved using crack.

"Ai'ight, one mo' stop, Tina," Bumper said.

"One mo' hit then."

"Goddamn, Double Bag, we gotta supply ya habit, put petro in this gas-guzzlin' muthafucka, feed ya, fuck ya ... we ain't no paymasters, ya foot-draggin' ass hoe!" Skat snapped from the captain's chair behind Bumper.

Before PopTart Tina could fire back at Skat, Bumper readily tossed a dubb rock into her lap. "Slide through Downtown Projects."

"Nigga, is ya ... well, I know ya crazy. But we can't be fuckin' 'round in DTP this time of day! Ain't no tellin' who we'll bump into. Please, don't get us merked ova no pussy, bro." When Bumper didn't say nothing back, Skat added, "Awww, man, here we go. I'm all in when we have a fightin' chance, but'chu 'bout ta send us on a suicide mission." He then slouched back in his seat frustrated.

PopTart Tina, meanwhile, was on her own mission. Multitasking, the seasoned crackhead continued to steer with her knee to Bumper's destination all while retrieving her "shooter" and lighter, loading up, and blasting off without breaking any traffic laws, or breaking a sweat.

199

With Tina in a blissful place, Bumper fantasizing about his next score, and Skat in a grumpy mood, silence filled the van.

Nobody had mentioned RahRah's name in days.

Ever since RahRah had left Bumper and Skat high-and-dry before vanishing the day they shot up the Lexus, which they still didn't know why they Swiss-cheesed the car, bringing up his name was a sure way to receive "fuck that nigga" as a response. They felt RahRah had betrayed their friendship, betrayed them "from sunrise till SunSet," like the motto they lived by dictated. And although they weren't downright looking for RahRah, they swore that if he ever showed his face, it would be a murder on sight.

"Yeah, I'm 'bout ta break this bitch, Yo'Ma back, Durt," Bumper disturbed the peace as PopTart Tina turned into the NO OUTLET projects.

"Yo'Ma! Really? I heard that bitch got that ninja."

"Keep rite on bumpin' ya gums, lil nigga, an' talk yaself outta some pussy."

"What pussy?"

"Yo'Ma cousin, Merdrea, ova there wit her."

"Bump, that fat, ugly bit ..."

At once, they both saw him, leaving out of the projects, by himself.

It was Eddie G.

Cooler than a polar bear's paws, Bumper said, "Follow that whip that just passed by us."

Still stoned, PopTart Tina mumbled, "What? Why? I thought you ..."

Not in the mood to play any games, and not wanting their duck to get away, Skat pulled a Model 1911 from his waist and placed it to the side of PopTart Tina's dome. "Turn this bitch around an' follow that car. Now!"

When she felt the pressure from the barrel digging into her temple, she frantically bust an illegal one-eighty in the two-lane road and began pursing Eddie G's Mazda 626.

"Drive carefully," Bumper said as Eddie G's car came into view. "Keep some distance until I tell ya ta get closer."

Whimpering, PopTart Tina soberly said, "Can you please take the gun from my head, Skat? Please, I'm doin' everythin' you say just like I always do."

"Put it down, Durt," Bumper said.

"Ai'ight. But, if I have ta put it back, ya brains goin' on da dashboard. An' ya' know I ain't bullshittin'."

They tailed Eddie G's car through the gridlocked streets of West Palm Beach's evening rush hour. Their opening presented itself finally about ten minutes later when Eddie G travelled down a back road that had minimal structures and was sparse with traffic.

Approaching a four-way stop sign, Bumper reached under the passenger seat and pulled out a Colt .45. "Speed up an' pull up next ta him so that he on my side," Bumper instructed. "We gon' wet him up, then you gon' burn off like nuttin' happened, Tina. Got that?"

To make sure that she had heard clearly, Skat tapped PopTart Tina's temple with the pistol. "Like nuttin' happened, okay? Don't fuck around an' make this a double homicide."

PopTart Tina, in all her years, had never been in a predicament like this one before and she had never been so nervous. Although she had been in many life-or-death situations in her walk of life, she had never thought that she would be an accomplice to murder. And with her life being threatened, she had never thought that she would be so happy to play ball with the Pleasant City Slumpers that were in her van.

As if she had practiced the maneuver a dozen times in advance, PopTart Tina nimbly swerved into the opposite lane just as Eddie G stopped at the stop sign.

What ensued next sounded like someone was three months late celebrating the Fourth of July.

201

Eddie G never knew what hit him. Still, with a dozen slugs lodged in his body, his motor reflexes caused him to speed off before he crashed into a telephone pole directly across the street.

PopTart Tina, on the other hand, immediately fell to pieces. Her motor reflexes, however, prompted her to smash the gas, catapulting the rickety van pass Eddie G's mangled, bullet riddled Mazda.

"Slow da fuck down, bitch!" Skat hollered as they barreled down the street.

"Calm down, babygirl," Bumper spoke at ease. "It's ova wit, Tina, so ya can slow down. Trust me, we …"

Whoop – whoooop

"MUTHAFUCKA, IT'S ONE-TIME!" Skat broadcasted the obvious. "Stupid, bitch, this all yo' fault!" He then raised the gun and aimed it at PopTart Tina's head.

POP

"What da fuck is you doin,' Durt?" Bumper immediately nutted up after swatting Skat's hand and sending the bullet intended for PopTart Tina through the van's ceiling. "She drivin', you dumb-ass nigga! You want us all ta die?"

"We dead anyway, cuz we ain't gettin' away in this piece of shit."

"Nigga, we dead when I say we dead. Now, follow my lead." He ejected the spent clip and popped in another. "An' Tina, you drive this bitch like ya stole it. An' when we make it home, you'll neva have ta buy anotha rock again." Then, he proceeded to climb out of the passenger's window and opened fire on the lone WPB police cruiser.

In a wink, Skat slid open the sliding door, got ahold of the handle attached to the roof with one hand, hung out the open door and let loose on the cop car as well.

They peppered the cruiser's windshield, quickly causing the pursuing officer to career off the road and decelerate. As the cruiser became smaller and smaller in their wake, their hopes of escaping began to increase.

"You doin' a good job, baby girl," Bumper assured Tina about one minute after making sure the coast was clear. "Look at me real quick." Clearly rattled to the core, she cautiously glanced in his direction. "Breathe, Tina, breathe. Slow down an' calm down." As she began to do as he directed, he added, "There ya go. Breathe."

"Yeah, bitch, breathe," Skat added his two cents.

"We good now. Just ..."

Bumper spoke a little too soon.

Straight ahead at the next intersection, there were at least four WPB patrol cars blocking the crossing.

Noticing that PopTart Tina was slowing down to a stop, Skat responded by maneuvering behind her seat, wrapping one arm around her neck, and putting the gun back to her head for a third time. "Bitch, you gonna ram them or I'ma kill you!" Seeing out of the corner of his eye that Bumper had something to say, he barked, "Please, Durt, don't make me bust ya ass rite now cuz I will. I got nuttin' ta lose."

Bumper merely shrugged, then he leaned back into his seat and fastened his seatbelt.

Boo-hoo crying, PopTart Tina gunned the 4.3-liter V6.

Twenty-seven traumatic seconds later, two of the four cop cars had extensive front-end damage from the collision that occurred.

Luckily, the cops dove safely out of the way before impact.

The GMC Safari Minivan, however, with two of its tires flat and steam billowing from the squashed radiator, teetered forward at a snail's pace before coming to a complete stop in the middle of the road. Oodles of shiny silver Pop Tart wrappers previously strewn about inside the van were now floating and settling around the wreckage. And sad to say, none of the van's occupants were moving.

The sun had set, although there were still a couple hours of daylight left before actual nightfall.

Chapter Twenty-three

December 30, 2010 8:19 pm

West Palm Beach, FL

Cat and mouse.

Hide and seek.

But this was a two-way game.

Rather than being good clean fun, the new version of these old pastimes now being played were deadly. This game should be called *Kill-or-Be-Killed.*

Neither side had gained any significant ground since the game began. Yet, neither side had any plans of quitting the game. Both sides, nevertheless, knew that this was a game to the death. And both sides, at all times, were seeking out ways to gain an edge over the other, because it was sure as hell game over for the one that wasn't on top of their game.

Bizzy felt confident that he would defeat his now-estranged sister in the end. With the Clean-up Crew at his disposal, he could put all his focus on what was most important, which was gearing up for the grand opening of Gold Coast Pain Management Center in West Palm Beach. He recalled having recent visions of following in his father's footsteps, reopening the "furniture stores" Demetrius once "monopolized." But seeing his own brainchild come to life in the exact same spot where his father did business was legendary, to say the least.

He was glad he and fate were on the same wavelength when he flipped that coin, because he would've felt miserable moving onward without obtaining that specific store. While it might not have been a golden spot for his father, he set out to break that stigma by turning the spot into a gold mine.

His plans of opening the store the day after New Year's Day was on schedule. The clinic's floor space was nearly twice as big as the one in Prichard. Instead of employing the same set-up as in

Prichard, he took advantage of the extra space by commissioning five doctors and hiring two receptionists, all of whom were under an identical contract as the personnel in Alabama, except they would work twenty-four-seven, three hundred sixty-five days a year in staggered shifts. Besides, the more legit the clinic appeared in the bustling city, the better the chances the clinic stayed open long enough to make him a nine-figure nigga.

And with Da Bottom Boyz movement having gone under so soon, as well as the heads of Triple S being cut off not too long ago, it was a lot easier for him to extract all illegal monies from the streets of PBC. With nobody in his way, and a loyal pack of killers on hand, he even had serious thoughts about dibbling and dabbling with weed, coke, heroin and meth, now that the streets were all his to control. He would strongly consider doing so only after his pill mill took flight and soared like an eagle, however.

Other than the score he had to settle with Devon, which was an issue that constantly bothered him for different reasons, and the opening of his newest clinic, Bizzy didn't have much of a personal life. Since he didn't know exactly what level of danger he was in, he stayed on his toes and kept in limited contact with his aunt Sheryl, his BM's and his sons through snail mail. He heard through the grapevine that the feds had contacted quite a few of his family and friends. Outside of those people mentioned, the only person in his life he'd spoken to during the past few months was Shan.

Shan helped him blow off steam and unwind from the annoyances of his currently tangled life. Although Shan had been slightly on his ass about them hooking up, he stuck to his guns of overseeing his plan's success without any hinderances, and promised they would do lunch some time right after New Year's Day. And from their freaky conversations, he couldn't wait for that day to cum, pun intended.

At the present time, he and Skinny-O were getting ready to deliver seven hundred fifty thousand to Adrian as a small payment on the ten-million-dollar debt. Although he had been expected to set up a second clinic by mid-September, he informed Adrian in all honesty why he didn't make that happen on time. After Adrian relayed Bizzy's anticipated news to Cesar, the top dog's response had been that he understood family matters needed handling first and foremost, sometimes.

However, Cesar demanded a payment of seven hundred fifty thousand before the year was out and ordered the West Palm Beach clinic be opened as planned and on time, or there would be terrible consequences.

In addition to dropping off Cesar's money, Bizzy would also be making arrangements with Adrian, who was somewhat bitter that he and Bizzy weren't making the deals themselves, about when and where he would pick up the two hundred thousand pills Cesar agreed to pay for once a second clinic had been opened.

Yes, the original agreement had been that Cesar would only pay for the two hundred thousand opiates *after* the opening of a second clinic in the agreed upon time. But Cesar gave the young go-all-out entrepreneur a little wiggle room since he respected how Bizzy was taking care of business and doing the best with what he had on short notice.

And to make sure that he could put a little something in his pocket, too, Bizzy had a side deal with Rusty in the making. The day of the grand opening of the clinic, he planned on copping from Rusty one last time before he began purchasing all of his pills from Cesar, for a third of what he was currently paying. That would be one dollar and sixty-five cents per pill.

Because he damn well knew Cesar's two hundred thousand pills would be dispensed in less than a month, he planned to spend his last hundred and fifty grand to purchase forty thousand pills from Rusty. Rusty would be selling him each pill for three dollars and seventy-five cents this time instead of five dollars, because Rusty claimed to be in a festive mood. Moreover, Bizzy also knew that after paying his staff and other overhead, he would make a huge profit if he bought the extra forty thousand pills from Rusty.

Then, when it was time to procure his pills from Cesar, the profit he made would be reinvested. And by his estimations, he would be able to pay off the ten-million-dollar debt in less than five months, just from the second clinic alone!

Between both clinics, I'll be able to stuff at least twenty-five million into my Sean John jeans by the end of 2011, Bizzy brainstormed as he and Skinny-O loaded the duffel bags full of dead presidents into the back of a rented Ford Explorer. *And then I'll flip that into over a hundred million by the end of 2012.*

*****

During the intervening time, at the Paul G. Rogers Federal Building in downtown West Palm Beach, Agents Dino and Raw Deal had been summoned for an urgent meeting with their commander.

When Dino and Raw Deal waddled into the commander's office at the same time, the top brass could clearly see the agents had just rolled out of bed. Before the rumpled agents could sit down, he began his tirade. "Jesus H. Christ, you boys look like shit. Did I wake you two up as y'all lay nice and comfy next to y'all better halves?"

He paused briefly as if waiting for an answer, then he blurted out, "Well, I'm tired, too. I'm goddamn sick and fuckin' tired of you two lollygagging and dragging out this Byron Woodson case. Now, I want a full report right this second, or your asses are fired! You hear me? If you don't tell me something good, tomorrow morning you'll be waking up jobless. And do you know what the trouble with unemployment is? You're on the fuckin' job as soon as you wake up, that's what. Now, report!"

Little did their commander know how hard they had been working on the case. Ever since they lost track of Bizzy back in September, they had backtracked and combed through every piece of intel and evidence they had on Bizzy. They had spent countless hours in the field, sometimes going days with no sleep. They were authentically exhausted, but their super-sized egos would not let

207

them cop out. They were determined to crack the case. When they revisited the shooting that killed Bizzy's cousin, Chad, they uncovered something they had overlooked.

Since Agent Zimmerman was the senior officer, and he had a rapport with the commander, he took the lead. After running a hand over his unshaven face and digging the crust from his baggy eyes, he sarcastically said, "Nice seeing you, too, boss. By the way, can I go grab a cup of coffee for me and my partner first, at least?"

His boss stared daggers at him.

"Ooo-kay...well," he clapped his hands and rubbed them together. "As you can see, we've been working to no end on this case. The only reason why we haven't reported anything recently is because we have been following up on a major lead."

"Cut the bullshit and get to it, why don't you?" the commander ordered.

"We're actively tracking a person-of-interest that may very well lead us to Mr. Woodson real soon." Dino then fast-forwarded to the night of Chad's murder. Although there wasn't much evidence at the scene that resulted in Chad's killer being arrested, they were able to recover one cell phone that night, which belonged to Dayvan Stubbford, aka JuneBug. JuneBug lawyered up ASAP, but, after they obtained a warrant, a search through his contacts yielded Bizzy's number.

They soon learned Bizzy had discarded his cell phone. From there, they obtained a warrant to get Bizzy's phone records. They checked out as many of the contacts as possible, mainly relatives and a slew of female acquaintances, and came up with nothing promising. Back at square one, they decided to ruffle the feathers of small-time dealers to see who would give up something of consequence. They got a lucky break when they intruded on a Halloween party and rounded up a dozen partygoers that had illegal substances in their possession.

Out of the dozen they nabbed, a teenaged white boy that had been caught with two Blues on him, provided them with a name in exchange for clemency, and that name was Russell Weiss, aka Rusty. At that time, Rusty's name had failed to ring any bells, but he became recognized the second time they rifled through Bizzy's phone records. Since Rusty had no criminal record, and Bizzy called him infrequently, they had disregarded him and never contacted him the first time they inspected Bizzy's phone records.

Identifying Rusty wasn't exactly the nail in the coffin, but it had been a new lead for them to see about. They then went out on the limb and got a warrant to gain Rusty's SIM card information so they could clone his phone and monitor it meticulously. Then, whee doggie, their nonstop sleuthing had finally paid off when Rusty received a casual text from Bizzy a day after Christmas, stating that they needed to meet real soon.

"And that's where we're at now, just waiting for more details so we can take them both down. So, until that time, can me and my partner get out of here and get our beauty sleep, please, sir?"

The commander pursed his lips and drummed his fingers on the desk. He then cocked his head to the side like a curious dog, and said, "One week. If you don't have that sneaky son-of-a-bitch Woodson in federal custody in one week … Just put it this way, don't bother trying to use me as your reference on your next job application, because I'm going to tell whoever it is that you two guys are useless pieces of shit. Now get out of here and find this ass wipe. You can sleep when you're dead!"

"And you have a lovely night, too, sir," Dino said satirically. He nodded to his meek partner. "Let's roll because somebody in here needs alone time to cool off before they go nighty-night."

While walking to their respective personal vehicles in the parking lot, Raw Deal finally spoke. "How can he give us one week when we're so close to detaining our man? How can he just fire us? Can he even do that?"

"Stop stressing, Holmes. I've been fired at least ten times by Dyker. His threats are empty. They're supposed to motivate us to move faster. *But*, I feel that in less than one week, we'll have our man in a pair of extra small cuffs."

"How can you be so sure?"

Dino simply looked at his partner and winked. "Goodnight, buddy." He then broke off from Raw Deal and headed towards his car while whistling.

Flame

Chapter Twenty-four

January 2, 2011 7:42 am

Lantana, FL

In the obituary section of *The Palm Beach Post...*

Jefferson, Fredrick.

Fredrick Allen Jefferson, 23, passed away on New Year's Day in West Palm Beach, Florida. He was born on June 9, 1987, in Boynton Beach, Florida, to Michael Jefferson and Sylvia Phelps. At an early age, it was evident that he was going to be special because he enjoyed creating and designing items from scratch. As a gifted adolescent, he attended Palm Beach School of the Arts, with dreams of becoming a world-famous clothing designer.

He graduated salutatorian in 2005. He was beloved and respected by all who truly knew him. He loved to dance, eat Twizzlers, laugh and cheat at any game that he played. He was really adored for his sense of humor. One of his favorite pastimes was to hang out with his friends and talk until it was time to part ways. Fredrick is survived by his brothers, Richard and Derrick Jefferson, his three sisters ...

Devon closed the newspaper with hot tears in her eyes. Even though she had heard the horrible news first on *FaceSpace* yesterday, actually reading about her friend's death in the local paper was beyond sad and difficult to process. But what really pained her the most about the sudden, tragic passing was that she had saved her unique friend's life a year ago to the day, which led to them becoming bosom buddies.

According to this morning's newspaper article in the local section, Shan had been shot to death while attending a New Year's party at Illusions Night Club. It was believed Shan had been murdered after becoming heavily intoxicated and deceiving a young man into thinking "he" was actually a "she." The police had a suspect in custody and was charging him with a hate crime.

This would've never happened if StudioX was open, Devon thought while remembering the good times she shared with her rambunctious girlfriend. *This, and what happened to Miracle, could've all been avoided if I never made that damn tape.*

Not only had Devon lost a good friend sooner than expected, she had lost the most valuable asset in her conspiracy to murder Bizzy. She had to return back to the drawing board once more, but only after she properly grieved for her dear friend first. "You promised me, Shan, that'chu wouldn't slip again," she mumbled to herself before sighing.

Just before Shan's premature demise, Devon had been certain that she would checkmate Bizzy any day now. Because she had Rhapsody and JJ on her squad as well, she didn't have to think about ways to set up her alienated brother every second of the day. Instead, she thought about Miracle as much as possible. It was tortuous not being able to be by Miracle's side when she wanted, so she reminisced and fantasized about her baby girl. While it might not have been an appropriate time to be daydreaming about the future, she began to make plans of returning back to Queen City ... with both Miracle and Kamani.

As Rhapsody and JJ remained passed out asleep in their room, Devon, who was in the living room, continued to stare off into space as sun rays trickled through the small gaps in the closed blinds. She hadn't slept at all after learning about Shan's misfortune. Her stomach growled steadily because she hadn't eaten, either, since receiving the bad news. She just sat in the loveseat, stroking her reliable .380 as if it were a loyal pet.

Phone rings

Lately, she was quite skeptical to answer her phone. Although she hadn't received any threatening calls, and she knew she had yet to do anything illegal, her hesitation stemmed from her being contacted by a federal agent named Holmes not too long ago. Agent Holmes had called to establish a connection between her and Bizzy. From the little the agent had revealed in the beginning of the call, she was almost certain the agent wasn't aware that she and Bizzy were related.

Therefore, she informed Agent Holmes that she and Bizzy only spoke about him wanting to invest in her gentlemen's club. The Q and A ended after she denied knowing Bizzy's location, prompting her to believe the agent bought her story. Still, that phone call raised a red flag, and she speculated that the feds were eavesdropping on her calls.

She grabbed the ringing phone off her lap, looked at who was calling her so early in the AM, and answered after identifying the caller.

"Wassup, my favorite white boy in da whole wide world?" she said in a laid-back manner.

"Not too much," Rusty replied. "I just wanted to holla at you first about this new shipment I got in, since you my best customer."

"Hmmmm … I-I dunno. Rite now ain't a good time. I got some shit I gotta handle first. But I'll hit'chu up ASAP when I'm back on my feet."

"I kind of figured you were going to say that since I noticed your club has been closed. But, I still had to reach out to you first, since you my dawg and all."

"Good lookin' out, Rusty. I appreciate it, tho'."

"Alright. You let me know if I can help you in any way. You know I got you, okay?"

"I'm good. It's a small thing to a giant. I'll be straight real soon."

"Well … my bad for disturbing you so early."

"It's *nathan*," he replied, using the slang for *nothing*.

"Bet."

Just when Devon was about to end the call, she heard low indistinct gibberish. She soon realized Rusty had resumed talking. "Hello?"

"I thought you hung up."

"I was just about to until I heard ya still speakin', so what's good?"

"I need a small favor."

"What'chu need?"

"I need to get a message to your brother."

"RahRah? I ain't seen or spoke ta —"

"Who is RahRah?" Rusty interrupted.

"My big bro."

After a few seconds, Rusty said, "Oh yeah, I know of him. But I'm talking about Bizzy."

Hearing Bizzy's name caused Devon's blood to run cold. Then, in a fog, she said, "How do ya' know—" A light bulb suddenly lit up in her head. "Actually, I do need ta see ya 'bout those stripper fits. Like I said, I'ma be hella straight soon, so I might as well see what'chu workin' wit. An' we can talk 'bout that favor ya need me ta do when we link up, ai'ight?"

"Okay. Cool."

Not wanting to be too specific for fear of her phone being tapped, she immediately said, "We meetin' in da usual spot, ai'ight? Say no mo'."

"At what time?"

"You in da city?"

"No, but I can be in an hour or so."

"Well, I'll be there at nine."

"Bet."

Devon ended the call smiling and shaking with excitement. *I don't know who to thank, my guardian angel mother or my new guardian angel Shan, or simply God, for this divine intervention,* she thought as she madly gathered what was needed before leaving to meet up with Rusty at the 45th Street Flea Market, *but I know wholeheartedly this plan I'm concocting on the fly will soon be ending the mayhem and madness in my favor.*

"This is it," she declared as she slammed the house door behind her.

January 2, 2011 6:02 pm

West Palm Beach, FL

Just so my name wouldn't be attached to either of my clinics, I spent a lot of extra money and time greasing palms in order for all my business dealings to appear legitimate, Bizzy said to himself as he exited Gold Coast Pain Management Center with a small duffel bag in hand and discreetly walked to his chauffeured car. *But I should've spent a few racks on advertising for this clinic and buying a mobile MRI Unit.*

Unlike his Prichard clinic, which was all set from the jump to be profitable due to it being located in an unkempt part of Mobile, his clinic in the inner city of West Palm Beach was being passed by because it was situated in a dense, vibrant section. While Prichard's clinic stuck out like a sore thumb, West Palm Beach's clinic was far from being the first of its kind.

The Prichard clinic needed no marketing at all because the sign itself was like a bug zapper, attracting all the maggots and cockroaches as soon as the doors opened. The West Palm Beach clinic, however, should've been promoted ahead of its opening since it was amongst a vast amount of big name, prominent businesses.

Although the grand opening didn't flourish as he previsioned, one rocky day wasn't enough to determine the overall success of the clinic. From this minor hiccup, he learned businesswise, that all business plans weren't two of a kind. Even if two businesses were managed by the same proprietor and exploited the same goods, each business needed to be handled differently, because each city, county, and state were demographically not alike. *I could've done much better if I would've took the necessary steps to market this clinic properly,* he concluded before instructing Skinny-O to head home so he could prep for his transaction with Rusty later on tonight. *And yet I still shelled out close to twelve thousand pills since opening at nine this morning.*

With a little over fifty stacks in the duffel bag, Bizzy would've loved nothing more than to touch base with Rusty and make swift arrangements to purchase additional pills with the money he had just picked up. It was a long shot, however, since he had to jump through a few hoops just to communicate with Rusty safely. He could make use of every pill he could get his hands on but rushing to order more pills at the last second could easily spell disaster.

Other than that, he was totally focused now. One of his New Year's resolutions was that he would deal with every situation he faced in the future on a day-to-day basis. He would prioritize and compartmentalize all of his matters from here on out. Some of his other resolutions were that he would no longer be impulsive when it came to planning, no longer stress over situations that were out of his control, and no longer trust his judgment of people he truly didn't know.

That last resolution, it was mandatory he held fast to it. It was one thing to be deceived by his own flesh and blood, even if he barely knew Devon, but it was even worse to have a con "man" run game on him. When he had gotten word of what happened to … *Fredrick* … he couldn't fucking believe how he let … *him* … eat through his ability to decipher people.

Consequently, he simply made up his mind to put his trust in nobody, not even a little bit, because openly trusting in people would destroy the main reason why he got into this *man's game* in the first place… to gain full custody of his sons, Bilal and BJ.

217

Chapter Twenty-five

January 2, 2011 9:30 pm

West Palm Beach, FL

Operation *HIT ROCK BOTTOM (HRB)*
The time was close.

After losing the elder Woodson to an unexpected death, the current mission was to take down the young Woodson alive so he could die in prison in his father's place. Over the course of four years, the DEA had spent a ton of taxpayer's money on manpower and resources while investigating the underworld activities of the RockBottom Family.

Although the tight-knit organization had dominated the streets of PBC, along with the surrounding areas, for nearly three decades with their criminal operations and legal businesses, the few members that remained at large after Demetrius' death were still a threat to society. Only after every component of the sinister enterprise had been eliminated would the streets be a little bit less corrupted. And taking down Byron Woodson would be the straw to break the camel's back.

The overseer of Operation HRB was Agent Zimmerman. It was T-minus fifteen minutes and counting before he and his brigade of highly trained agents launched into their assignment. Until then, Agent Zimmerman proceeded to fire up the troops with a final briefing.

"Tonight," Dino began his address, "we take down the demon seed of the diabolical, savage piece-of-shit formerly known as Demetrius Woodson. The rotten apple recognized in the streets as Bizzy didn't fall but a few centimeters from the poisoned tree. He was relatively unknown until he came into contact with an affiliate of his father last March. Once on our radar, one of my C.I.'s confirmed that the young Woodson aspired to take over his father's disarrayed crime ring.

218

"Further surveillance eventually placed him in the company of Adrian Mendoza, the Peruvian kingpin's middleman. That meeting alone gave us reason to pick him up for conspiracy and violating his federally supervised release. Yet, we let him continue to dig a deeper grave. Soon after the meeting with Mendoza, the murder rate in Palm Beach County skyrocketed and my C.I. mysteriously disappeared, and it was all attributed to Byron Woodson. We then made plans to arrest him, but unfortunately, one event transpired suddenly—the death of his cousin —and we lost our man.

"Me and my partner, Agent Holmes, then spent the last four months actively tracking this asshole down. We finally hit pay dirt not too long ago, and that got us where we are now. From our investigative work, we've learned about a drug transaction between our intended target and another punk named Russell Weiss. So, at midnight tonight, we will be swooping in on the transaction that's taking place at a vacated business on Martin Luther King Boulevard.

"With there being a few vacated businesses on the three MLKs in PBC, one in Boynton Beach, another in Delray Beach, and the third in Riviera Beach, the men here will split into three teams in order to cover the locales. This is a coordinated strike, with Team One being led by yours truly and Team Two led by Agent Holmes. Agent Ellis will lead Team Three. You are to treat these assholes like *America's Most Wanted*. Let's bag 'em, tag 'em, and hit up the nearest titty bar afterwards. Now mount up and let's take this Woodson scumbag down for good so we can give order back to the streets! What say you?"

The officers cheered in unison as if they were the San Francisco Giants, the new World Series champions.

January 2, 2011

9:42pm

Lantana, FL

"But why?"

"It's too dangerous, that's why, Kiki," JJ answered.

"I undastand that it's dangerous," countered Rhapsody, "but I played a major part in helpin' you ..." She took notice of Devon standing nearby. "... I mean *us* ... I helped to get y'all where we at now. Y'all can't leave me behind. That's not fair. An' what if y'all need me? What if sumthin' happens? What if—"

"Keema, da man is rite," Devon interrupted. "It's just not safe. We gon' be on point. You just hold da fort down till we get back, okay?"

Rhapsody folded her arms across her chest and grimaced.

JJ casually approached a seething Rhapsody. He then grabbed her by her hips and planted a kiss on her lips as they stood in the middle of the living room. While looking into her eyes, he proceeded to whisper so Devon couldn't hear what he had to say. "Ya' know why ya can't come, Kiki." He gently touched her belly on the sly. "If sumthin' does go wrong wit'chu there, it'll fuck wit me fo' da rest of my life. So stay put, Mama KiKi, an' daddy will be back as soon as I take care of both of these lames," he concluded with a wink.

With a concealed smile, she then muttered, "I love you, Javon. You do what needs to be done an' come rite back home. You hear me? Rite back. I'm not losin' you again."

As Devon stood out of earshot, watching the touching scene between Rhapsody and JJ, her skin began to crawl. A bad feeling in her gut increased more and more as the time drew near. While it had been a team effort to get to where they were now, she somehow felt as if Rhapsody and JJ were the dynamic duo, Jordan and Pippen, and she was Scott Burrell, an expendable. *I got to keep a close eye on this crazy nigga tonight,"* she said to herself while inspecting her .380, *because I'll be damned if I let him murder me on the humbug.*

Flame

Chapter Twenty-six

January 3, 2011 12:03 am

Vero Beach, FL

Bizzy's text said, *I'm 5 mins away.*
I'll b there n 10 mins tops, read Rusty's reply.
Nothing more had to be said.
However, Bizzy could've talked to Rusty for as long as he wanted now without feeling uneasy. After learning that the feds had reached out to most of the people he knew a little while ago, he sent Beetle on a mission to locate Rusty PFQ, pretty fucking quick. Once Beetle tracked down Rusty, Beetle passed on his message. And that brief message informed Rusty to get a second prepaid phone for only them, to do business. Additionally, the message informed him not to get rid of the phone that he currently owned, because the feds would become suspicious if the phone suddenly was no longer in use.

For that reason, tonight's transaction should go down without a hitch, all thanks to Bizzy's ingenious thinking. More than likely, he put the feds on a wild goose chase by sending a detailed text message to Rusty's original phone about the deal happening in an abandoned parking lot on MLK in Palm Beach County. He felt he could rest assured knowing that the Alphabet Boys were sniffing on a fake trail. And with Skinny-O accompanying him to the exchange, he most definitely had nothing to sweat about.

My father once told me that good judgement comes from experience, and experience comes from bad judgement, he thought reflectively, *so I can no longer use ignorance as an excuse when I personally saw what my father endured, not to mention, the little storms I've suffered the past two years.*

I'm at da spot now, read Bizzy's text.
Rusty's reply was, *I'm almost there.*

Usually, Bizzy would've been ticked off having to wait in an unfamiliar city with a hundred-fifty grand in the car with him. Even though he was comfortable with the exchange spot he and Rusty had agreed upon, and even more comfortable having a hardened killer looking after him, this was the first time he'd beat Rusty to the spot, causing him to feel bad vibes as a result.

"Park rite there," Bizzy instructed, pointing to a desired parking space while trying to keep his mounting anxiety in check. "Back in, kill da lights but keep da motor runnin'."

*****

Meanwhile ...

"Yeeeaaahhhhh," JJ broke the silence with his raspy voice. "Oh, let's do it!"

Upon seeing the lonesome headlights that swiftly pierced the night, Devon's heart leapfrogged in her chest. She could feel herself getting cold feet as the vehicle slowly rolled into the conveniently empty parking lot. The unsteady and powerful beating of her heart was either due to apprehension or excitement, but trying to figure out which of the two she was experiencing was purely pointless at this time. All that really mattered now was there was no aborting the homicide in the works.

Besides, even if something impromptu were to take place that could cause them to call off the mission, Devon sure enough sensed there wasn't enough money in the world to dissuade her bloodthirsty and raring-to-go accomplice crouched at her side. *Fuck it, it's kill or be killed,* Devon concluded while glancing purposely to her left and getting a load of the satanic smirk on JJ's scarred face. *And I'm definitely not trying to play the victim tonight ... or any other night.*

The vehicle eventually materialized to be a SUV. It soon parked. Then, the headlights cut off, but the engine could be heard running still. The SUV was too far away to clearly see who was inside. And it was too far away for Devon's Baretta .380 to be effective. However, distance didn't matter for what JJ had in mind with the MAC-10 in his hands.

"Is that'cha cracka?" JJ asked.

"Naw, that ain't him. He ain't comin' till I send him a text."

Without further ado, like a demented jack-in-a-box, JJ sprang out from behind the city dumpster that concealed them. Garbed in all black, he immediately revealed his position with short bursts of rapid fire while converging on the idling SUV, and Devon, who also wore all black, followed a few feet behind him without firing once. The SUV suddenly took off, but instead of fleeing, the vehicle charged at JJ and Devon. JJ then proceeded to unload his clip and Devon finally began to fire, and the two of them perforated the SUV's hood and windshield. Regardless, the SUV never veered off its course, and JJ and Devon eventually had to lunge out of its path.

The SUV skidded sideways to a halt about fifty yards away from the ambushers' position, then two figures exited the vehicle, took cover behind it and returned fire.

Once the return fire ceased, JJ yelled, "I wuz prayin' you wouldn't make this easy, Byron!" While harboring behind a tree, he reloaded, then continued, "You can fight, but eitha way it go, you gonna die tonite, nigga. That's on my mama!"

"Is that'chu, JJ?" Bizzy hollered back while hunkering down behind the passenger side wheels of the SUV with Skinny-O.

"Yeah, bitch, it's me. But tonite, I'm God, so prepare ta meet ya maker, fuck boy!"

"Bring it, sweet-ass nigga! An' I'ma make sho' you dead-dead this time!"

After releasing a battle cry, JJ jumped back into the fray, firing short bursts again while moving low toward Bizzy's position, like a Navy SEAL storming a terrorist stronghold. As bullets zipped past him, his determination to kill Bizzy caused him to black out in rage. He had tunnel vision and Bizzy was at the end of it.

Devon, on the other hand, listened to the exchange of gunfire as she cowered behind the concrete pedestal of a broken parking lot light. As bullets pinged and ricocheted off everything around her, she closed her eyes tightly and began to pray aloud for God to save her.

Seconds later, Skinny-O was hit after popping up to shoot back at an encroaching JJ. He fell to the ground on his back next to Bizzy and placed his left hand over the hole in his right shoulder. "Run, young blood," he directed Bizzy. "Get outta here an' live ta fight anotha day. We got ambushed but I'll hold'em off." He gripped the 9mm Ruger tightly in his right hand. "Now go. RUN!"

Hunched down by Skinny-O's side, with a hail of bullets still whizzing overhead and thumping the truck, Bizzy knew exactly what needed to be done for him to have any chance of surviving tonight. He made up his mind right then and there as to what his next course of action would be. He quickly decided to take a stand against JJ, because running tonight would only prolong this beef.

Bizzy then checked how many rounds he had left in the extended clip of his Glock 17. When he saw he had eight bullets remaining in the only clip he had, he asked Skinny-O, "Quick, how many slugs ya got?"

"I gotta full clip. I just relo ..."

That was all Bizzy needed to hear. He then snatched the heat out of Skinny-O's hand and drew up a quick game plan. With JJ firing in a steady pattern, he was able to figure out the perfect time to counterattack. *There were two shooters at first, so the other one must be down since JJ is the only one still firing,* he gathered as JJ's assault grew way too close for comfort. *I got to make my move ... now!*

During the brief pause in JJ's rhythmic shooting, Bizzy arose from cover at the perfect time and began to clap back with both semi-automatic pistols in JJ's general direction. His defensive surprise sent JJ tumbling backwards. Then, seeing a window of opportunity, he finessed his way around the front end of the SUV and advanced forward while tactfully firing at JJ, keeping him disengaged.

225

"Aaaaaahhhhhh," JJ screamed as a bullet ripped through the tissue of his calf, causing him to fall on his ass and drop the MAC-10.

The sight of an unarmed JJ made Bizzy grin instinctively.

"Look at'chu, nigga," Bizzy said as he approached his ex-homie, who was writhing in pain. "You *still* can't get shit rite, lil nigga." He shook his head in mock disappointment. "But I gotta admit, I thought you were KFC'd that nite wit ya old girl. You most definitely got da will ta live. It's just too bad that all you did ta get here amounted ta nuttin'. Nice try, tho!"

"Fuck you, pussy!" JJ then attempted to grab the MAC-10.

Bizzy hurriedly kicked it out of his reach. "You really deter-mined ta off me, I see." He sighed sincerely. "Damn, JJ, we ... we could've been kings in these streets. You were my road dawg. But noooo, you had ta go an' play wit my paper. What happened ta Miss Sadie is all on yo' head. If ya wouldn't have ran off wit my dough, thinkin' I was a cold lame, then er'thang woulda been super straight. Now look at'cha, hellbent on gettin' back at me, goin' ta great lengths just ta avenge ya mama."

He sighed once more. "Altho' I wouldn't have took ya bread, especially not after ya got outta prison, I admit, bruh, I woulda went through all that'chu did ta kill da muthafucka that fucked ova my peeps ... As a matter ah fact, I'm doin' all that'chu did an' mo ta find out who smoked my pops."

JJ suddenly started to laugh.

"What da fuck?" Bizzy said with a look of confusion on his face. He then took aim at JJ with one of the guns in his hand, and added, "What da fuck can be so funny at this moment? Is it laugh now, die later, huh? Cuz you sho' 'bout ta die real soon."

JJ's laughter grew louder, filling the cool night's air.

Then, Bizzy realized he had disregarded something real im-portant. As he surveyed his surroundings, he said, "Where's da otha shooter that was wit'chu?"

JJ stopped laughing, then replied, "Ya mean ya sista?"

That startling revelation caused Bizzy to lower his weapon.

"Yeah, nigga … ya sista round here sumwhere. She prolly got da drop on ya rite now." He laughed a little more. "Yeah, she 'bout ta kill her faggot-ass brotha just like she killed her weak-ass Pops, but she ain't gonna tape yo murder tho' … at least I don't think so. Ha-ha! So kill me, becuz as long as she kill you, usin' her as bait worked out perfectly." He laughed some more, then added, "Don't look so stupid, nigga. Ya need ta thank me, cuz you woulda never known who murked ya Pops if it wasn't fo me. If it wasn't fo' me, you'd be chillen wit da bitch that slumped ya punk-ass Pops." More laughter.

Bizzy had heard more than enough. He simply raised his Glock and squeezed the trigger.

Click

In the split second it took Bizzy to realize his Glock had mis-fired, JJ seized the moment. Before Bizzy could up the 9mm in his other hand, JJ had snatched a small .25 from his waist and fired five times.

Sprawled out now on the ground, Bizzy had been hit by three bullets.

JJ struggled to get to his feet. "Well, well, well," he taunted Bizzy as he limped over to him. "You shoulda killed me. Now, unlike all that unnecessary talkin' you did, all I gotta say is sayonara, pussy."

Here I come, Pops, Bizzy thought, *I know you didn't expect to see me so soon.*

When the smoke cleared, nothing would be the same.

227

Chapter Twenty-seven

January 5, 2011 9:11 am

West Palm Beach, FL

"So that's it, huh? Just like that?"

"Yep. Just like that."

"What about Byron Woodson? Kelly Kronkite? Adrian Mendoza? Do they just get off that easy?"

Dino felt very bad for playing a major part in tarnishing his partner's reputation in the department so soon. Raw Deal's valor and true grit were needed qualities for taking down the ruthless, predatory criminals in the streets, he knew. He also knew the collapse of their last assignment would haunt, yet motivate, Raw Deal for quite some time, if not forever. But, for now, he had to put Raw Deal's concerns to rest about the future of their investigative work on the Woodson case, for they had been reassigned.

As the pair walked side by side after their removal from the Woodson case by an extremely infuriated commander, Dino said, "Kelly Kronkite ... his indictment for insider trading will result in him spending three, maybe four years behind bars. The reason why he isn't facing any drug charges at this time is because he has no co-conspirators linked to his case right now and there just isn't enough evidence on him. However, his indictment can be superseded once the department arrests ..."

He grunted. "Anyway, Mendoza ... honestly, he'll only face major charges when we nab the *ghost* in Peru. Until then, the agency won't waste taxpayer's money on some pretty boy Latino with no criminal record that mainly talks drugs but is never caught or seen with them. He'll manage his legit boutiques until his pompous ass runs out of luck." He shrugged. "And Woodson ... I don't even want to talk about that jinxed nigger."

About ten seconds of silence slipped by before he spoke again. "And for what it's worth, I'm sorry, Holmes, for muddying your name already. You have a promising career in the agency, and you'll soon get another shot to prove that you're a top-flight agent ... just like I *was*."

Raw Deal smiled. "It's no big deal, Zimmerman. And I apologize, too. Although I didn't get you killed, I did help kill your career in the field by sending you out in a blaze of glory." He paused to think for a second. "Hmm, that didn't come out right. What I meant was ... "

"Don't sweat it, rookie. I understand what you meant. But understand this, we did our job ethically and with integrity, unlike Agents John Reid and Ken Brunel before us."

"Why do those names ring a bell?" Raw Deal asked with a puzzled expression on his face.

"They're the agents that bungled the DOJ's first case against the elder Woodson by testi-*lying*, fabricating evidence and coercing witnesses to lie on the stand. And for that, they're still serving time in the system."

Silence.

"Alright," Dino said as he prepared to part ways, "I'll see you tomorrow, partner. We've got a new mission to tackle before I retire, so let's get to it."

"Yes, sir, we do. I can't wait to execute a search warrant on some teenaged pothead's high school locker."

They both laughed ... to keep from screaming in defeat.

January 5, 2011 10:39am

West Palm Beach, FL

Palm Beach International Airport

Lying.
What is the true purpose for telling untruths?

Nobody had been truly taught to lie. No parent, in their right mind, educated their child in dishonesty. Yet, somehow, lying had been learned. Who was to blame for babies finding out how to lie? TV? Magic? Jokes? Or was it simply them becoming mindful of their surroundings?

Lying.

What is the true reason for lying?

Of course, once a baby becomes conscious of their actions, they will lie out of fear after getting caught doing something wrong, and that gimmick will remain until death, a majority of the time. Some are led to the art of lying in order to protect themselves against a bigger, stronger person that threatened to take from them, or even harm them. On the other hand, they will learn to lie to get something they aren't entitled to or do not deserve. Eventually, they will use lying as a way to protect a loved one from the truth, to make someone feel better during difficult times (a white lie), or even to hurt someone's feelings purposely. Indubitably, they just might learn to lie for no apparent reason.

Nevertheless, to ascertain whether or not there is a true purpose for lying depends on who was asked. However, self-interest could be regarded as the main reason why people lied.

And it was self-interest that caused Bizzy to now despise his once beloved father.

"... an' I put that on my life," Devon ended her full explanation as she sat behind the wheel in the parking lot at Palm Beach International Airport.

In the passenger seat, Bizzy calmly said, "Like I said back at da telly, I believe ya. But thanks fuh tellin' me da whole story just then."

Devon had just wrapped up telling Bizzy exactly why she had killed their father. There were so many things in her blow-by-blow story he had never known, as well as so many things his father was dishonest about. It was truly disturbing when he first found out nearly two years ago Demetrius had lied about him being an only child and that his mother went to Mexico to start a new family.

But it hadn't been enough for him to condemn his father. He felt like those lies were to protect him in a way.

However, when Devon just disclosed that Demetrius had indeed murdered their mother after he had raped her, he nearly threw up. Then, only after she made it very clear to him that knocking off Demetrius was the only way to get over her obsession of avenging their mother, did he deem her actions justifiable.

Getting that story directly from Devon was a stroke of luck, but he was forced to hear her out after she had become the unlikeliest of heroes.

When JJ had him with nowhere to go but to hell a few nights ago, he had known for sure he was a goner once he heard that single gunshot. However, the following sound of something hitting the pavement had been the only indication he was still alive. Subsequently, seeing Devon standing over JJ's crumpled body left him unsure of what would happen thereafter. He had not been sure if Devon planned to kill him next, but he figured that his time had finally come when she unexpectedly extended her arm towards him. Instead of drawing down on him, though, she had actually offered to help him get to his feet. Lucky for him, JJ had been a terrible shooter, grazing his left hip once and hitting him on the left hand and forearm, so she was able to help him and Skinny-O get away with the hundred and fifty thousand before the cops arrived.

Since he knew Devon had been well aware of what he planned to do to the person that killed Demetrius, Bizzy couldn't help but ask her why she chose to save him. Her explanation for that was, as she hid behind the base of that light pole, she had heard JJ basically confess to breaking into her club, stealing the murder tape and leaking it for all to see. At that time, she understood it was JJ's fault that a million-dollar reward had been put on her head, so she killed him because he had made the last seven months of her life a living hell.

And immediately after she had whacked JJ, she felt that saving Bizzy's life finally gave her the opportunity to actually tell

him the whole truth about what happened between her and
Demetrius. So, when it was all said and done, everything worked
out for the best. They were reunited, and there were no hard
feelings.

"Are ya sho' ya gotta go so soon?" Devon asked sadly. "Ya
sho' ya don't need ta heal up first?"

"Yeah, sis, I gotta bounce. Ain't no tellin' how close da feds
are from my ass. I already did sixty-eight days in da feds befo',
an' I ain't tryna go back ta spend anotha day in that hell hole. So
yeah, I gotta get ghost ... ASAP."

"Why Puerto Rico, tho'?"

"That's just da first stop. I plan on island hoppin' till I reach
South America, then I'm off ta Peru."

"Peru?"

"Yeah, I gotta job proposition." He winked.

"What about Aunt Sheryl? You talked ta her yet?"

"Negative. But when ya swing up that way ta see her an' our
G-Ma..." he sighed, "...just tell her I'll be in touch, okay?"

Devon nodded.

"Anyways, you just make sho' you don't fa'get about a nigga,
okay?"

Devon frowned. "Biz, look ... I know it's hard fo' ya ta trust
people. Hell, when big bread is involved, it's wise not ta trust
anybody. But there's no point in buryin' da hatchet if we're gonna
put a marker on da site. If we killed da beef, then it's dead.
Actions speak louder than words tho'. So I'll prove ta ya that I
got'cha back. I'ma take care of ya jits like ya asked, so don't
worry 'bout them, an' I'll send ya bread whereva an' when ya
need it. Just hit me up. Bet?"

"Bet."

"An' besides, that's da least I can do fo' da nigga that gave me
a crib. I wanna thank ya once again fo' that. When my girl get out
da hospital, I'ma sell my club an' Mobile is where we gonna start
ova at."

"No need ta thank me. It was eitha give it ta you or my BM in Orlando. An' since my BM is ratchet as all outdoors, givin' it ta you was da wisest choice."

They smiled before giving each other dap.

"Ouch!"

"What?"

"Fuck! That bitch-ass nigga shot da tip of my pinkie off, that's what! I should go dig his black ass up an' shoot his damn pinkie off."

Imagining Bizzy doing exactly what he just said caused Devon to laugh. Then she said, "Well, ya gotta get goin', playboy. Ya plane leavin' soon."

"Help me wit my bag, please. I can't do much wit my arm in this sling." He got out and limped to the trunk. He watched as Devon struggled to remove his large rolling suitcase from the vehicle. Once he was ready to roll, he said, "I'll be seein' ya soon … Devona. An' hopefully, you'd have grown ya dreads back by then." He grinned. "Altho' you can rock waves betta than most niggas."

"Hopefully, I won't have ta change my appearance no mo', cuz I shouldn't have anymo' enemies out ta kill me." She chuckled. "Well … I hate ta see ya go so soon, Deltoine Scott."

Bizzy shot a sly smile her way after hearing the alias that he was flying under. "Ai'ight, you be safe an' keep pimpin', pimpin'."

They shared a brief hug, then Bizzy wobbled into the airport with his luggage trailing behind him.

January 5, 2011 1:09 pm

Riviera Beach, FL

As Devon neared the entrance to St. Mary's Hospital, she was startled by someone she hadn't seen in almost four months.

"What'chu doin' here?"

"Damn, I thought you'd never show up," said RahRah as he approached Devon. "I been campin' out in this baser's quail fo' da last few days, lookin' fo' ya. I ain't bathe or brush my teeth, real shit. But I knew you'd sho' up eventually."

She didn't know if RahRah was joking or not about not washing his ass and brushing his teeth. However, she casually said, "What da beat is? Is er'thang good wit'cha?"

RahRah had heard the bad news about Miracle a while back. He soon came to the conclusion that she was in the hospital because of him, indirectly. When he realized at the last second whose car it was travelling down Beautiful Avenue that unforgettable day, it had been too late. Although he never bust his gun, he felt just as guilty as if he had. And fear hadn't been the reason why he left Bumper and Skat, it was regret.

Since that day he bailed out on his homies, he had ducked off in Quinterria's crib. From there, he continuously tried to figure out who the strange sounding female had been that called him with that information which led to Miracle being shot. With the caller's number no longer in service, he ran into dead end after dead end. But he still vowed he would eighty-six whoever it was, male or female, that tricked him into setting the lick up.

At the moment, he was at a crossroads. He couldn't just come out and tell Devon Miracle had been shot and was in a coma because of him. However, it was hard facing her when he knew who was really responsible for Miracle's predicament. And although he learned that both PopTart Tina and Skat had been killed by the police and Bumper was locked up, telling her that his one-time homies were the culprits still didn't sit right with him.

RahRah sighed. "Yeah, er'thang grizzy. I-I … I heard 'bout Miracle an' … I just wanted … I want ta see her. But I didn't know her real name, so I been waitin' fo' ya ta slide through."

Devon could sense that her brother was holding something back. But instead of seeking out the truth, she replied, "We gotta go then, cuz viso ain't that long. Most of her family prolly up there now, so we only gon' have a few minutes ta see her."

"How ... how is she tho'?"

"Last I heard, she was still in a coma. But she stable."

RahRah inhaled deeply and exhaled sharply. "Damn."

Then, they entered the hospital, signed in and headed for Miracle's room. As expected, they weren't the only visitors. After Devon introduced RahRah to some of Miracle's family members, and they had waited their turn, they were finally escorted in.

"Hey, baby," Devon said a bit gleefully as she stood by Miracle's bedside. Miracle was looking much better than the last time she saw her three months ago. She saw the bruises had faded and the swelling had gone down, yet most of the bandages remained. "You lookin' good, Marie." She stroked her cheek. "An' look, I brought someone ta see ya." She motioned for RahRah to come closer. "It's RahRah."

The pitiful sight of Miracle lying motionless in the bed with all types of medical machinery hooked up to her nearly broke RahRah down. Not only was he feeling guilty, seeing her laid up in that bed reminded him of when he had visited his grandmother Miss Candace, in the hospital before she passed. At a loss for words, he merely uttered, "Hey, Miracle."

Then, the miraculous happened.

"Nurse!" Devon yelled when she saw Miracle's eyes struggle to open. She yelled even more as Miracle began to move slightly. "Help!" Once two distraught-looking nurses arrived, she ecstatically said, "She's movin'! She's movin'!"

The nurses rushed both Devon and RahRah out of the room. When she and RahRah were gathered with Miracle's family again, she told them the wonderful news, but none were happier than Devon.

That's my girl, she said to herself as the plans she had made for her and Miracle became closer in view. *Now get better soon so we can get you out of this miserable place and live happily ever after.*

After several hours of waiting around, Michelle approached Devon. With a beaming smile on her face, she said, "She is fully awake now. She can also speak, but only a few words at a time. And I want you to know that all she keep saying is your name. So go and see her, Devona. That will make her happy."

"Can my brotha come wit me?"

Michelle nodded.

Once again, Devon and RahRah were escorted to Miracle's room. When they entered this time, they could feel the energy in the room was different, it had transitioned from funeral-like to Christmas-y.

Upon seeing Devon's face, a misty-eyed Miracle smiled faintly. "D-D-De ... "

"Shhh. Don't speak, baby. I know. I love an' miss you, too. An' I'm so, so sorry." Devon grabbed Miracle's hand as if it were made of tissue paper. "Just get betta so we can go home, okay?"

Miracle swallowed hard and closed her eyes. After a few seconds, she reopened her eyes and, instead of a smile, a frown took form on her face. Then, she strained to say, "R-R-Rha ..." She paused to gain her strength. "Rhap ... Rhap ..."

"Rhapsody?" asked Devon. When Miracle nodded her head a little, she added, "What about her?"

Rather than exhausting herself further with trying to speak, Miracle slowly lifted her hand and fixed her fingers into the shape of a ...

For what felt like a century, Devon stood tongue-tied by Miracle's side with tears of anger streaming down her face. She incessantly attempted to erase from her mind the *gun* gesture that Miracle had made. As she agonized over Miracle's condemning revelation, she gradually began to hear the clamorous, recurrent sound of her mother's deadly gunshot, which soon brought sad thoughts of a woman she scarcely knew to mind. Suddenly, her thoughts shifted to what she planned to do once she got her hands on Rhapsody.

Little did she know, however, that RahRah was already on top of it. Because when she turned around, RahRah had disappeared.

Epilogue

January 5, 2011 3:02 pm

West Palm Beach, FL

County Jail

"What's good, Blue?"

"Ain't too much goin' on. It's da same clown-ass niggas out here, just a diff'rent tent."

Fuck, I can't stand seeing my nigga behind that plexiglass, Blue thought, *I can't wait for my dawg to jump.*

JuneBug had been incarcerated ever since the night Chad was killed. First, he had spent a little over a month in the hospital, healing from two shots to his stomach, before he was discharged and sent straight to lock-up. Although he hadn't been charged with Chad's murder, he was charged with the QP of weed that had been found in his 'Vette, however. And with his record showing two prior possessions of marijuana over twenty grams, he was facing up to a year in jail when he went for sentencing next week.

"I appreciate da bread that'chu been puttin' on my books," Bug said, looking more upbeat than usual.

"Get da fuck outta here wit' that bullshit, bruh." Blue grinned, flashing the four open-faced golds on his top row of teeth. "How many times I gotta tell ya that'chu don't have ta keep thankin' me, ole sentimental-ass nigga. Ya' know how we rock. I'ma take care of ya, unlike da rest of these flaw, perkin' niggas that claim they fucks wit'cha. Besides, I don't mind lookin' out fo' a real nigga that put me on my feet when I was on my dick. Cuz if it wasn't fo' you, I'd be ..."

"Say less." Bug smiled. "Anywayz, when I get outta this bitch, I'ma take care of ya. I got some shit I'm schemin' on now. These streets gon' be ours."

"Nigga, you buggin'."

"Naw, fo' real." Bug shifted in his seat, then said through the phone, "I just learned that …" He suddenly halted to look around to see if anyone was watching him. "Da streets of Palm Beach are up fo' grabs. An' I'm already plugged in, so it's easy pickings."

"If it's like ya say it is, then I'm down like four flats. Do ya need me ta do anythang while ya in here?"

"Yeah."

"What's dat, bruh?"

A big goofy smile took shape on his mug, then he said, "Be patient."

The End

Lock Down Publications and Ca$h Presents assisted
publishing packages.

BASIC PACKAGE $499
Editing
Cover Design
Formatting

UPGRADED PACKAGE $800
Typing
Editing
Cover Design
Formatting

ADVANCE PACKAGE $1,200
Typing
Editing
Cover Design
Formatting
Copyright registration
Proofreading
Upload book to Amazon

LDP SUPREME PACKAGE $1,500
Typing
Editing
Cover Design
Formatting
Copyright registration
Proofreading
Set up Amazon account
Upload book to Amazon
Advertise on LDP Amazon and Facebook page

***Other services available upon request. Additional charges may apply

Lock Down Publications
P.O. Box 944
Stockbridge, GA 30281-9998
Phone # 470 303-9761

Submission Guideline

Submit the first three chapters of your completed manuscript to ldpsubmissions@gmail.com, subject line: Your book's title. The manuscript must be in a .doc file and sent as an attachment. Document should be in Times New Roman, double spaced and in size 12 font. Also, provide your synopsis and full contact information. If sending multiple submissions, they must each be in a separate email.

Have a story but no way to send it electronically? You can still submit to LDP/Ca$h Presents. Send in the first three chapters, written or typed, of your completed manuscript to:

LDP: Submissions Dept
Po Box 944
Stockbridge, Ga 30281

DO NOT send original manuscript. Must be a duplicate.

Provide your synopsis and a cover letter containing your full contact information.

Thanks for considering LDP and Ca$h Presents.

<u>NEW RELEASES</u>

LOYAL TO THE SOIL by JIBRIL WILLIAMS
A GANGSTA'S PAIN by J-BLUNT
MONEY IN THE GRAVE 2 by MARTELL "TROUBLESOME"
BOLDEN
THE BRICK MAN 2 by KING RIO
A DOPEBOY'S DREAM 3 by ROMELL TUKES
CONFESSIONS OF A JACKBOY II by NICHOLAS LOCK
A GANGSTA'S KARMA 2 by FLAME

Coming Soon from Lock Down Publications/Ca$h Presents
BLOOD OF A BOSS VI
SHADOWS OF THE GAME II
TRAP BASTARD II
By **Askari**
LOYAL TO THE GAME **IV**
By **T.J. & Jelissa**
IF TRUE SAVAGE **VIII**
MIDNIGHT CARTEL IV
DOPE BOY MAGIC IV
CITY OF KINGZ III
NIGHTMARE ON SILENT AVE II
By **Chris Green**
BLAST FOR ME **III**
A SAVAGE DOPEBOY III
CUTTHROAT MAFIA III
DUFFLE BAG CARTEL VII
HEARTLESS GOON VI
By **Ghost**
A HUSTLER'S DECEIT III
KILL ZONE II
BAE BELONGS TO ME III
By **Aryanna**
KING OF THE TRAP III
By **T.J. Edwards**
GORILLAZ IN THE BAY V
3X KRAZY III
STRAIGHT BEAST MODE II
De'Kari

KINGPIN KILLAZ IV

STREET KINGS III

PAID IN BLOOD III

CARTEL KILLAZ IV

DOPE GODS III

Hood Rich

SINS OF A HUSTLA II

ASAD

RICH $AVAGE II

MONEY IN THE GRAVE II

By Martell Troublesome Bolden

YAYO V

Bred In The Game 2

S. Allen

CREAM III

By Yolanda Moore

SON OF A DOPE FIEND III

HEAVEN GOT A GHETTO II

By Renta

LOYALTY AIN'T PROMISED III

By Keith Williams

I'M NOTHING WITHOUT HIS LOVE II

SINS OF A THUG II

TO THE THUG I LOVED BEFORE II

By Monet Dragun

QUIET MONEY IV

EXTENDED CLIP III

THUG LIFE IV

By **Trai'Quan**

THE STREETS MADE ME IV

By **Larry D. Wright**

IF YOU CROSS ME ONCE II

By **Anthony Fields**

THE STREETS WILL NEVER CLOSE II

By K'ajji

HARD AND RUTHLESS III

THE BILLIONAIRE BENTLEYS II

Von Diesel

KILLA KOUNTY II

By Khufu

MONEY GAME III

By Smoove Dolla

JACK BOYZ VERSUS DOPE BOYZ

By Romell Tukes

MURDA WAS THE CASE II

Elijah R. Freeman

THE STREETS NEVER LET GO II

By Robert Baptiste

AN UNFORESEEN LOVE III

By **Meesha**

KING OF THE TRENCHES II
by **GHOST & TRANAY ADAMS**

MONEY MAFIA II

LOYAL TO THE SOIL II

By **Jibril Williams**

QUEEN OF THE ZOO II

By **Black Migo**

THE BRICK MAN III

Flame

By King Rio
VICIOUS LOYALTY II
By Kingpen
A GANGSTA'S PAIN II
By J-Blunt
CONFESSIONS OF A JACKBOY III
By Nicholas Lock

Available Now

RESTRAINING ORDER **I & II**
By **CA$H & Coffee**
LOVE KNOWS NO BOUNDARIES **I II & III**
By **Coffee**
RAISED AS A GOON I, II, III & IV
BRED BY THE SLUMS I, II, III
BLAST FOR ME I & II
ROTTEN TO THE CORE I II III
A BRONX TALE I, II, III
DUFFLE BAG CARTEL I II III IV V VI
HEARTLESS GOON I II III IV V
A SAVAGE DOPEBOY I II
DRUG LORDS I II III
CUTTHROAT MAFIA I II

KING OF THE TRENCHES
By **Ghost**
LAY IT DOWN **I & II**
LAST OF A DYING BREED I II
BLOOD STAINS OF A SHOTTA I & II III
By **Jamaica**
LOYAL TO THE GAME I II III
LIFE OF SIN I, II III
By **TJ & Jelissa**
BLOODY COMMAS I & II
SKI MASK CARTEL I II & III
KING OF NEW YORK I II,III IV V
RISE TO POWER I II III
COKE KINGS I II III IV V
BORN HEARTLESS I II III IV
KING OF THE TRAP I II
By **T.J. Edwards**
IF LOVING HIM IS WRONG…I & II
LOVE ME EVEN WHEN IT HURTS I II III
By **Jelissa**
WHEN THE STREETS CLAP BACK I & II III
THE HEART OF A SAVAGE I II III
MONEY MAFIA
LOYAL TO THE SOIL
By **Jibril Williams**
A DISTINGUISHED THUG STOLE MY HEART I II & III
LOVE SHOULDN'T HURT I II III IV
RENEGADE BOYS I II III IV
PAID IN KARMA I II III

Flame

SAVAGE STORMS I II
AN UNFORESEEN LOVE I II
By **Meesha**
A GANGSTER'S CODE I &, II III
A GANGSTER'S SYN I II III
THE SAVAGE LIFE I II III
CHAINED TO THE STREETS I II III
BLOOD ON THE MONEY I II III
A GANGSTA'S PAIN
By J-Blunt
PUSH IT TO THE LIMIT
By **Bre' Hayes**
BLOOD OF A BOSS **I, II, III, IV, V**
SHADOWS OF THE GAME
TRAP BASTARD
By **Askari**
THE STREETS BLEED MURDER **I, II & III**
THE HEART OF A GANGSTA I II& III
By **Jerry Jackson**
CUM FOR ME I II III IV V VI VII
An **LDP Erotica Collaboration**
BRIDE OF A HUSTLA **I II & II**
THE FETTI GIRLS **I, II& III**
CORRUPTED BY A GANGSTA I, II III, IV
BLINDED BY HIS LOVE
THE PRICE YOU PAY FOR LOVE I, II ,III
DOPE GIRL MAGIC I II III
By **Destiny Skai**
WHEN A GOOD GIRL GOES BAD

249

A Gangsta's Karma 2

GANGSTA SHYT **I II &III**
By **CATO**
THE ULTIMATE BETRAYAL
By **Phoenix**
BOSS'N UP **I , II & III**
By **Royal Nicole**
I LOVE YOU TO DEATH
By **Destiny J**
I RIDE FOR MY HITTA
I STILL RIDE FOR MY HITTA
By **Misty Holt**
LOVE & CHASIN' PAPER
By **Qay Crockett**
TO DIE IN VAIN
SINS OF A HUSTLA
By **ASAD**
BROOKLYN HUSTLAZ
By **Boogsy Morina**
BROOKLYN ON LOCK I & II
By **Sonovia**
GANGSTA CITY
By **Teddy Duke**
A DRUG KING AND HIS DIAMOND I & II III
A DOPEMAN'S RICHES
HER MAN, MINE'S TOO I, II
CASH MONEY HO'S
THE WIFEY I USED TO BE I II
By Nicole Goosby
TRAPHOUSE KING **I II & III**

KINGPIN KILLAZ I II III
STREET KINGS I II
PAID IN BLOOD **I II**
CARTEL KILLAZ I II III
DOPE GODS I II
By **Hood Rich**
LIPSTICK KILLAH **I, II, III**
CRIME OF PASSION I II & III
FRIEND OR FOE I II III
By **Mimi**
STEADY MOBBN' **I, II, III**
THE STREETS STAINED MY SOUL I II
By **Marcellus Allen**
WHO SHOT YA **I, II, III**
SON OF A DOPE FIEND I II
HEAVEN GOT A GHETTO
Renta
GORILLAZ IN THE BAY **I II III IV**
TEARS OF A GANGSTA I II
3X KRAZY I II
STRAIGHT BEAST MODE
DE'KARI
TRIGGADALE I II III
MURDAROBER WAS THE CASE
Elijah R. Freeman
GOD BLESS THE TRAPPERS I, II, III
THESE SCANDALOUS STREETS I, II, III
FEAR MY GANGSTA I, II, III IV, V
THESE STREETS DON'T LOVE NOBODY I, II

Flame

BURY ME A G I, II, III, IV, V
A GANGSTA'S EMPIRE I, II, III, IV
THE DOPEMAN'S BODYGAURD I II
THE REALEST KILLAZ I II III
THE LAST OF THE OGS I II III
Tranay Adams
THE STREETS ARE CALLING
Duquie Wilson
MARRIED TO A BOSS I II III
By Destiny Skai & Chris Green
KINGZ OF THE GAME I II III IV V VI
Playa Ray
SLAUGHTER GANG I II III
RUTHLESS HEART I II III
By Willie Slaughter
FUK SHYT
By Blakk Diamond
DON'T F#CK WITH MY HEART I II
By Linnea
ADDICTED TO THE DRAMA I II III
IN THE ARM OF HIS BOSS II
By Jamila
YAYO I II III IV
A SHOOTER'S AMBITION I II
BRED IN THE GAME
By S. Allen
TRAP GOD I II III
RICH $AVAGE
MONEY IN THE GRAVE I II

253

A Gangsta's Karma 2

By Martell Troublesome Bolden
FOREVER GANGSTA
GLOCKS ON SATIN SHEETS I II

By Adrian Dulan
TOE TAGZ I II III
LEVELS TO THIS SHYT I II

By Ah'Million
KINGPIN DREAMS I II III

By Paper Boi Rari
CONFESSIONS OF A GANGSTA I II III IV
CONFESSIONS OF A JACKBOY I II

By Nicholas Lock
I'M NOTHING WITHOUT HIS LOVE
SINS OF A THUG
TO THE THUG I LOVED BEFORE

By Monet Dragun
CAUGHT UP IN THE LIFE I II III
THE STREETS NEVER LET GO

By Robert Baptiste
NEW TO THE GAME I II III
MONEY, MURDER & MEMORIES I II III

By **Malik D. Rice**
LIFE OF A SAVAGE I II III
A GANGSTA'S QUR'AN I II III
MURDA SEASON I II III
GANGLAND CARTEL I II III
CHI'RAQ GANGSTAS I II III
KILLERS ON ELM STREET I II III
JACK BOYZ N DA BRONX I II III

Flame

A DOPEBOY'S DREAM I II III

By **Romell Tukes**

LOYALTY AIN'T PROMISED I II

By Keith Williams

QUIET MONEY I II III

THUG LIFE I II III

EXTENDED CLIP I II

By **Trai'Quan**

THE STREETS MADE ME I II III

By **Larry D. Wright**

THE ULTIMATE SACRIFICE I, II, III, IV, V, VI

KHADIFI

IF YOU CROSS ME ONCE

ANGEL I II

IN THE BLINK OF AN EYE

By **Anthony Fields**

THE LIFE OF A HOOD STAR

By Ca$h & Rashia Wilson

THE STREETS WILL NEVER CLOSE

By K'ajji

CREAM I II

By Yolanda Moore

NIGHTMARES OF A HUSTLA I II III

By King Dream

CONCRETE KILLA I II

VICIOUS LOYALTY

By Kingpen

HARD AND RUTHLESS I II

MOB TOWN 251

THE BILLIONAIRE BENTLEYS

By Von Diesel

GHOST MOB

Stilloan Robinson

MOB TIES I II III IV

By SayNoMore

BODYMORE MURDERLAND I II III

By Delmont Player

FOR THE LOVE OF A BOSS

By C. D. Blue

MOBBED UP I II III IV

THE BRICK MAN I II

By King Rio

KILLA KOUNTY

By Khufu

MONEY GAME I II

By Smoove Dolla

A GANGSTA'S KARMA I II

By FLAME

KING OF THE TRENCHES II

by **GHOST & TRANAY ADAMS**

QUEEN OF THE ZOO

By **Black Migo**

BOOKS BY LDP'S CEO, CA$H

TRUST IN NO MAN

TRUST IN NO MAN 2

TRUST IN NO MAN 3

BONDED BY BLOOD

SHORTY GOT A THUG

THUGS CRY

THUGS CRY 2

THUGS CRY 3

TRUST NO BITCH

TRUST NO BITCH 2

TRUST NO BITCH 3

TIL MY CASKET DROPS

RESTRAINING ORDER

RESTRAINING ORDER 2

IN LOVE WITH A CONVICT

LIFE OF A HOOD STAR